I0575458

The First Contact

Written By: Michael Bills

Edited By: Alexandra Pini

Preliminary Editor: Cathy Bills

This book is dedicated to: My dad, Robert, for supporting me on my journey. My brother, Jason, for always being there for me. The Bills and Schmidt family, the best family anyone could ever ask for. Dusty, my purrrfect companion. My best friends Lindsey H. and Brandon S. for reinvigorating my passion after it had faded. My best friends Andrew B. and Pat M. for putting up with me since middle school. Caleb B. and Mike D. for letting me edit their work, challenging me to write my own body of work. A huge thank you to my mom, Cathy, and cousin, Ali, for taking the time to give me huge constructive feedback and a long list of editing notes.

Thank you! All of you mean so much to me! I literally couldn't have finished this without you.

- Michael Bills

CHAPTER LIST

1. SELENE

"Good luck out there," a man whispered in Selene's ear. "I was nervous my first time too. Just remember to stick to the script."

The sun was setting in front of Selene as she nodded to the man, never making eye contact. She was nervous, not knowing what she was getting herself into. Selene was standing at the cave entrance, looking out at the ravine, taking in the beauty of the vast green blanket of evergreens covering the planet. She could hear loud screeches coming from deep within the jungle.

This cave where she stood was home to all the people living on this green planet. The large cave system granted them protection from the dangers dwelling outside. The original settlers named it Quaketown.

Selene took one last glimpse at the sunset as she walked backstage. The sunlight danced across her pale face, which was pasted with white makeup. Her jet black hair glistened. She peeked around the brown tarp at the large audience. The citizens of Quaketown were sitting patiently in the dark, dreary cave. There were dozens of families holding lit candles waiting for the show to begin.

Selene spotted her mother, Mona, laughing, most likely at a joke that her father, Aqib, told to the group around them. *Just look at them. They look so happy. Mother looks so beautiful tonight.*

As if her mother had just heard her thoughts, she looked directly into her big emerald eyes and waved. Selene, overwhelmed with joy, smiled and gave her mother two thumbs up in return.

Mona tapped Aqib's broad shoulder and pointed at her. He said something Selene couldn't hear but she could read his lips, "I love you my little sweetheart." It was a phrase he used quite often.

Selene continued looking around at the audience and spotted her best friend, Kelly, the most popular twenty year old girl in Quaketown. From what Selene could see, she was flirting with three older boys. They seemed to be interested in the conversation. Kelly had gorgeous blue eyes and long blonde hair that flowed just past her shoulders; she had brains *and* beauty.

Kelly was one of the best engineers in Quaketown. There were very few engineers because it was a rare skill to have since there was no need for them until recently. A giant spaceship sat across the ravine, next to Quaketown. It had been sitting there for two centuries. Kelly hid her oil pasted hands into her pockets as she continued to talk to the three boys. Selene knew Kelly didn't want them to know how dirty her profession made her. She had been a miner before she was granted this engineer position which was slightly less dirty.

It was almost showtime, but Selene was still searching the audience for someone in particular. She wanted to see if *he* made it this afternoon. He promised he would come and watch her performance.

The last row of seating was in front of the cavehomes where everyone lived. The cavehomes were chiseled out from the cave's walls, each one containing one wooden door and one window with a giant leaf in front of it for privacy. As she scanned the back row, she spotted a boy with dark, overgrown, ratty hair. He was wearing black and green camo paint on his face; it was Sarva. Her heart skipped a beat. She fell in love with him exactly one month ago. She adored his fierce dark eyes and strong physique.

There were two major professions in Quaketown; hunting and mining. Hunters traveled outside the cavehomes to catch the local wildlife and pick edible vegetation. They used modified bows equipped with a device that increases their range and accuracy. Sarva was one of their best hunters.

Selene was a miner. Miners dig deep into the caves to find natural gases, metals, and blue crystals.

The gases powered the generators that kept the caves warm.

The metals supported structures within the caves, provided protection at the safe haven out in the wild, and to make jewelry.

The blue crystals powered the laser drills, also known as melters. Even though it doesn't produce any heat, the melter can easily shave off layers of soil and stone, appearing to melt whatever surface it touches. In reality, the laser deconstructs soil and soil into sand. The powder can then easily be shoveled out of the caves. When miners find something valuable, they must turn it in to be put in storage.

Mr. Bradham, the director and Selene's acting coach, finally walked past the brown tarp and onto the stage. He had a big smile on his face, which stretched from ear to ear. As he walked, his chubby cheeks bounced up and down. The audience's chatter came to an abrupt halt at his presence. As head of the Council, he was well-respected in their community.

"Good evening ladies and gentlemen. Welcome to the show," Mr. Bradham sang loudly so the back row could hear him. "We have a very special show for you tonight. The two hundredth anniversary of our arrival on this planet is coming up in just two months. In preparation for our town's anniversary, we have decided to put on a magical show for you tonight to acknowledge our journey and celebrate the history that lead us here."

Selene heard cheers in the crowd as she walked over to the side of the stage to compose herself. She began to pray to the Ancients.

The stage crew turned knobs and flipped switches to start the special effects on the transparent screen in front of the stage. The special effects are projected onto the screen during each show to enhance the performances and the story. The actors performed behind the screen along with the special effects. Apparently, it was similar to what they once called movies back on Earth.

A blue spotlight shone down on Mr. Bradham, as he theatrically announced, "And without further ado, I introduce to you the young and talented Selene as she transports us two hundred years into the past, to where it all began." Mr. Bradham bowed and walked to stage left. He shouted excitedly, "Enjoy the show!" The spotlight switched off.

Right on cue, the sky outside the cave began to darken. It was the perfect weather for a show. Two boys snuffed out the torches nearby the stage while the audience members collectively blew out their candles. The stage was lit perfectly for Selene's first performance. Giant white text was superimposed across the transparent screen, which read *Our History*.

One of the crew members working on the special effects said, "Break a leg" to Selene. Apparently that's what famous people said to each other back on Earth as a sign of good luck. She didn't understand it though, why was breaking a leg good luck?

When the small orchestra on stage right began to play, Selene strode on stage to the beat of the drums with confidence as the audience roared. This was the moment she had been waiting for her entire life. Even though she was a miner, her dream was to be the most famous and beloved actress in the universe.

Selene first fell in love with the theater at a very young age. Her first memory was of watching Claire Altaïr give a moving performance of the first venture out of the spaceship and onto their planet. Sure, the strobing lights of the special effects dazzled her, but even more so by the electric and kinetic performance of her idol, Claire. Since that night, Selene has been captivated by the shows and one day wanted to be an actress just like Claire, or better. She also wanted to become a princess like the fairy tales her mother told her, but knew that was a reach. Maybe one day she could play a princess in a show.

The title on the transparent screen faded. It was finally her turn in the spotlight. Between her and the audience, the special effects screen magically came to life. She watched as the 2D space station floated across the screen, with its name *The New Frontier*, painted boldly on the side of it. The space station had a spherical chamber in the middle surrounded by five spaceships, each attached by a singular bridge. The spaceships differed slightly in size and shape, but the main difference was each of their colors.

The New Frontier was drifting in space when it came to a stop. Suddenly, the five spaceships detached themselves from their bridges and blasted off into five different directions, away from the center chamber.

Small script appeared at the bottom of the screen that only Selene could read. To the audience, it just appeared to be a little scribble, a possible error in the projection.

Selene read off the prompter, narrating the scene. "It was a little over two hundred years ago that our people left Earth to find a new home. Our ancestors were forced to discover this planet we live on today. Camilla Quaketon was the first to step foot outside of the ship and into the caves. In fact, she stepped directly into this very cave where we sit."

The screen showed the spaceship landing right next to the cave. Selene walked in place behind the air-lock door of the 2-D spaceship to imitate Camilla's movements.

"It took many years to establish roles and carve out our homes," Selene continued. "Many risked their lives journeying outside the safety of the caves and into the jungle. Some unfortunate souls didn't survive." The 2-D screen showed people in the jungle, Selene being one of them, surrounded by scabites, the most feared animal ever encountered on their planet. Selene stood in the center and acted scared as the scabites moved in closer and eventually pounced on top of her. Selene fell into the fetal position on the stage floor.

Scabites were ape-like creatures, but with a smaller head and longer arms. Instead of hair, they had a skin disease that covered them with scabs from the tip of their pointed head to the soles of their wide padded feet. If a person were to touch one, even for a split second, they would contract the skin disease called scabitus. At first, the infected start to lose their hair. Eventually scabs start to cover the infected body. Once their entire body was covered, they died an excruciating death. There was no cure, nor did they have the scientists to produce one.

Selene skillfully pushed herself back onto her feet. "This is why only the bravest of our community become hunters to traverse the jungles." Selene instantly thought of Sarva.

A 2-D bow appeared on screen. She skipped up to the bow and pretended to pick it up. She drew the bowstring back and fired it at one of the holographic scabites. The arrow hit the scabite, causing it to fall backwards off the screen.

"Hunters are very important to our survival. Not only do they make sure we are safe, they provide food on a daily basis." The bow disappeared from her hands and in its place, appeared a pile of meat and vegetables. A bonfire was projected next to her as she brought the food up to her lips.

"Miners also have an important job," continued Selene, as she walked across the stage to the 2-D cave that expanded as she stepped closer. She pretended to pick up the 2-D melter that was floating on the screen. "Miners work tirelessly every morning to expand the living environment, find natural resources, and create new technology." Selene pretended to fire the melter and a blue beam of light shot around the screen. She heard *oohing* and *aahing* from the audience at the special effects. Selene could only see part of the show since she stood so close to the screen.

"In the two hundred years we have been living in Quaketown, we have had our struggles adapting to this new way of life. Despite these disadvantages, we ultimately ended up thriving. But it is almost time for…" Selene paused and stared at the prompter. She became confused and then quickly looked over to the side of the stage, where Mr. Bradham now stood.

Selene could see sweat glistening on her teacher's forehead. He shook his head up and down with a nervous look, signaling for her to continue.

In disbelief and shock, Selene looked out into the audience. First, at her lovely parents who's faces were illuminated by the reflection of the lights from the projection screen. Then she looked over at Kelly who was now more interested in the show than in the three boys. Finally, Selene looked over at Sarva way in the back and she noticed he was looking straight into her eyes, even though she wasn't currently the center of attention.

The show would continue whether she said the next line or not. She looked at the screen, which started to depict what she was afraid to read out loud.

Chapter 1

People began boarding the spaceship.

Selene gave Sarva an awkward smile and he shrugged his shoulders.

Determined to remain calm and professional, she whispered to herself. "Okay Selene, just say it and get it over with. Be brave like Claire. Don't let them know you're scared."

The prompter reversed and then paused at the sentence where she left off. Selene took a deep breath as the prompter began to scroll again.

Walking over to the spaceship that was now displayed on screen and dreading the audience's reaction, Selene read the script out loud. "But it is almost time for us to travel back to *The New Frontier* and reunite with our people from Earth."

The audience let out a huge gasp. Selene wasn't surprised at the audiences reactions because she felt the same way. She could tell the audience members feared what the images on the screen meant, just as she did seconds before.

Now that this plan was revealed to them, their expressions became more intense. A couple of her neighbors jumped up and threw their hands in the air in disgust. Others swore in their seats, while the rest of them started gossiping with the people around them.

She knew everyone felt safe and peaceful here. Finding out there were plans for them to join the other people from Earth was a scary thought. They hadn't seen the others in over two hundred years, but had heard horror stories of war, violence, and troubled times on Earth from their ancestors.

Selene decided to continue reading the script

9

anyways because she thought it was her duty to inform regardless of what was happening.

"In exactly two months time, our people will leave Quaketown on our spaceship to join the other four civilizations who left Earth all those years ago."

The screen showed *The New Frontier* again, but this time, the five spaceships were reconnecting with the central space station.

"The Five Ancients will awaken for our return and lead us to a more habitable planet that will allow us to grow and thrive. The Five Ancients will also teach us the ways of the past and how to get along well with the other civilizations."

Selene thought of the many shows she watched when she was little about people from the other civilizations. She remembered being terrified of some of them because they were depicted as monsters. Others made her laugh because they looked goofy and had exaggerated features.

These unacquainted humans were mainly the evil ones who interfered with the princesses in the fairy tales her mother told her when she was younger.

Selene wasn't looking forward to this reunion and she knew the citizens of Quaketown weren't either. The crowd continued expressing their dissatisfaction.

Sensing the growing hostility in the crowd, Mr. Bradham ran on stage, coming to Selene's rescue and interrupting her performance. "Unfortunately this is the way things have to be," Mr. Bradham announced. "We have been given strict instructions about how to prepare for our journey back."

Selene watched as her neighbor, Gratius, who had a dirtied shirt and long greasy hair, stood up and threw a jennybob, a green circular vegetable that tastes sweet and watery, at the screen right in front of Mr. Bradham. Some others joined him in this shameful act by throwing other vegetables.

Instead of seeing this as an act of retaliation, Selene pretended they were throwing flowers at her for her great performance. "Don't break character," she said through a fake and uninspired smile.

Gratius' face turned red as he aimed another jennybob at Mr. Bradham. "Oh yeah?" yelled Gratius. "Instructions from whom?" He wound his arm back.

Mr. Bradham calmly replied. "From Jonathan Quaketon, one of the Five Ancients."

At the mention of Jonathan's name, the crowd significantly calmed down. Gratius lowered the soggy jennybob. The citizens of Quaketown prayed to the Five Ancients as if they were Gods. Jonathan, the one who directly spoke to them through pre-recorded messages on the spaceship, was their distant ancestor from before the destruction of Earth.

"The Five Ancients are looking out for us and know we are having a tough time down here," said Mr. Bradham. "In two months time, we will finally leave this scabhole and find a home just like Earth once was. We will be free to do the things our ancestors once did."

A good portion of the audience took offense to this, Gratius grumbled the loudest.

"We can discuss things in later," Mr. Bradham finally said, this time directed at Gratius. "As of now, this show is over." He walked off stage. The special effects immediately went off and the torches were re-lit along the cave walls.

Selene was alone on stage again. She felt a huge knot in her stomach and tears started to well up under her eyelids. She refused to cry in front of her audience and quickly ran to the opposite side of the stage from Mr. Bradham. The projector hummed and crackled behind her as one of the crew members used a pulley to roll up the transparent screen.

As Selene walked around backstage the stars were shining through the Quaketown exit. She worked her way her way towards the cavehomes. Part of the audience hung around to discuss the news they had just received. Some of them, people she has never even seen before, gave her dirty looks. Disappointed faces were everywhere. She hurried over to her parents who were still sitting down, waiting patiently for their daughter.

"Mom! Dad!" Selene ran up to her parents, finally allowing the tears to fall down her cheeks. The white-powdered makeup she was wearing for the show smudged across her right cheek as she wiped her face, revealing a dark birthmark.

"My little Selene," said Mona tenderly. "You shone like Earth's moon up there."

"That *is* what you named me after, mom," Selene said as she hugged her mother.

On the side of Selene's face, next to her emerald right eye, just like her beautiful mother's, was a black birthmark the shape of a crescent moon. Her left eye was brown, like her father's. Both features made her stand out in a crowd.

Her mom had explained to her many times she was named after the moon that orbited Earth. She says that it shone many times brighter than Selontris, the moon orbiting this planet. Selontris orbits around the planet so there is a single moonrise and moonset each day.

Elias, one of the Elders of Quaketown, said a long time ago the surface of Selontris was bombarded with space rocks that had chiseled it down on multiple sides, carving it into its irregular shape.

Aqib joined in on the hug. "Great job today, sweetheart." After a few seconds went by, he let go. "I will have to have a word with Stefano later." He shook his head. Stefano was Mr. Bradham's first name. "What was he thinking, having your first performance be one like that? I'm sorry it went that way, honey."

"No," sniffled Selene as she used her sleeve to wipe her tears away. "No, Dad, it's okay. I'll be fine." She had thought hard about this already and figured it was better to put on a performance like she just had, so shocking and memorable, rather than a dull performance such as teaching young kids about the professions.

Aqib looked worried.

Selene confirmed what she said. "Really, dad, I've already made peace with it."

Mona replied. "That's perfect, Selene, because we wouldn't want that to sour your birthday."

She had forgotten during the show because of all the adrenaline coursing through her body. "That's right! It's my birthday today."

They laughed.

It wasn't just any birthday, it was Selene's twenty-first birthday. This birthday was special to all young women of Quaketown because the Elders of the village held a *Chosen Ceremony*. The Elders would choose their future husbands at midnight, who they called the *chosen*. Selene hoped the Elders would choose Sarva for her tonight. Selene had already pictured a full life with him. She wanted two kids, an older daughter and a younger son. She wanted to be a famous actress at night while providing for her family by mining in the morning. Sarva would be the most fearless hunter and would only bring home the biggest meat for their family, although now she wasn't sure what the future held. She couldn't wait for the ceremony to begin at midnight.

"Happy birthday, sweet Selene," her parents cooed lovingly as she stared off in the distance.

"Thanks mom and dad. I appreciate everything you have done for me over the past twenty-one years." Selene hugged them again.

Out of nowhere, Sarva walked past them. "Sarva!" Selene shouted excitedly and waved her hand in the air. "Over here," she motioned.

Her parents shared quizzical looks and looked at the boy with the unkempt hair, baggy clothes, and camo face paint. Judging by the look they gave him, they had already formed opinions of him. Selene noticed her parents seemed to recognize him. They were acting suspicious.

Sarva waved at Selene and gave her parents a devilish grin. "Yo, Selene, what's up?"

Again, Mona and Aqib exchanged looks.

"Did you like my performance?" asked Selene.

"We will discuss that later," replied Sarva. He seemed anxious to leave, rubbing the bottom of his arm. He was probably nervous because he had not met her parents yet and they were giving him strange glances. "I am needed somewhere else. I gotta go," he said.

"Before you leave, I have to tell you something important." Selene grabbed his arm as he turned away. "You see, today is my birthday. My twenty-first birthday."

Sarva stopped dead in his tracks. "Oh yeah? Well, happy birthday, then." He turned his head towards Selene. "Maybe you will get lucky at midnight." He winked and headed toward the cavehomes.

Her parents looked at her, disappointed.

"What?" Selene cried out.

"That boy," said mother. "Sarva, was that his name? He seems charming…"

Selene detected sarcasm.

"What are you doing with him?" her mother demanded.

Selene looked down at her feet. Her parents had warned her on numerous occasions not to fall in love with anyone because she would only be heartbroken when her chosen was named. It's rare for two love-birds to end up together. Others are torn apart when they discover they can't have who they want. Her parents were one of those lucky few couples. They had been best friends since childhood and all Selene wanted was a loving relationship like theirs.

"I started hanging out with Sarva after I watched him at target practice after work about two months ago," confessed Selene. "I was standing by a tree alone when he approached me and we just started talking. At first it was little things. Then I noticed we have a lot in common…similar plans for our future."

"I can only imagine what plans he has for his future," her father interjected.

Selene glared at him. "What's that supposed to mean?"

"You might find out about Sarva one day," her father warned her. "Please, just be careful around him."

Selene sensed pain on her father's face and this confused her. She continued to glare at her father and then turned to look at her mother, who nodded her head in agreement.

"I can't believe you guys," Selene whined. "You are supposed to support me, especially on my birthday." Selene started to get frustrated. She felt her blood boil.

"We are," said both of her parents harmoniously. "We…"

Selene stopped them before they could continue. "No, you know damn well you aren't. I am of age now and I will make my own decisions."

"Young lady, do *not* use that fowl language around us," Mona said sternly. Her face was bright red. "Apologize to us immediately!" she yelled.

Selene noticed people around them stop their conversations about the show and look directly at them.

"I am not arguing with you any further," Selene told her parents, "I'm going home to take a nap. Wake me up when it's time for the Chosen Ceremony." She stomped her feet, leaving her parents behind.

She overheard her father say, "What has gotten into her? I hope she doesn't act like this from now on."

Like a whisper, she barely heard her mother reply, "Let's just see what tonight brings us. Hopefully a nice gentleman will be chosen for her. Praise the Five Ancients, hopefully it's anyone besides…"

Selene was too far away to hear her mother's exact words, but she knew her sentence ended with a single name. Sarva.

2. WAKAN

The red sands blew across the dunes as the intense sun set on the horizon. Several mountains and volcanoes could be seen in the distance. A small, light green lake gently flowed downstream. Crabbing nets and workbenches were laid out on the beach, next to a spaceship. People peeked out of their caves patiently waiting to begin their day.

The blazing sun physically hurt Wakan's eyes as he limped towards his cave's entrance. His three children were still asleep. The sun was setting and Dunestone would soon be bustling with life. Wakan was wearing his usual baggy tan shirt with a ruffled blue tie, and his brown worn out jeans, with several patches. They had been passed down to him over four generations. He watched as the sun finally fell below the dunes.

Wakan took his first few steps outside the cave. It was dark but the light of the stars kept everything visible. The soles of his feet burned on the piping hot, red sand. He heard the volcanoes churning lava miles away, beyond the expanse of mountain ranges. Wakan looked at the spaceship next to his cave. People had already stormed the beach with metallic pieces of the spaceship strewn across the sand. They were testing out their inventions made from the scraps.

One man, wearing a white lab coat flowing in the breeze, was standing next to a tank filled with the lake's green water. He was wearing thick glasses and had his hair slicked back. He was measuring out different liquids and chemicals in test tubes.

"Good morning, Rufus," said Wakan.

The man named Rufus set down his test tubes onto a workbench and gave Wakan a handshake. "Good morning, Wakan. How was your night?"

On Dunestone, the time when the sun was up was considered night and the time when the sun was away was considered day. The temperatures exceeded one hundred and forty degrees Fahrenheit when the sun was out, making outside mostly inhabitable.

Families lived in their own caves that had been naturally formed in the ground before they arrived. The sun remained in the sky for thirteen hours, allowing everyone time to spend with their family and rest. The sun stays hidden for fourteen hours, where the temperatures are sixty degrees less, around eighty degrees Fahrenheit. The people of Dunestone called each day "a change in the sun."

"My night wasn't too bad," answered Wakan. The children mostly rested the entire time, which was a blessing. You know how they can be."

Rufus chuckled. "Your children are something else. It seems every time I see them, they are exploring something new."

"Tell me about it." Wakan rubbed his left leg. "My leg has been acting up again. I think I'm getting too old."

"You and me both," Rufus said. "Time hasn't been kind to us. You should go get that checked out. I heard Memphis has a healing cream that works wonders." He picked up the test tube with the green lake water in it and dropped something small in. The water began to fizz.

"I appreciate your concern, Rufus," said Wakan. "As for now, I have some more important matters to attend to."

Rufus chuckled again. "You and your stories. Are you ever going to run out of them?"

"Never," said Wakan with a smirk and a wink. "I'll catch you later."

Rufus waved goodbye. "See you."

Wakan continued walking along the beach, greeting people and stopping occasionally when he spotted an invention that looked promising. He looked out into the vast green lake.

Two men and a woman cast a crabbing net and hauled it in. Wakan stepped closer to his friends. He counted only a few crabs in the net; not as many as he was hoping for.

"Hey, Copper," Wakan said to the man with red hair and a short beard. He was wearing large wader boots. "Hopefully today brings better luck."

"It's not looking that way," said Copper. He had a deep voice. "With this long drought, all the crabs are hiding deeper within the lake."

"That's unfortunate," said Wakan. He stroked his gray beard that grew down to his chest.

"Has anyone thought of something to help us out?" asked Copper.

"Not yet," said Wakan. "I'll let you know as soon as someone does. Trust me, you'll be the first crabber I come to."

Copper smiled and patted Wakan on his shoulder. "The clock is ticking, my friend." Copper grabbed on to the net with the two other people, Copper's brother, Silver, and good friend Sistine, and started walking towards the lake. "Take it easy!" He yelled back to Wakan as they cast out the crabbing net into the lake.

Wakan waved at them. "Good luck. You're gonna need it."

Wakan made his way up the hill and suddenly his leg started to spasm. Luckily, it went away rather quickly. This had become a common occurrence. He reached the top of the hill, slightly out of breath.

The village center was packed with people. There were trading markets, food halls, and art performers. Most of the people surrounded a bonfire at the very center. They were talking loudly as Wakan made his way through the crowd. He stood near the bonfire and the crowd quieted down. They sat down on the sand and waited for him to speak. One person yelled out his name.

Wakan stroked his blue tie dangling around his neck. Then, he stomped his good foot on the ground. "Good morning laddies and lassies," said Wakan with a mysterious voice. "Are you ready for today's story?"

The crowd cheered.

Wakan composed himself and slowly circled the bonfire so everyone could see and hear him.

"Long ago, the human beings lived together in harmony on a distant planet called Earth. Then, everything changed."

Wakan heard a woman in the audience speak to the woman sitting next to her. "I love this one."

This gave Wakan confidence. Wakan continued his story. "Tensions arose between our ancestors. The humans formed groups and started attacking each other. Each group thought they were superior to the other. The fighting turned into battles. The battles turned into wars. It became a global conflict."

Wakan gestured wildly to further entertain his audience. "The hate for one another became so immense the humans became blind. They could not see into the future of how this fighting would affect us. The death toll kept rising quickly. Finally, the governments around the world held a top secret conference and created a new separation law. The five main groups were sent to different corners of the world, limiting contact with each other to zero. This is when peace and harmony began again."

A man with an enormous pointy nose whispered excitedly to the little woman next to him, "You're not going to believe what happens next."

"But the peace didn't last very long. News spread that two asteroids were headed directly to Earth," Wakan continued. "The asteroids were going to hit the Earth on its two poles, perfectly on opposite sides. They had two and a half years to prepare themselves. For the first year, all five groups broke the separation law and invaded each other. This war would be the bloodiest in human history, known as the Pangaean War. Corpses piled up in the fields and the entire

Earth smelled of rotting flesh."

The crowd squirmed at the thought of this. The light from the bonfire danced and swayed across their uncomfortable faces.

"One day, the heavens opened up and down flew five distinct spirits," said Wakan. "Each group was visited by a different spirit and given an ultimatum: to stop their fighting and join together to build a giant spaceship. The groups, fearing their end, agreed. The spirits gave them blueprints to their spaceship to assist them. For the next year and a half, the five groups worked together to build the spaceship. It consisted of one central space station with five surrounding spaceships, one for each group. Tensions were still high. The occasional clash between warring groups was immediately stopped by one of the spirits. They finished with no time to spare. They painted *The Final Frontier* on the side just before blasting off."

Wakan pretended his arm was the spaceship as he raised it through the air to help his crowd visualize. He noticed a man *glaring* at him with a nasty look. Wakan paused for a few seconds and the man pulled a hood over his head and walked away, out of the village center. He found this quite strange. Who was this man and why had he never seen him before? He pushed this thought to the back of his mind as he continued with his story.

"On the morning of their second day in space, they felt a strong force move past their spaceship," continued Wakan. "It was one of the asteroids that was predicted to hit. Everyone watched out the bay windows as an asteroid hit Earth while another hit the other side. The Earth's crust broke apart and the planet split up into billions of pieces. The explosion reached them within seconds and people held on for dear life, hoping they built the spaceship strong enough. The five spirits revealed to the five groups that once they reach a certain spot in space, the five spaceships would be launched into different directions to planets they thought were habitable."

Some people shuddered at that.

"After thirteen years of space travel, we were beginning to run low on supplies," said Wakan. "Thankfully, the spirits announced our arrival to the spot where we would split. We would only need to travel eight months each to the individual planets. The spirits gathered in the space station and were put into cryosleep, waiting for our return. They sent us pre-recorded videos that would display in each spaceship every once in a while. Recently, we have received a video announcing the two-hundred year anniversary is coming up and we are to prepare to rejoin the others back on *The New Frontier*."

Wakan saw disbelief in the young faces in the crowd. They must have never seen him tell stories before.

Wakan was the designated storyteller and speaker in Dunestone. Many looked up to him. Growing up, he became fascinated by the stories left behind through word of mouth. He decided to memorize each one and started out telling the stories back to his parents. At the age of twenty-six, he began telling the hundreds of stories he had learned around a bonfire in the center of the village. As the years went by, the crowd grew as he perfected his craft. At this moment, Wakan was fifty-two years old and everyone regarded him as the best storyteller in their history. He would disagree with them as he thought his wife, Sapphire, was much better. She had been his inspiration.

"Our people set off on a new journey and ended up here, on Dunestone," said Wakan. "Daisy Powers took a leadership role and led us to the caves where we would set up our houses. Brent Hawk used his fisherman expertise from Earth and taught everyone how to catch crabs. Jason Boone created a large device that could filter water, making it was drinkable. Every single one of our people contributed to our survival here on Dunestone. I would now like to have a moment of silence for our ancestors who paved the way for us nearly two hundred years ago."

The people in the crowd lowered their heads. Others kneeled. People even held hands with those close to them. A couple young children couldn't understand and continued to make noise. A moment went by until Wakan began to speak again.

"I appreciate everyone who decided to hear me speak this morning. If anyone would like, I will be…"

A loud alarm interrupted his speech. It was coming from the spaceship. It echoed three loud beeps, paused for five seconds, and then repeated.

"Scratch that," said Wakan over the alarm. "It appears that we have a message from the five spirits." Wakan headed in the direction of the spaceship, limping through the crowd. "Duty calls."

Wakan left the village center and went down the hill onto the beach. He passed the scientists working on their inventions. Rufus seemed ecstatic. Maybe he had a breakthrough with whatever he was working on this morning.

Wakan passed his cave and on the other side was the spaceship. Wakan and his family had moved into the cave at the far end of the village since he took up the leadership position.

The red lights on the outer walls of the spaceship were blinking along with the beeps. Wakan trudged up the long ramp and entered the spaceship.

Right inside were the living quarters. The room was big enough to house four hundred passengers. Bunk beds and metal trunks filled the room. This is where the injured and sick were held. The doctors and nurses lived in the living quarters with their families. Wakan's middle child, Triss, was studying to become a nurse.

In the center of the room, there was an opening in the ceiling. This was for people to quickly traverse the spaceship when in zero gravity.

On the far side of the room was a stairway leading up to the crew deck. No one, not even Wakan, was allowed inside. There were knobs and buttons which should not be tampered with.

In the highest room, beyond the crew deck, was the observatory. At the top of the spaceship, there was a giant high pressure resistant glass window. Birthday parties and special occasions were held up in this room.

The stairs led down to the old recreation room and break room. It was now used for storage; they kept food, water, and important supplies there.

The storage room and the fuel room were on the bottom floor. In the storage room, they kept barrels of fuel and the rest of the supplies overflowing from the rec and break rooms. The fuel room was where the spaceship was refueled, but obviously no one has filled it since they arrived. They were told they would not need fuel for the journey back since a powerful magnet linked directly to *The New Frontier* would pull the spaceship.

Wakan walked to the right and pressed the big red button blinking on the wall. He looked at the video screen where a woman's face appeared. There were four people standing far enough behind her that they were in the shadows. Wakan couldn't make them out, always trying to guess who was who based on their silhouettes. Wakan had come to know this woman in front as one of the spirits from *The New Frontier*. He listened as the spirit recited her message.

"Greetings," she said. "It is I, Cersei, speaking. This message is for the leaders of this planet. It has come to our attention that two hundred years have gone by. It is almost time to join back together to reunite the human race."

There was a small crowd forming outside the spaceship door. Wakan focused on the video while people peeked inside, trying to get a glimpse of the video screen. Little children ran inside. Wakan smirked.

"In fifteen days, prepare to board the spaceship," Cersei said. "Your spaceship will not be big enough to carry all your people. I would recommend sending half your leaders and as many helpful and intelligent citizens on the first trip. The young, wounded, and medical professions should stay behind with a family member. The trip to *The New Frontier* should take approximately eight months. Shortly after, we will send the spaceship to bring the rest of your people.

For now, prepare for the journey. I wish you luck."
With a loud "fzzzt," the screen went blank.

This had been the latest in similar messages the spirits had sent. They have been told to prepare to leave for the last year. Each announcement only updated the timeframe.

Wakan was excited for this new adventure. He thought of all the new stories that would emerge and the new people he would be able to share those stories with.

The people of Dunestone already nominated him to be their leader. It was already decided his children would stay behind. The three of them wanted to hone their skills before they left and Wakan agreed.

Wakan's oldest child, Star, was eighteen years old. She was bright and hoped to be a scientist.

His middle child was Triss; she was clearly caring and compassionate at a very young age, which complemented her goal to become a nurse.

Zato was twelve years old and the youngest of the family. He liked playing with crabs. Wakan always found him wandering off, going on solo adventures on the dunes. He always made to sure keep an extra eye on his only son.

Wakan pressed the red button to stop the flashing lights. The video screen shut off and a wall closed down over it. Wakan picked up one of the children that was running around inside and brought her to the entrance.

"I'm sure you all are aware what is coming," said Wakan. "We have around fifteen changes of the sun to prepare. Good thing we already started putting stuff in storage."

Wakan saw the child's parents and set her gently into her mother's open arms. The father put his hand on her head and ruffled up her hair. She didn't like that. Wakan laughed with joy.

"The most important action we have to take now is to catch all the crab we can or else we will be short on food," he said. "The crabbers aren't catching much out there these days." He pointed at six people with multiple pockets on their pants. "Why don't you guys and girls grab a dozen nets and go see Copper down by the lake. He'll need all the help that he can get."

"Yessir," a man said. "Right away, sir."

Wakan pointed at three people dressed in white lab coats. "You guys should go help Rufus out. This morning, he was pouring some chemicals into the lake water. On my way to the spaceship, it looked like his idea was working. Whatever it was it looked promising. Hopefully he has something to help with our crab shortage."

The two women and one man wearing lab coats took off towards Rufus. Halfway there, he noticed one of the women wasn't with the other two people. Where had she gone?

The rest of the children in the spaceship ran outside past Wakan.

"Hey! Aren't you whippersnappers supposed to be stargazing?" he asked. "Where's Pai?"

Wakan started making his way down the ramp. The children followed him. One toddler was holding on to his pant leg. He must have been afraid. They reached the bottom and a short young woman wearing a pink dress ran to Wakan. Her hair was back in a bun. It was Pai.

"Wakan!" said Pai, out of breath. She stopped, bent over, and put her hands on her knees.

"Good morning, Pai," said Wakan. "It's good to see you. I was afraid I was going to have to take care of these little children all day." He laughed. Wakan noticed a worried look on Pai's face. "Hey, what's wrong?"

Pai caught her breath before she answered. "Your children," she said. "All three of them have suddenly become ill."

"Where are they?" The tone of Wakan's voice dramatically changed from jolly to frightened.

"They are in the gardens." Pai started running away from the lake. "Follow me. Hurry!"

Wakan ran as fast as his bad leg could take him, pushing his body's limit to get to his children. They ran down the beach and curved towards the caves. Across the way were the gardens that were used to grow vegetation. Wakan saw a small group of nurses huddled around the perimeter of the gardens. He could tell they were in shock. He ran up to them, out of breath and leg throbbing, and saw his children lying on the ground. He barely noticed his own pain. They each had a wet rag on their foreheads.

"What happened?" Wakan asked one of the nurses desperately. "What's wrong?"

A nurse by the name of Christine spoke up. "They just collapsed; all three of them at once." Christine was thin, taller than everyone there, wearing a white and red medical dress, which revealed her big chest. She had a jet black badge on her right shoulder, signifying her importance in the medical field. Many men in Dunestone fancied her.

"They were fine when I left this morning," said Wakan. "Any idea what caused this?"

"Early evidence suggests that they have been infected by the burstfly disease," said Christine. "They have puncture marks on their arms. It's strange though. There haven't been any burstfly sightings lately. I had my assistant interview the surrounding workers and none of them can even remotely tell us what has happened to your children."

Wakan was devastated. He knew what this meant. Burstflies were similar to the flies that once lived on Earth, except these ones thrived in hot temperatures. Burstflies infect the host through a puncture bite. The disease slowly dehydrates the body from the inside out. If caught early, symptoms could easily be treated. Symptoms include high fever, dehydration, loss of function in major organs, blindness, and potentially some other long-term effects. Serious cases can cause death in a matter of months. Since Wakan saw with his own eyes how bad his children were, he already knew this was serious.

"Memphis has already gone to check on our medicine supply to see if we have any rosena petals," said Christine optimistically. She looked behind her. "Here he comes now."

A tall man wearing a white hat with a red stripe and no top came barreling down to them. His white and red apron blew in the slight breeze. He greeted Wakan with a sympathetic nod.

"Doctor Memphis," Wakan greeted the man. He waited for him to say something in return. Wakan noticed Memphis' hands were empty. Wakan's face and shoulders dropped.

"I'm sorry, we are all out of rosena petals," said Memphis, "the most important ingredient needed for the cure."

Wakan knelt on the ground and held on to his three children.

"We must have used the last of our supply recently," said Memphis. "We haven't journeyed up Mount Crimson in a while. We stopped going about six months ago once we found out we were leaving the planet soon. The journey is just too dangerous. I am so sorry."

Wakan set his hand on Zato's forehead. It was burning up. Zato coughed. "Papa, it hurts," said Zato.

Wakan picked up his son. Memphis picked up Star and Christine picked up Triss. They made their way back to the spaceship. On their way, Wakan's friends Copper and Rufus saw Wakan struggling with his son and beginning to break down into tears. They joined up with them and helped carry his children up the ramp. They walked inside and set them down on separate bunk beds.

Wakan overheard Memphis explain to the nurses what was happening. They replaced the rags on their foreheads with fresh ones. Wakan put his face in his hands. He felt Copper and Rufus rub his back.

"It'll be alright," said Copper.

"If there's anything that we can do for you, just let us know," consoled Rufus.

Wakan wiped the tears off his cheeks with his forearm. He looked at his three children lying in bed; they looked helpless. This couldn't have come at a worse time. He was supposed to leave in a little over two weeks. He couldn't leave his children like this.

Wakan leaned his back against the wall. He was deep in thought when a plan came to him.

He tapped Copper and Rufus on their shoulders. "Would you two like to come with me to Mount Crimson?"

3. BRANT

On this planet, there was nothing but darkness. Hidden within the darkness, there was a large glass dome which housed the entire population of people living on the planet. This glass dome was named "The Eye" by its inhabitants simply because it acted as an eye of a hurricane. Everything on the inside was calm while the Outside presented dangerous conditions.

The sky was pitch black and the land lay barren. The infinite fog loomed around with high gusts of wind every so often. One couldn't see even a few feet in front of them without a source of light.

The elements weren't the only hazardous obstacles that laid in wait for a lost soul to venture out of "The Eye." The crying and suffering of small prey could be heard all around and yet not a sound could be heard from the predator cautiously stalking and ruthlessly attacking.

Many poor souls have been lost forever in the Outside. Including Brant's parents.

Brant just finished his schooling as he walked down the dimly lit street towards his house near the edge of the dome. He was wearing his signature neon red and black cloak with the hood covering his short dark hair and concealing his face in shadow. Around his neck was a silver necklace in the shape of two crossed daggers. The arms of his cloak were lazily torn off revealing his tattoos. On his right arm was a black dragon that slithered down the entire length of his arm with its boney face, sharp blue eyes, and a grisly grin that sat in the palm of his hand. On his left shoulder were two thick blue arrows pointing towards each other.

There was a group of men standing menacingly in Brant's path. "Here we go again," said Brant, rolling his eyes. If the men looked close enough, they would see a smirk under Brant's hood.

"Show off!" yelled the pot-bellied bald man with a gap between his two front teeth.

"Never show yourself in class again, ya hear?" the taller man with a green Mohawk and purple leather jacket filled with patches shouted threateningly. He tossed a metallic object at Brant, striking him on the chest, "Or else we'll run you out of town! Back to where you belong, in the Outside!"

The other gangly men wore frayed purple leather jackets with the letters GG sewn into the back. They filled in behind their leader with the patches. There were upwards of fifteen men but Brant didn't bother counting.

Brant spit in their direction. "Beat it, punks," he said and continued walking while the group of men stared on in disbelief. Brant knew these guys were all talk and no action. He had been dealing with them for as long as he could remember; the big popular boys picking on the small meek loner. Well, he wasn't so little anymore and he could defend himself…and they knew it.

"Yeah, go cry to your fake mommy and daddy, Brant," the purple leather jacket man spat.

Brant had never cried a day in his life, but Brant did make this punk cry once and not too long ago. His name was Arnold, but everyone called him Patches, and his pot-bellied second in command was Hanks.

Patches led a group of guerrillas called the Greasy Gangsters. They contributed nothing to society. They were a waste of time and space.

Brant left them behind as he heard them prey on their next victim. By the high-pitched tone of the boy's voice, it was most likely Sylvester.

Opening the door to his house, Brant stepped inside. His adoptive parents, Elijah and Phoebe, were nowhere to be seen. Brant bolted to his room. He treasured the time he got to spend alone.

He summersaulted across his bed and landed in front of his dresser. On top sat a green glowing cube with a hole on each side. Next to it were two blue instruments that looked similar to screwdrivers. Brant picked up a blue visor from his chair and put it on his face. This was one of Brant's few hobbies.

Using his Virtuvisor and DigiPens, Brant created digital images in a virtual reality zone and once he finished, the Projectocube could project his creations into the real world.

Brant created this technology by himself, spending many lonely nights alone at home. He firmly believed this tech could save people's lives if they ever had to spend long hours in the Outside.

Time flew by as Brant lay in his bed, tampering with his most recent creation. Looking up towards the ceiling, Brant used the DigiPens to draw, erase, copy, and paste into the virtual world. He swished and flicked the DigiPens around in the air as he created something that looked humanoid.

Brant was lost in thought as his adoptive parents barged into his room.

"Howdy, son," said Elijah. He was a handsome man who looked intelligent. He wore round glasses and a neon orange and black coat.

Startled, Brant reached for his Virtuvisor and his hand slipped, gouging his fingernail into his forehead, drawing a thin line of blood. Wincing in pain, Brant sat up and knocked the Virtuvisor off. It flew into the air, almost touching the ceiling and landed safely on the mattress.

"Didn't notice you two came back," said Brant angrily. He smeared his forehead leaving traces of blood on his cloak. "Doesn't hurt to knock."

Phoebe sat down on the mattress next to Brant, her long, red hair seemed redder above her neon yellow and black robe. She took out a rag, licked it, and proceeded to wipe the blood smear. Brant crossed his arms and turned his head away in protest like a child. "Brant, please let me do this," she said.

Brant loosened up. "It's not often you come into my room." He looked back and forth at Elijah and Phoebe, trying to read the expressions on their faces. "What is it you want?"

"We just came back from the town meeting," said Elijah. "There's something important that we need to tell you." He paused and looked at his wife.

"Well if it's so important just spit it out already," said Brant anxiously. He leaned in.

Brant felt Phoebe lightly touch his hand. "Brant," she said. "You remember that spaceship that was supposedly buried under "The Eye"?"

Brant nodded.

"Well, we will be excavating it soon," she said. "It is almost time to reunite with the Others in the Up Above."

Elijah picked up where his wife left off. "We were offered two seat tickets for the departure. Your mother and I had to fight hard for this third ticket." He showed Brant the bright gold tickets. "You wouldn't believe what we had to go through to get these."

Realizing where this conversation was going Brant spoke up. "Are you kidding me?" Brant unconsciously grabbed onto his silver necklace. "Why would you think I want to leave?"

"You don't exactly have any friends here," Elijah started under his breath.

"Oh, taking the high road I see," Phoebe fired back towards her husband.

Brant stood up off his bed and grabbed his gray handbag. He started packing up his tech.

"Look what you've done now," said Phoebe to Elijah. She put her hands over her open mouth.

Brant stomped over to the bedroom doorway. He turned around and faced them. His hand was still gripping his silver necklace. The daggers glistened. "How do we even know there is a spaceship under the city?" asked Brant. "Even if there is, it probably doesn't work. It has been centuries since it has seen the light."

"The plans have been set in place," said Phoebe. "We have to trust the ones that have come before us."

His father stood up. "Look, you obviously have nothing good going on here. It's time to move on and get a life."

Brant's eyes were as wide as hailstones and his nose flared like a mushroom on a rainy day. "Leave then!" he yelled. "Go on without me! I am doing just fine by myself, thank you very much. Just know that if you do leave, I hope to never see you two ever again."

With that, he stormed out of the house and he could hear both of them gasp and then possibly Phoebe smacking Elijah on his cheek.

Brant was back again in the dreary streets of "The Eye." He immediately took a left towards the northern side of the city. The last thing he wanted to do was to bump back into Patches and his Greasy Gangsters.

Brant scurried off the streets into the dark alleys and lifted his hood back over his head. He ventured this way nearly every day. For years, Elijah and Phoebe thought he came this way to visit with his match, Persephone, but to their disappointment, this was not the case. He was training to become a Master Assassin.

With high precision and extraordinary ease, Brant ducked underneath heating pipes and hurdled over sewer containers in the pure darkness. His heart was healthily beating as he made it to the other side of the alleyway back into the dimly lit streets.

People gathered around the corner to his right. Brant heard a loud woman demanding something. He slowly walked over to see what the commotion was about.

There was a circle of people protesting in the middle of the street. Most of them were women. They wore neon pink and black clothes.

Brant knew the woman who was leading the chant. It was Lizbeth, a girl he knew from schooling. They were friends when they were younger but they had parted ways right after puberty struck. She had blonde curly hair with a scar on her neck. Brant never found out how she got the scar. She just came into schooling one day showing it off with a low-cut neckline. She displayed her scar as if it were a trophy.

Brant stayed in the back of the crowd as he tried to interpret what Lizbeth was chanting.

"There's no way we're going to go to the Up Above!" she announced. "We have everything that we need right here! They simply can't make us dig up the spaceship! If they really want to, they can dig it up themselves!"

"Same old Lizbeth," said Brant. "Trying to get herself in trouble while bringing down everyone else who was foolish enough to follow her."

Brant walked away from the protest. He heard Lizebeth yell some more as he left the construction site. "The Pretty Pranksters won't stand for this!"

Brant laughed out loud. Lizbeth wasn't very good at coming up with names for her unlawful activity groups. Clearly she copied the name from the greasy gangsters. "The posse of privileged pretty pranksters," Brant snickered. "What a riot."

Brant came up to a house that looked spooky and unwelcoming and he knocked on the door three times. He waited on the doorstep until he heard creaking steps beyond the door. There was a pause and then he saw the doorknob turn. The door swung open half a foot and a wrinkly hand appeared from within the shadow of the room. The wrinkly hand greeted Brant.

"Welcome, Brant," an elderly voice came from the apparition now in front of him. "Come in," it said. Brant grabbed the hand and was led inside. The lights turned on by themselves. Brant never understood how the lights worked that way.

"Meditating in the dark again, Alexis?" Brant asked the female figure.

"Always," she said.

Alexis was wearing a maroon cloak just like Brant's, except it lacked a hood. Instead, she wore a black headband. She was an old and wrinkly woman with a buzz cut. She was currently training Brant to become an Assassin. Assassins acted as bodyguards for people who traveled into the Outside and protected anyone who was a paying customer. Alexis was one of the six Master Assassins in "The Eye" and was known for only training one apprentice at a time. She had taken Brant under her wing only two months ago but had never offered him an apprenticeship. He had been waiting ever since for her to announce it.

"I hope you brought everything I've asked for," said Alexis. She saw his handbag and pointed at him to see what else he was storing.

Brant moved his cloak to the side revealing two daggers attached to his hips.

"Great, then we must leave at once," she said. "Follow me. Quickly." She handed Brant a pouch.

Brant followed Alexis through her house and out the back door, which bypassed the glass dome and let out directly into the Outside.

Alexis took out an illuminating object from her pouch and held it in front of her. She took out a spool of yarn from the box that was attached to her waist and tied the end of it to the stake waiting just outside the door. She set the spool back inside the box and closed the lid.

Brant took out his Projectocube, which also lit the way with a dim green light. He attached it to his waist using a chain. He could see nothing but dense fog and darkness upon the forbidden barren landscape.

"What's our mission for today?" asked Brant, "Off to save another pathetic soul?"

Alexis sighed, "No, just an easy one for today. We will be hunting specterlings for their meat."

Brant looked through the endless fog. "Finally. Something I'm good at."

"We will sell the pelts to the black market and give the meat to the homeless," stated Alexis.

"Fine with me," said Brant. "All I want is to get some practice in and some time away from home."

They both walked quietly into the flat uncharted landscape. They stopped every once in a while to listen for their targets. They raised their lights in every direction. Every so often Alexis checked to see if the yarn was still unwinding behind her.

Dozens of minutes passed by and neither of them made a sound. Brant had to turn around every once in a while to see if Alexis was still following him.

Alexis halted and broke the silence. "Look," she whispered ever so gently. "I didn't bring you out here tonight just to hunt."

Brant rubbed his hands together with excitement. "Oh yeah? What else are we doing?"

"I have to discuss something important with you Brant," she replied. "The higher ups recognize what I do for the city and they want me to go to the Up Above with them."

Brant rolled his eyes.

"And I want you to come with me as my full-fledged apprentice," said Alexis. "I want to continue training you in the Up Above and beyond. You will be the first Assassin to travel to other worlds."

Brant stood there deep in thought. Finally, he could become her apprentice, but at what cost? That seemed ridiculous.

"So this is why you brought me out here? Isn't it?" he whispered. "So you could lay this news on me while we are surrounded by wolfwraiths. Great. Just great."

Brant continued to keep his voice low and soft even though he was annoyed. He faced Alexis and pointed at her threateningly. With his other hand he grasped his silver necklace.

"Well guess what?" he continued, "Elijah and Phoebe already offered me a ticket and I refused." Brant's voice rose a little higher. "I ain't going no matter what."

Suddenly, Brant heard light skittering footsteps across the way. He must have startled whatever it was. He stood completely still.

Alexis must have heard it too, because she looked in the same direction. She raised her finger over her mouth warning him to be quiet and to be still.

There were more tiny footsteps coming from the same direction. Alexis pointed at Brant to signal for him to get ready.

Brant reached down for his daggers, brought them up, and stood in a fighting stance. Both dimmed their illuminating objects and hid in the foreboding fog for the prey to come to them. The skittering moved closer and closer. Brant readied himself for the attack.

Small ugly creatures as big as a winter hare appeared underneath him. He raised his daggers and slashed down at them. Blood squirted everywhere as the specterlings squealed out in agony. Brant aimed for their throats like a tiger pouncing on its prey. With precision, he killed every last one. Alexis did the same.

"Very well done," she said, with her daggers already cleaned off and sheathed. "Let's go back before the wolfwraiths get here."

"I never want to see one of those," said Brant.

Alexis bent down to grab the five specterling corpses and stuffed them in her pouch. She took out the spool from the box and pulled the yarn upwards.

Brant wiped off his daggers and picked up the three bloodied hides. "Too easy," Brant frowned. "I was planning on testing out my new projections tonight."

"There will come a time," whispered Alexis as she started walking and winding up the spool. "Now, hurry up."

Brant followed Alexis. Alexis followed the yarn. There was silence once again. Neither of them wanted to bring up the conversation about the spaceship. On the walk they heard some disturbing noises coming from ahead of them but neither wanted to find out what it was.

It was a long walk until Brant bumped into Alexis. She was untying the yarn from the stake. They were back at Alexis' house. Brant set his Projectocube into his handbag.

Alexis opened the door for Brant. He walked into the kitchen and unloaded his kills onto the table. She set her pouch on the counter. "I'll cut them up tonight and pay you tomorrow."

Brant paced around the room with his head hung low. He was deep in thought.

"We can talk about it later," said Alexis.

Brant gave her a dirty look.

Suddenly, Brant heard shouts in the city. "Damn those pretty pranksters!" he threw his hands up in the air. "They just formed today and are already getting on my nerves!"

"The who?" asked Alexis.

The ground shook as they both heard explosions in the west side of the city. They looked at each other and ran outside. Flames and screams filled the streets. There was panic all around. "What the darkzone is going on out here?" said Brant.

An out-of-breath passerby heard and answered Brant. "Somehow a pack of rabid wolfwraiths broke into the city and started attacking!"

Brant took off his hood and started to run towards the chaos with Alexis. Brant grabbed her hand and snuck her off into the alleyway. "Are you crazy?" asked Alexis, "It's pitch black in there."

"Just listen to what I say." Brant made his way through the alleyway while dragging Alexis behind him. He spoke instructional cues to alert her of the upcoming obstacles. "Duck. Over. Duck. Duck. Side.

Duck. Over." They came out the other end and the street smelled of burning flesh and death. There was no one to be seen. Hopefully everyone got out alive.

Brant and Alexis ran up towards his house. There was rubble displayed across the front. A giant hole was on the side of the house. "Mother! Father!" he yelled. This was the first time he called them that in years. "Mother! Father!" Brant gasped for breath as the smell started to get to him. He put his arm over his nose.

Alexis put her hands on his tattooed shoulders and turned him around. "Let's get out of here," she said. "We need to get help and put out the fires."

"No," said Brant. "I need to find them."

Brant moved the rubble that was blocking the door to his house. The massive stone must have weighed over three hundred pounds. He opened the door while Alexis hung back.

Brant entered the house and immediately saw blood spattered across the walls. He put his hands over his open mouth. He looked around in horror. He stepped into the kitchen and overturned the upside down table that was thrown in the middle of the room. He pushed it aside as he slowly crept towards the back of his house. There were deep scrapes in the floor. He peeked into his bedroom, which was untouched.

A ghastly odor was coming from his adoptive parents' bedroom. He stood there, unmoving. Brant was afraid to look. He grasped his silver necklace, took the deepest breath that he could muster, and stepped into the room.

Brant immediately regretted his decision. The scene was worse than he could have ever imagined.

His father's body lay upside down with his head on the ground and legs on the bed. His torso was ripped wide open. Puncture marks could be seen all over the body, which could have only come from the fangs and claws of a wolfwraith. His entrails had been dragged across the floor.

As for his mother, she was ripped to pieces. Or at least that's what Brant thought was spread across the ground. Parts of her scalp with blonde locks were hanging off a chair.

Brant could do nothing but stare. Instead of sorrow, he felt anger. Instead of fear, he felt rage. He wanted revenge.

Brant knelt on the ground. He spotted something within the gruesomeness. He picked up the object that was covered in blood and was warm to the touch. It was a toe, but not the toe of a human. It was furry and had a long claw, several inches long. The claw of a creature that haunted his nightmares; A wolfwraith. Brant deduced that it was hacked off by a sharp object judging by the edge of the bone and gristle. Someone must have put up a fight.

Looking over the room, he spotted something. Over by Elijah's body, was the golden ticket that was to be given to him. Next to that was a kitchen knife.

As Brant knelt in his home, he felt a hand touch his shoulder, which brought him back to his senses.

"Brant, it's time to go," said Alexis. There was pain and sadness in her voice. This is ultimately what broke Brant.

As they headed out of the house, Brant threw up remembering everything single detail of the horror he just witnessed.

"I'll go," he said.

"What do you mean?" asked Alexis.

"I'll train with you as your apprentice and travel with you on the spaceship," he said. "I will become the best assassin this, and any other planet, has ever seen. I can promise you that."

Surprised, almost as if this came out of nowhere, Alexis asked, "Where did all of this come from?"

Brant thought long and hard. Even though he got into heated arguments with his adoptive parents nearly every day, he still loved them and they were really the only people in his life besides Alexis. His match, Persephone, probably wouldn't even notice if he were to disappear. Brant held on to his silver necklace.

"It was their last wish for me to be aboard that spaceship," said Brant. "I was against it, but now I have to live out their wish for me."

4. JAYLIN

The blue waves of the vast ocean churned and crashed into the sides of the floating city. Hydronia was home to the entire population of humans on this planet. Around the city, people geared with aqua-breathers and force spears swam deep into the oceans to provide food for each other. Whistles were chirping during the many competitions being held outside. Inside the city, buildings spanned upwards touching the clouds.

Everywhere, builders made their personal touches on Hydronia. Every so often, tsunamis and hurricanes destroyed parts of Hydronia, which was why the builders of the city were always busy.

Seven moons spanned across the sky; each one was named after one of their Gods. Just below the surface of the middle of the city was a spaceship.

The Annie Edison School sat in the middle of Hydronia and was where all the eighteen year olds were currently gathered. The school was holding a ceremony in the auditorium lead by Principal Jeffery Edison, a tall good looking man.

Twins, Jaylin and Akeer, were sitting next to each other as they intently listened to the announcement in progress.

On the big screen played a pre-recording of one of the Sleepers aboard *The New Frontier*, discussing the reunion of the separated humans.

The man speaking was currently in cryosleep along with the other four Sleepers. He was the only Sleeper Jaylin had ever seen. The man never revealed his name. The voices of the other Sleepers could only be heard off screen.

To Jaylin's knowledge, each planet had their own Sleeper that gave each colony their own set of instructions on how to prepare for the coming meeting. She had no clue what the other planets were doing or even if they were still alive.

Nearly two hundred years had passed since their last contact with the others. Literally anything could have happened within that time. The Sleeper announced this would be his last video and would welcome them as they arrived on *The New Frontier*.

The video ended as Principal Edison continued the presentation. "So it is with my greatest pleasure to announce, this afternoon we will know who our Ambassadors are!" exclaimed Principal Edison. "As you know, only two people from each age and gender will be chosen. Sort of like that old guy and his ark, but instead of animals, it's humans from each age."

Jaylin shook her head in embarrassment at this reference.

"These two Ambassadors will be a few of the lucky individuals that will travel into space on the two hundredth anniversary of our arrival," he continued.

"We have narrowed down our candidates to just a handful of students. We are locked in a heated debate but be assured we will have our two Student Ambassadors chosen by tonight. This last minute competition we are about to hold will help us make our decisions faster. We have decided to test two important criteria for the competition. An exam to measure intelligence and a race to test endurance. The exam portion will begin shortly. Again, I thank you all for gathering here this morning. Please grab some grub and refreshments on your way out. That is all, have a swell day!"

Jaylin Robins had long braided hair, dimples, and an athletic build. She remained in her chair as her classmates behind her stood up, ready to leave the auditorium. Her twin brother, Akeer, had short hair with a lanky build and glasses. He held his face in his hands and sighed.

Jaylin noticed his disappointment and put her arm around him. "Looks like I'll be going on that space trip, little brother," said Jaylin. "Everyone knows I will crush the competition in the endurance test. The teachers must have already chosen me, they just want to see me win again. I just have to nail the exam and my dreams will finally come true. No more boring days in school. No more fighting for my own food. Student Ambassador, here I come."

Akeer took his face out of his hands, looked at her, and bowed to her as if she were royalty.

"Too bad the second test didn't showcase building skills," said Jaylin. "You would have won that one. Oh wait, you don't care about becoming the Student Ambassador anyways." Jaylin laughed at her brother.

Akeer spoke up, "I just can't wait for you to leave Hydronia, Jaylin, so I don't have to come in second anymore."

Jaylin was the first born. She had been better than Akeer at nearly everything that was tested in school. Jaylin was better than most people. Akeer was nearly as smart as her and nearly as strong as her but no one seemed to notice. Jaylin created a big shadow and Akeer had always been in it since he was born. He had only even been recognized as a great builder, the one thing he had been better at than Jaylin. Akeer had no doubt his sister would become their groups Student Ambassador.

"Second?" asked Jaylin. "You're lucky to place in the middle of the pack, little brother. Keep dreaming and maybe when you look up at the moons, I'll be up there and I'll grant you your wish." Jaylin lightly hit Akeer on his shoulder. "Chin up," she said. "Get your head in the game. We have a quiz to take."

The twins stood up from their seats and headed outside the auditorium. "I wonder who the male Student Ambassador from our class will be?" Jaylin said insensitively to Akeer.

They passed a tall strong teenager and Jaylin eyed him. "Will it be Thomas?"

Another strong teenager walked passed them and brushed shoulders with Akeer. He flinched and said, "My bets are on Julius."

"Does it matter?" said Akeer. "They all pale in comparison to you," he said sarcastically.

"Do my ears deceive me?" asked a grinning Jaylin. "Was that a complement?"

Akeer gave her a dirty look.

They made it to the academic section of the Annie Edison School and continued their way to their assigned classroom. Since the teachers organized the rooms by last name, Jaylin and Akeer were headed to the same room.

"I wonder what they will be quizzing us on," wondered Akeer.

"Who knows," said Jaylin. "Probably anything and everything. Ah, here it is. Room 628."

Akeer opened the door for Jaylin. She walked in and noticed all the desks were full except for two in the back. She hated sitting in the back. She walked past Charlize sitting in the front desk and gave her the evil eye. Charlize looked intimidated.

Akeer strolled in after Jaylin and quickly sat down in the back.

The teacher was in the front of the room. Jaylin recognized her as Ms. Britta from force spear training. Ms. Britta waved at Jaylin and smiled. They had been good friends. Jaylin sat down next to her brother.

"Since we have everyone in the room, I'll start passing out the exam," said Ms. Britta. She weaved up and down the rows of desks, handing out the quiz. One was set in front of Jaylin.

There were four pieces of paper stapled together, with questions on both sides. As she turned it over to the back, she could smell the fresh ink from the printing press in the school's basement. The last question had the number 80 on it.

"How long do we have?" asked Jaylin.

"The endurance test takes place in two hours so anytime before that unless you want to fail," said Ms. Britta. "Now, no more talking. The exam has begun.

Keep your eyes on your own paper. If I catch anyone cheating you will automatically fail. I personally will withdraw your entry as a Student Ambassador. Plus you will have to swim twenty-five laps with me. Comprende?"

Some of the students groaned. "I could easily do twenty-five laps," Jaylin whispered to herself. She flipped the packet back to the front and read the first question.

Question 1: How many days have gone by since we landed on Hydronia?

Jaylin wrote down *365 x 200*. 365 for days in a year and 200 for how many years have gone by. She made sure to carry over the 1 both times and came up with the answer *73,000*. Then, Jaylin subtracted 14 from her answer because the spaceship will be leaving in two weeks. The final answer Jaylin jotted down was *72,986*. 72,986 hours? 72,986 seconds? 72,986 armored fish? She made sure to write down *days* after her answer or else she knew it would have been marked wrong.

Easy math to start off. So far so good.

Question 24: What is the main producer of oxygen on Hydronia?

Jaylin remembered being fascinated by this topic. She wrote down, *The moon phytoplankton absorb energy from the moons and gain nutrients from the ocean to undergo a process called moonlight photosynthesis. Since there are seven moons revolving around our planet, the moons reflect the sun's light on to the moon phytoplankton so they can thrive under these harsh conditions. There are large pools around Hydronia with phytoplankton living in them.*

Question 36: List the names of our Gods and Goddesses and their titles.

So far, Jaylin thought this was the easiest question. Everyone on Hydronia knew who the Gods were. The Magnificent Seven. These Gods were the first settlers on Hydronia. They were mortal, but by paving the path of their new civilization, they were immortalized. Historians created mythology surrounding them and named the seven moons after them.

She began to write her answer. *1. Stonewall – God of Destruction.* Stonewall Jones had a major part in protecting the lives of the early settlers. He built structures to counter the terrifying tsunamis that once devastated their relocated home.

2. Jersey – God of Life. During the brutal first years, Jersey saved countless lives from drowning. He invented an apparatus that would inflate if it detected danger. Jersey became a life guardian.

3. Namorita – Goddess of Water. Namorita was the greatest swimmer. She taught her people how to swim and how to hold their breath to maximize their lung capacity.

4. Miss Ippi – Goddess of Fish. Zelda Ippi, also known as Miss Ippi but pronounced as one word, was a tour de force when it came to catching the native armored fish.

5. Franz – God of Waves. Franz was known for the supports he built all around Hydronia to keep the city level and sturdy as the waves flowed underneath the floating city.

6. Jezebel – Goddess of the Deep. Jezebel invented the aqua-breathers that allow us to swim deep underwater.

7. Argo – God of the Moons. Argo's real name was Jason but he preferred to be called Argo after the Greek mythological tale of Jason and the Argonauts. Argo studied the seven moons and recorded their paths and their effects on Hydronia.

The Magnificent Seven were important historical figures on Hydronia and were everyone's role models.

Question 57: Two side supports and a middle support hold up a fourth support above them. What is the middle support called?

This was a builder question. Jaylin took a peek at Akeer, risking her neck, but she had been good friends with Ms. Britta and didn't believe she would squeal on her. She saw her brother was only on the third page. She thought hard to remember what the answer was.

Jaylin tilted her head down and looked at the ground. The girl in front of her was tapping her foot up and down fast. It annoyed her to no end. Jaylin lightly kicked the girl's heel to make her stop, which she immediately did. Jaylin tapped her pencil on her desk until it dawned on her. She laughed and wrote *Achilles Heel* and moved on to the next question.

Question 63: How do force spears work?

Jaylin used force spears all the time. She wrote down, *Pressure builds up in the shaft of the spear and as you jab it forward, the pressure is released in a short burst of force which is powerful and sharp enough to pierce through the armor of a fish.*

At this point, Jaylin noticed people starting to finish. How did they complete it so fast? Do they just not care and sped through it? They better not distract her.

Eventually, Jaylin was on the last question.

Chapter 4

*Question 80: What would you do if you became
Student Ambassador?*

This wasn't really a question. She didn't have to
think hard about it as she had thought about what she
would do on a daily basis. She wrote, *If I were to
become Student Ambassador, I would do everything to
the best of my ability.* Jaylin figured the teachers
would understand what she meant by this. She was
good at everything, so why go into detail about
everything she would do?

Jaylin stood up and turned her quiz in to Ms.
Britta. She gave her a thumbs up and left Room 628.
She headed towards the gymnasium where the
endurance test was going to be held in twenty
minutes. Akeer better hurry up or else he would miss
the big event.

The gymnasium was a wide building with a low
ceiling. The tallest of people would have to slightly
bend to fit inside. There were thousands of holes in
the floor leading directly into the waters below.

Aqua-breathers sat on the table at the entrance.
Jaylin grabbed one and proceeded to search for an
unoccupied watering hole.

In the center of the gymnasium, Jaylin found a
group of empty watering holes and dipped her legs in.
The water was room temperature. She tuned out the
crowd by meditating and focused on her breathing.

Ten minutes later, Jaylin was still working on her
breathing when Akeer startled her.

"May I sit here?" asked Akeer.

Jaylin opened her right eye and peered at her
brother. "Do as you must," said Jaylin. She closed her
eyes again.

"That quiz was pretty hard," Akeer stated. "It covered almost every topic. There's no real way to study for it unless you have a photographic memory."

Jaylin smirked with her eyes still closed.

"What are you smiling at?" asked Akeer. "How do you think you did?"

"Let's just put it this way," said Jaylin. "If I don't win this endurance test, which is extremely unlikely considering who I am going up against, I still think I have a pretty great chance at becoming the Student Ambassador." With that she opened her eyes and was ready to race.

Six students filed into the watering holes next to Jaylin and Akeer. They whispered to each other and pointed at Jaylin.

The shortest girl spoke up. "Aren't you Jaylin, the best in our class?"

"I am in fact this Jaylin you speak of," responded Jaylin with a smug grin.

The fat boy took his turn speaking. "I have been waiting a long time to finally meet you, Jaylin!" he said loudly.

The blonde girl had her chance. "Can we have your autograph please?"

"I don't see why not," responded Jaylin.

All six students handed them an object for her to sign. A towel, a hammer, two sandals, and two books.

"You're giving out autographs now?" chuckled Akeer.

"And who are you supposed to be?" said the boy with the beard. "Her wimpy bodyguard?"

"I happen to be Jaylin's brother," said Akeer. "Her *twin* brother."

The group of six took a step back and stared at him. "You could have fooled us," they all said at once.

"It was nice to finally meet our star Student Ambassador," said the girl with the hammer as all six prepared themselves for the endurance test.

Akeer rolled his eyes. "They are already calling you the Student Ambassador."

"You better get used to it," said Jaylin. "My time has finally arrived."

"When will this end?" he wondered out loud. "Just please leave Hydronia already so I can live in peace."

It was time to start the endurance test. The teacher closest to Jaylin and Akeer explained to them the rules of the race. "The main objective is to dive deep into the ocean to find buoys that are either hidden on the ocean's floor or strung up in the currents. Your goal is to collect a total of five buoys. You must bring up one at a time and under no circumstances are you to interfere with or harm a fellow student. There will be guards stationed at each outpost to observe. On the sound of the scalehorn, you may begin. Good luck."

Jaylin put on her aqua-breather and jumped in the watering hole. She dipped her head underwater three times. Carbon dioxide bubbles came out of the end of the aqua-breather. She was ready to begin. Jaylin rested her hands on the edge of the watering hole and waited for the scalehorn to sound.

This was it, her moment to shine. Time to put her best skill to the test. For what felt like an eternity, Jaylin rest her lips on the aqua-breather and took one final breath.

The scalehorn blew and Jaylin dove into the ocean. Her eyes already adjusted to the water. She could see all around her in the calm, clear water as she dove as fast as she could with no one in front of her. She was diving deeper and faster than everyone else. Not even the referees had made it down yet.

Jaylin looked around her for the buoys. She saw some of them tied up within the currents. They were bright orange.

As she dove, she formulated a plan. She would gather five buoys on the ocean floor and hide them in a good hiding spot. Jaylin chose the buoys on the ocean floor because she knew they were going to be easier to gather than the ones trapped in the current. She also knew most of the other contestants weren't strong enough to make it all the way to the ocean floor because some student's bodies hadn't been formed to properly deal with the vast amount of pressure. She could hide her buoys out of reach from nearly everyone.

In a matter of minutes, Jaylin rested her feet on the ocean floor, stirring up the silt. She looked up and saw most of the students were going for the buoys in the currents. She had been right. Now she had time to execute her plan.

The first buoy she found was wedged underneath a boulder. She used her body weight and momentum to knock the boulder a few inches to gather her first buoy. As she gathered each buoy, she tied it to her belt.

The second buoy was hidden inside a narrow crevice. She had to squeeze through a tight opening to obtain it.

The third was in the middle of the armored fish nesting grounds. These types of fish lay semi-hard eggs with shells that were made out of a material that allowed water and oxygen to pass through. The buoy was in a nest with other eggs. Jaylin had to knock away a couple armored fish with her arms, receiving a few scratches to get it.

The fourth buoy she found was peeking out under a ledge. She wouldn't have seen it if she hadn't come from the nests.

The fifth and final buoy was hidden at the bottom of a crater.

Jaylin quickly swam back to the place where she found the fourth buoy under the ledge. She figured this was a perfect hiding spot for the buoys because it was hard to see underneath. All she had to do was swim towards the nests and look at the crater to find them again. Easy, she would finish the endurance test in no time.

Jaylin grabbed her first buoy and swam up towards the watering holes. She found her designated hole and popped out. Jaylin placed her buoy on the surface. She noticed some had already gathered two but she wasn't worried.

Jaylin dove back down and passed others. She headed towards the armored fish nesting grounds. Once there, she turned towards the crater and saw her remaining buoys. She gathered her second buoy and swam back up to deliver it. She saw the students who had gathered two buoys still only had two. No one she could see had three yet. *Perfect*!

Jaylin followed the same steps for the third and fourth buoy. As she brought the fourth one up, she noticed Akeer had gathered three while others still had two. "I got this one in the bag," she said out loud.

Jaylin dove back in to gather her fifth and final buoy. On the way down to the ocean floor, she noticed someone swimming towards her. As the student swam closer, Jaylin noticed it was Akeer. Had he been also searching on the ocean floor? She swam to the nesting grounds only to discover her last buoy missing. "That damn brother of mine," she cursed.

Jaylin swam as fast as she could to Akeer. She caught up to him in no time and bumped into him with her shoulder. She pushed him away and wrestled with him to gain possession of the buoy. She wound her fist back to punch him when a strong hand prevented her from doing so. Jaylin turned around to see two referees. They both shook their heads and pried her off of Akeer.

That's not fair. That was my buoy and he stole it from me. Why does he get to keep it? He didn't work hard for it, I did!

The guards held on to her as Akeer swam the rest of the way to the surface. That buoy was Akeer's fourth one. She better hurry and find her last before anyone else does, especially her brother.

Swimming back and forth on the ocean floor, Jaylin attempted to find her last buoy. She wasn't having any luck and started to get frustrated.

Suddenly, it dawned on her. The buoys in the currents were much closer to the surface than the ones on the ocean floor and she could spot them easier. She was a strong swimmer too so all she needed to do was to find one and she would be finished with the endurance test. She looked above and all around.

To the south, she spotted a buoy strung up in the strongest part of the current. No one had dared to venture there yet.

Jaylin quickly swam underneath the strong current until she was directly underneath the buoy. She cut the rope with her belt and played tug of war with the current to obtain the buoy. She won and tied it to her belt.

Jaylin passed everyone up to the surface and pulled herself out of the water. She slammed her last buoy down on the ground. A teacher marked down her time. She took off her aqua-breather and laid down, her chest rising and falling fast. Her heart rate was up.

Jaylin looked over and saw Akeer's four buoys. She noticed that she was the first one to finish.

After a minute or two, Akeer emerged from his watering hole with his fifth buoy. Jaylin was surprised and impressed by her brother. Not even a tenth of the students had finished yet and her brother had made it before top swimmers and divers.

Jaylin sat up and patted Akeer on his back, noticing that he was out of breath. "Congrats little brother," said Jaylin. "Although that move was totally illegal."

"The rules hadn't mentioned stealing other's buoys," said Akeer. "It was tempting since you hid them all in one spot."

"You were watching me the entire time, weren't you?" asked Jaylin.

Akeer nodded.

"You slippery solefin," said Jaylin.

The same teacher who discussed the rules with them announced once they were finished with the endurance test, they were allowed to head back into the auditorium. Once all eighteen year olds finished, Principal Edison would announce the final Student Ambassadors after a deliberation.

Jaylin and Akeer turned in their aqua-breathers at the door and walked outside. The tall skyscrapers covered with scaffolding surrounded them on all sides. One blue moon was out; Jezebel.

"It will be nice to finally graduate and become a full time builder," said Akeer.

"You will accomplish great things, little brother," said Jaylin. "I look forward to coming back and seeing what you have built for our people."

Akeer looked up at the buildings and stared off into the future.

Jaylin and Akeer made it inside the auditorium and sat down. An older age group had just left.

They discussed the exam and endurance test with the group surrounding them until the auditorium became full. Jaylin wasn't surprised when most of her classmates thought they were hard. When the speakers came on, everyone quieted down and turned to the front. Principal Edison walked out on stage and held up a microphone. He cleared his throat.

"After a long debate," started Principal Edison, "...calculating the exam and endurance test results, the teachers and I have found two standouts from your class who have excelled in all criteria."

Jaylin leaned forward.

"These two students who I am about to name will exceed our expectations as leaders and will have a great impact on the future of humanity."

Jaylin couldn't sit still.

"Without further ado," boomed Principal Edison, "our two Student Ambassadors are…"

Jaylin began to stand up as Principal Edison announced the two names.

5. CEREMONY

There was a knock on the worn wooden door, waking Selene up. She rolled over across her right side to face it. There was white makeup smeared on her pillow. She forgot to wash it off before she took her hour-long nap. She could see torchlight shining underneath the door and a dark shadow in the center. Selene noticed there were two feet on the other side. She was expecting her parents but the shadow was only the size of one person.

"Be right there," she called. Selene propped herself up on her leaf bed and slipped on her moccasins. She was still wearing her clothes from the show. While strolling to the door, the mysterious guest knocked again. Selene undid the lock and opened the door. It eerily creaked open, revealing a disheveled young man. His dark eyes gleamed from the candles.

"Sarva!" she exclaimed. "What are you doing here so late? Aren't you supposed to be out on a hunt?" Selene allowed Sarva to step inside and she closed the door behind him.

"I just came from there," he said. Sarva held up a fresh kill. Blood dripped on the floor. "Have you been sleeping this entire time? Aren't you supposed to be at your Chosen Ceremony?"

"Oh gosh," Selene gasped. "What time is it?" She paced back and forth, confused on what to do. "Mom and dad must have gone back to work after the show." Both Mona and Aqib were on the Council, a high-ranking group of citizens in line to become the next Elders. She dusted off a chair for Sarva to sit down and stepped inside the changing closet. She pulled the leaf curtain shut. "We have to hurry."

"I'm positive everyone will be late tonight, with the all the ruckus about leaving the planet," said Sarva. "They will probably have us start working double shifts to provide for our journey to the space station."

Selene came out of the changing closet. She scoffed and rolled her eyes. This meant less time for acting. Selene definitely was not a fan of mining. It was boring.

Sarva was sitting on the chair as Selene sat on her bed. She brushed the leaves to knead out the wrinkles.

"I really don't care about anything we learned tonight," said Sarva. "About leaving and everything." He looked at her with his big dark eyes, expecting a reply.

Selene leaned forward on her bed towards Sarva. She was visibly confused but interested in what he had to say. "How can you not care?" she asked. "This is going to affect our entire lives. We will be leaving home and traveling into space. We will have to meet the Jambos and Sirfates." These were nasty terms a few people in Quaketown had given to the other people from Earth. A chill went up her spine and into her neck at the thought of this. "Once up there, we can find a more suitable home for all of us; for the entire human race."

None of this seemed to faze Sarva. He just sat there with the same look he always had on his face.

"Everyone can leave for all I care," he said. "I want to stay here."

Selene was taken aback, "Huh?"

"I want to stay here," replied Sarva, "…with you."

She froze to her mattress.

"I love you, Selene," Sarva confessed. "I have always loved you. I want to stay here on this planet with *you* and *only you*."

Selene had so many questions, but she couldn't physically speak. Her heart was pounding out of her chest, trying to escape her body. She was confused for a few moments until one emotion overwhelmed her; love. His response made her fall deeper in love with him. It reminded Selene of all the old fairy tales of princesses and true love her mother told her when she was little. Maybe this is what she was feeling; true love.

Selene looked under the wooden door to make sure the shadows of her parents weren't lurking around, listening and waiting to barge in and interrupt. Selene beckoned to Sarva. He slowly got up from the chair, walked to Selene's bed, and sat down.

So many things were racing through her head. *What was it that the princesses did in those fairy tales? Well, there was usually a kiss.* Should she kiss him? She had never kissed anyone before. Was there a different way to kiss a lover than kissing her parents? There has to be. She thought of how her parents kissed each other.

"Sarva," Selene shyly whispered.

"Yes?" he said.

"Can…" Selene hesitated. "Um, may I kiss you?" She blushed.

Sarva smiled. "Of course. Where do you want to kiss me?"

"Where do I want to kiss you?" She wasn't expecting that question so she repeated it back to him. "Where *should* I kiss you?"

"Neck up," he said with a devilish grin.

She figured this must be his neck, cheek, or lips. Maybe even his forehead. But princesses don't kiss anywhere except on the lips. Selene leaned towards Sarva and prepared to kiss him. She closed her eyes and pouted her lips.

"Neck up."

Selene paused. Sarva's voice started to sound more feminine. Her bed suddenly began to shake.

Selene slowly opened her eyes as she felt a soft hand on her shoulder. She groaned.

"Wake up." It was her mother.

As her eyes struggled to focus on her mother, she became disappointed. It was all just a dream. Selene felt startled and dazed.

Mona stared at her with emerald eyes. "Wake up, honey. You must get ready for the ceremony or else you'll be late."

Selene shot up out of bed. She was trying to make sense of reality as she tried to grasp on to her fleeting dream. She attempted to tell what time it was. The door was open and she could barely see light bouncing off from the mirrors, which reflected the moonlight and starlight into the cave. It had to be getting close to midnight.

"We better not be late tonight," said Selene.

Aqib was in the corner of the room with his hand on his forehead. He looked exhausted. He must have had a long talk with Mr. Bradham and the rest of the Council.

Aqib was the peacemaker of Quaketown. The Council trusted him to make the right decisions regarding important topics. By the look on his face, he must have agreed to pack up and move on from this planet. Most did not share his opinion.

Only Mr. Bradham was aware of these events prior to the show. He had been the only one who had access to the spaceship and had received instructions from Jonathan. Mr. Bradham then wrote the script and kept it sealed away in the underground vaults.

Aqib finally took his hand away from his face and looked at Selene. "Don't worry, I packed everything for you," said her father. "Your mother insisted we let you sleep until it was time to go." He stood up, grabbed the bag, and handed it to her. "Come on."

"Thank you so much, Dad!" said Selene lovingly. "You really didn't have to do that for me. I'm a big girl now," she half joked.

"You will always be my little girl, Selene," he said. It seemed like her parents had forgotten the argument they had earlier. Mona was waiting by the door. As they headed out, she handed them each a walking stick, which were tucked underneath the window.

On the way, they walked by Kelly pacing outside her cavehome. Kelly had her blonde hair tied in a high ponytail, which meant she was hard at work problem-solving. Selene thought it best to leave her alone. When Kelly gets like this, she's hard to talk to. She gets so focused on the task at hand, their conversation comes second. She just stares off into space until you leave her alone or when she discovers a solution.

However, this time Kelly spotted them. Selene saw her shake, literally snapping back to reality.

"Selene!" exclaimed Kelly. Selene turned around. "I'm *so* sorry I can't make it tonight." Kelly's beauty radiated off of her. Selene had always been jealous of her pretty looks.

Aqib and Mona headed to the Quaketown exit, which was just across from the stage seating nearby. "Make it quick," Mona said to them without turning around.

Selene hugged her best friend. "Oh, you don't have to be sorry, Kelly. I planned on having a small ceremony..." Selene knew Kelly could tell she was lying by the tone of her voice. In fact, Selene had told Kelly many times before explaining how she wanted her Chosen Ceremony to be the biggest ceremony of their lifetime. Ever since they were little, they revealed to each other their secret crushes and their hopes and dreams. They stopped hugging and stood face to face about a foot apart.

Kelly put both her hands on Selene's cheeks. "You know I wouldn't miss this for anything in the world," said Kelly. "But tonight, Akira gave me an important, time-sensitive task that I just can't spare any time."

Akira the Adventurer was an Elder and the main leader in Quaketown. He had discovered many safe havens out in the jungle for those who were lost. Once a week, a rescue group traveled to each safe haven to check if anyone was lost and to make sure it remained uncompromised. He had accomplished so many things on this planet in his sixty-seven years.

"Akira wants me to figure out the best way to clear the rubble and vines away from the ship so it won't get damaged during the excavation," said Kelly. "On top of that, he also wants me to find a fast and efficient way to make the land level underneath the ship. This will take up a lot of my time but I'm confident I can figure it out."

Selene could tell this meant a lot to her best friend, especially orders coming directly from Akira. He must see a lot of potential in her. "I'm so proud of you," Selene blurted out. "Bestie," she added.

Selene heard her mother yell out for her. She hugged Kelly one more time. Both had tears welling up in their eyes. "I love you," they said to each other.

"Best of luck tonight, grandma," Kelly joked with Selene, but then became more serious. "I hope you get hooked up with someone very special."

Selene laughed and waved goodbye. "Thanks!" She ran towards her parents, who were still waiting for her at the Quaketown exit. As she ran, she suddenly realized something; Kelly's twenty-first birthday will be months after they leave the planet. What will the Elders do about Chosen Ceremonies? Everything in their lives was about to change in just two months time. It will come fast. At least Kelly had her mind occupied for the time being.

Selene greeted her parents at the exit. Her mother and father introduced the two guards escorting them to the ceremony that was on top of Ceremony Hill in the jungle. Torches lighting the yellow brick trail scared off most of the predators but the guards were there as an extra precaution.

Selene recognized one of the guards. Lem was their neighbor and the eldest son of Gratius. She could barely see his eyes under the shadow of his big brow and bulbous forehead. He was intimidating.

The other guard she had never seen before. Lee was tall and handsome. He looked at her and gave her a toothy smile that made her blush. Lee had dimples that made her think for a split second that it would be okay if the Elders picked him to be her Chosen.

Lem carried a bow and had a quiver slung around his back. He also had a short blade attached to his side. Lee carried a longer blade, the size of his arm, and a rectangular shaped piece of wood as a shield. This was supposedly strong enough to withstand a scabite attack. Selene had never seen a real scabite before but she was familiar with the smell of the burning scabite bodies the hunters killed at night.

Lem and Lee led Selene across the yellow brick trail into the jungle. Her parents followed close behind.

She had only been out this far into the jungle a handful of times, mostly for weddings. The one other time, she was barely a teenager. Selene ventured out with Kelly and a boy they both had a crush on. She didn't remember the boy's name because Kelly won the right to kiss him after stepping farther into the jungle than she had. Selene had been too afraid.

The boy died a year later in the mines. An older man was using a faulty melter and wasn't aware he was pointing it directly at the boy. Selene wasn't there but she heard his bone-curdling scream all the way from the stage seating area, which is where the schooling was. She still heard that same scream very clearly in her nightmares.

They were walking around a bend when Selene heard a strange noise off in the distance; a yodel. She feared the scabites. The only one she knew who didn't was Sarva. Her mind began to play tricks on her but Lee sweetly reassured her the noises were just the guests at the ceremony. That must mean they were getting close. She could see Ceremony Hill. Torches illuminated the vegetation surrounding it. This must be their destination. The torches were spaced closer to each other the farther they walked up the Hill.

Finally, they reached the top. A giant circle was dug out of the ground with a stone wall surrounding its interior edges. A high altar sat at the far back within the circle. It was decorated with pink and orange flowers and wreathes.

The guards halted at the end of the path. Selene carefully stepped down the stone stairs into the circle. She saw familiar faces there, including Mr. Bradham, Gratius, her aunt and uncle, Luci and Tobe, and some of her friends, including Farhad. Her mother joined her sister, who looked just like her except her eyes were a different shade of green. Tobe had a big gut. Selene's father stood with them.

Akira stood at the opposite end of the circle with Sarva and eleven other boys. Sarva was there! He was good at keeping secrets from her.

Selene recognized all of the boys from the cavehomes but she never introduced herself to any of them. She wished she knew at least one of them personally because if they didn't pick Sarva for her, she would feel more comfortable with someone she had already knew. But unfortunately, that was not the case.

Akira was adding the finishing touches as Selene prepared herself for the ceremony; it was about to begin. She looked out into the crowd of happy faces and saw her parents, who smiled at her. This calmed her down.

Lem and Lee stood on each side of the altar. They simultaneously began banging on the drums at exactly midnight. Selene stood in the center of the ceremonial circle as the five Elders gathered in front of her.

Akira the Adventurer, was the leader of the Elders. He was old and wore a red robe. His jaw was freshly shaved. He was the first in line.

Fortuna the Healer, wore a blue robe. She was like a grandmother to Selene. Despite her old age, she only had a few wrinkles on her face. She had taken care of the young children of Quaketown for three full decades. Fortuna had established a small hospital for the sick and injured.

Elias the Great, a middle aged man with glasses, a receding hairline, and a green robe, chronicled the history of Quaketown. He established The Elias Library of Quaketown.

Christopherson the Cave Troll was a wide muscular man with a giant swirly mustache. He wore a big brown robe. Christopherson gave himself the title of Cave Troll just for laughs. He was the leader of the mining force. Selene had met him many times before in the mines, where he brought positive energy and motivation into the workplace. She could always tell where he was because of his jolly laugh.

Hazel the Valiant was the youngest of the Elders at only thirty-eight. She wore a purple robe. Selene couldn't help but notice the deep scar that extended from her nose, up across her left eye, and through her eyebrow. Hazel was the leader of the hunters. She was deadly accurate with a bow and could outrun everyone in Quaketown.

The drums fell silent. Only the crackle of the fire could be heard. "Happy twenty-first, Selene!" Akira congratulated her with a nod. The crowd cheered and clapped their hands. Akira raised his hands to the crowd, twisting his torso side to side. "Welcome to Selene's Chosen Ceremony," he said. "Selene, have you brought The Gift?"

The Gift was a piece of Selontris. Elias had explained this moon rock must have fallen to the planet's surface a long time ago because miners dug it up deep underneath the planet's crust. It had no use for them, but it looked cool and shiny, so one woman decided to give it to her newly appointed Chosen and the tradition had stuck ever since.

Selene reached into her bag and pulled out the moon rock. "I have," Selene responded as she gave Akira The Gift.

"Tonight we are gathered here to unite a daughter and a son of Quaketown," he said. "It is *my honor* to bring two young souls together since I have known and watched Selene grow and mature into a bright young woman."

Selene heard her mother start to weep. She blew her nose.

"Whomever is chosen tonight to be your Chosen will surely be lucky because you have a bright future ahead of you." Akira paused and then went off script. "We will be leaving this planet soon to search for a better home and I hope you and your Chosen's bonds will only strengthen on this journey."

Today had been the craziest day Selene had experienced in her entire life. She performed for the first time in front of an audience. She was about to potentially be paired with the man of her dreams. She had learned that in two months they will be leaving the planet and joining up with the other human beings to start a new way of life. Selene thought that after leaving, it was possible that she would never have to mine again, never get to follow her dreams as an actress, and maybe never even get to spend time with her new prince.

"Thank you," said Selene.

Akira nodded his head, signaling the next step of the ceremony.

Recognizing their cue, her mother and father started walking towards Selene, each carrying a rope that was one foot in length. They handed both ropes to her and walked back to their spot within the group.

Akira looked into the stars and recited, "The Five Ancients look down on us tonight. May they bless Selene, her Chosen, and both of their families." Akira walked up a flight of stairs and stood on top of the altar. He raised The Gift up high towards the sky.

"Ancients!" he exclaimed. "Selene has come here tonight on a very special date. Please choose a man for her that will compliment her and love her until the end of time. We await your answer."

The young men walked single file to the front of the stone wall. All light was snuffed out. A minute went by and the anticipation was bothering Selene. She didn't know if she was shaking from her nerves or excitement. Maybe both?

It was called the Chosen Ceremony for one reason; they believed the ancients chose the perfect man for the young woman by shining the most amount moonlight on him during the period of time just after midnight where Selontris hides behind the evergreens on the horizon.

Selontris began to rise over the horizon behind Selene. The rays of moonlight shone through the overgrowth of the jungle and onto her suitors. They all glistened and sparkled like the special effects on the translucent screen during a show. Selene saw three of the men were completely in the shadow. She forgot to pay attention to which position Sarva was in line before the torches went out and now she wasn't able to tell which silhouette he was. She prayed he wasn't one of the ones hidden in shadow. Six men had a few speckles of moonlight streaming across their bodies while the other two were fully lit up except for their faces. She silently prayed harder to the Five Ancients.

Eventually, the moonlight moved above the overgrowth and she could see everyone once again. Lem and Lee re-lit the torches. Akira stepped down from the altar. The Elders gathered nearby and discussed their interpretation of which man had the greatest amount of light on them. It felt like hours had passed as she awaited their decision.

Selene stood there as the men walked single file to the side. She turned around and saw her father give her two thumbs up as her mother put her arms around his neck.

Only a minute passed as the Elders returned to where the rest of the crowd was and Akira joined with Selene at the center to give her their decision.

"Selene," he said, "The Five Ancients have spoken. Will the future husband of Selene please join us over here?" Akira went over to the men and stood on the far left. He started walking slowly past each man as he teased them. If Akira moved on to the next man, they were to sit down immediately.

Sarva was towards the end of the line. One by one, Akira passed the men and patted them on their shoulders to comfort them.

The next in line was a short man with dyed green hair. The green hair made Selene remember this man. A couple years ago, there was a green-haired kid who was picking on a younger boy because he was overweight. The green-haired boy pushed him down and spit in his face. This must be that same kid all grown up. Selene breathed a sigh of relief as she watched Akira pass him.

Akira passed two more men and was finally standing in front of Sarva.

Selene pleaded with the Five Ancients. "Please please please," she begged. "Please choose Sarva."

Akira lingered on Sarva longer than any other man. She hoped this was a good sign. Eventually, Akira continued to the next in line.

Selene was devastated. Sarva sat down, slumped over, and crossed his arms. She felt like doing the same but she didn't want to embarrass her parents or disrespect the ceremony.

Akira extended his hand to the next man in line and led him to Selene. On his way over, Selene studied her Chosen. He was plain looking with wavy black hair and a goofy smile. He was average height and slightly overweight. If Selene had passed him in the cavehomes, she probably wouldn't even have noticed him. He was certainly no Prince Charming.

"The Five Ancients have chosen Miles for you, Selene," said Akira.

Selene hesitated, but gave Akira the two ropes. Selene stood facing Miles and she held his hands. She forced herself to make eye contact with him. Akira wrapped the ropes around their hands.

"I give you both the chains of marriage," said Akira. "Let the chains symbolize the two of you becoming one."

Akira then unwrapped the ropes and tied the ends of them together. He put one rope around Selene's wrist and then the other around Miles' wrist. Akira gave Selene her moonstone back.

Selene recited the traditional words. "With The Gift, I give to you my past, present, and future." She handed Miles the moonstone. The crowd celebrated.

"Now the Elders have something to give you for the start of your new journey together," said Akira.

Fortuna stepped up first. She set a plant that was used for healing on the ground in front of them. "Here is my medicinal herb to cure all illness. May your relationship be healthy." She stepped back.

Hazel was the next to step forward. She placed a blade on the ground. "Here is my sword to ward off all evil. May your relationship be strong." She stepped back.

Like a true gentleman, Christopherson waited for Hazel to step back before stepping forward. He gently placed a jar of moonbugs on the ground. Moonbugs were little bugs that light up at night. "Here is my light to shine through all darkness." He bowed. "May your relationship be safe." He stepped back.

Elias stepped forward. He placed a journal on the ground. It was thick. "Here is my knowledge to battle all ignorance. May your relationship be bright." He stepped back.

Finally Akira returned to Selene and Miles. He placed a compass on the ground. For some odd reason the compass pointed directly towards Sarva. "Here is my direction to conquer all obstacles. May your relationship be peaceful."

All the Elders stepped forward and clapped. "Congratulations you two on this momentous day!" beamed Akira.

"Congratulations," the Elders said in unison.

The audience cheered.

Aqib and Mona ran over to Selene and gave her a big hug. She gave them a fake smile.

Lem and Lee lit up the torches. They were lining everyone up for the journey back to Quaketown.

Selene looked all over for Sarva but he had already disappeared. The two guards must not have noticed or cared that he was missing. She looked down at her new boyfriend. Her first boyfriend. Her cheeks began to hurt from faking her smile.

"Hi," said Miles. He extended his hand and awaited a handshake.

Selene felt awkward. She just wanted to wake up from this dreadful nightmare and be paired with Sarva so she could spend the rest of her life with him instead of this joke of a Chosen. She wondered when her prince in shining armor was going to rescue her so she could finally have her happy ending.

6. THE FELLOWSHIP

"Would you two like to come with me to Mount Crimson?" asked Wakan a second time.

Copper and Rufus looked at him as if he were crazy.

Memphis overheard Wakan and walked towards him, shaking his hands back and forth like it was a problem.

"Are you crazy?" asked Memphis, incredulously. "First of all, it's a very dangerous journey. Second, I heard our spaceship leaves in fifteen changes of the sun. It takes seven changes of the sun to journey to the top of Mount Crimson and another seven back."

"Well then we better head out right away," said Wakan.

"Wakan," Memphis said gently as he stopped him from leaving by putting his hand on his chest. "Don't do this."

"I have to." Wakan's voice cracked. He broke free of Memphis' grasp. His hands clenched into fists. "My children are dying."

"He does have a point," chimed in Copper.

Memphis sighed. "You are supposed to lead us to our new home. We can't do it without you. If you go to Mount Crimson and don't come back, we will all be lost."

Wakan looked at the three men standing before him. Two of them were good friends. He then peeked over at his three children. Wakan knew what he had to do, what was more important.

"I'll go with him," Rufus said to Memphis. He looked at Copper. "What about you?"

Copper hesitated, then nodded.

Rufus then turned to Memphis. "I will make sure Wakan gets back in time. If we stray from the path at any point, I'll make everyone turn back."

Memphis hesitated and looked at each of the men.

Wakan knew Memphis had given up on trying to stop them just by looking at his face. Memphis tried to stall them to think of a plan. He nervously walked around in circles with his hand scratching his chin.

"We're going whether you like it or not," said Wakan. He sat down on a bed to rest his feet.

"I can send someone else to go retrieve the rosena petals," said Memphis. "Someone who isn't going off planet. That way you…"

Wakan angrily interrupted him. "They are *my* children. *I* have to do this. It has to be *me*."

Wakan didn't want anyone else to go because he knew whoever went wouldn't have the motivation to go all the way. He was afraid without him, they would turn around without getting the rosena petals just so they wouldn't miss the spaceship departure. He would be devastated if he had to leave Star, Triss, and Zato behind without knowing they had the cure.

Memphis sighed again. "Fine," he said. "But please take Christine with you. She knows what the rosena looks like." Memphis flipped through his files on his desk. "I may have a few others in mind to escort you on your journey."

Copper and Rufus were both elated. Wakan was pleased and wanted to head out right away. He stood up from the bed and limped over to his children on the bunk beds.

"Stay here. I'll be right back," said Memphis. "I promise." He left the spaceship to retrieve his people for the journey.

Wakan knelt down next to Zato first. "How are you feeling, Z?" He looked like a miniature and chubby version of himself, without the beard and wrinkles.

"I'm hot," said Zato.

Wakan patted him on his head. "I'm going out to find some medicine, okay? I need you to stay brave for your sisters. Can you do that?"

"Mhm," said Zato.

"That's my little man." Wakan gently straightened his son's messy hair and kissed his forehead.

Next, Wakan went to Triss. She seemed to be the most sick of the three. He held her hand. "How are you doing, honey?"

Triss coughed hard. Her throat sounded dry. Triss had her mother's blue eyes and his wide nose.

"Want some water?" he asked her.

She nodded.

Wakan got up, went over to a table, and grabbed three containers of water. He went back to Zato and handed him some water. He went back to Triss and helped hold the container for her as he poured some into her mouth. She licked her lips and gave a weak smile. "I love you, honey." He gave her a kiss on the forehead. "I'll be back."

Finally, Wakan knelt down by Star. His eldest daughter looked so much like her mother, Sapphire. Same eyes, shimmering blue. Same hair, jet black. Same smile, one that always cheered him up. He stared at her, missing his wife.

Star seemed to be a little better than she was when he found her in the gardens. He handed her the container of water. "Your sister doesn't look too well."

"She was the first to collapse," said Star. "I was going to get help but I suddenly felt steaming hot and then I passed out too."

"Do you have any idea how it happened?" asked Wakan. "Did you see the burstflies? Didn't you hear them coming?"

Star stared at the ceiling. "I can't remember anything that happened before passing out; just that I was playing in the gardens with Triss and Zato. Next thing I remember, Memphis was carrying me in his arms to the spaceship."

Wakan scratched his temple. There has to be a reasonable explanation as to how this happened, but what?

"Star, listen," said Wakan. "I am headed to Mount Crimson with some people to get you and your siblings ingredients for the cure."

"That's way too dangerous!" Star exclaimed. She started to cry, overwhelmed with emotion. "We need you here to keep us company."

"Hey, don't worry about me," said Wakan. "I can do it. Even if I'm not fast enough to make it back before the spaceship leaves, at least I will have the rosena petals to treat you three myself."

Star hugged him and gave him a kiss on his cheek. "We will miss you," she said. "Good luck. I love you, poppa."

"I love you too, Star." Wakan got off the ground and stepped back. "I love you all," Wakan said to his children. He waved goodbye to them and he headed towards the front of the spaceship.

Copper and Rufus were there waiting for him.

"Thanks for doing this for me," said Wakan as he patted them on their backs.

"That's what friends are for," said Copper.

Memphis walked up the ramp and stepped inside with two men.

"This is Bruce," introduced Memphis.

The short man had a sharp nose and pointed eyebrows. Bruce had some bags slung over his shoulder. Wakan shook his hand.

"Bruce has been to Mount Crimson many times. He knows the mountain terrain like the back of his hand."

Memphis introduced the man standing next to Bruce. "Tank is our expert survivalist. He will be able to keep you safe on your journey." Tank was a big round muscular man with a shaved head and strong jaw.

Wakan noticed that Tank's eyes were twitching constantly. He gave Tank a handshake, his hand crushed from his strength.

Tank grunted.

Memphis then waved down Christine. "Sorry, Christine, but I would like you to go to Mount Crimson with these guys. I trust you can differentiate between the flowers on top of the mountain and find the rosena, right?

"Of course," she said. "I understand completely." She noticed Tank and averted her eyes. "I would do the same if they were my children."

"Okay, let's grab everything we need and head out," said Bruce as he clapped his hands together.

The group started out the door but Memphis ordered Christine and Tank to meet with him inside before they left.

"Alright folks," said Bruce. Wakan figured he was in his late thirties, considering how the wrinkles on his forehead were visible but less defined than his own.

Wakan watched Bruce as he counted out on his fingers how many people were going on the journey. He was lightly counting to himself. He stopped at five until he remembered that Christine was also going and added another finger. "I'm going to gather food and supplies that should last us for fifteen changes of the sun."

"*Should* or *will*?" said Copper.

The group chuckled together.

"Ok," said Bruce. "*Will* last fifteen changes of the sun."

"Good," said Copper. "I wasn't planning on dying before I got a chance to travel into space."

Bruce gave Copper a dirty look. "Let's meet at the hill west of Wakan's cave in one half hour. Gather anything that you think we might need. It's going to be a long journey so we need to be prepared."

Tank came out of the spaceship and met up with them.

Bruce handed out a bag to everyone in the group and gave Wakan two bags, one for him and one to hold on for Christine. "See you soon."

Bruce pulled Tank aside. Wakan overhead Bruce say, "What in the inhospitable blazing dunes was that about?" before Bruce headed south to the village center. Tank rejoined the group.

Rufus spoke up first. "I will pack some of my inventions. I know a couple will come in handy." He laughed as he straightened his glasses. "I cannot wait to try them!" He headed east to his workbench.

Wakan wasn't thinking about what to bring. He couldn't help but think about his sick children. If he could, he would trade places with them. Wakan looked over the mountainous terrain and feared what lied ahead.

Tank's twitching eyes kept on distracting Wakan. He wondered what the cause of it was. Was it a neurological disorder or some sort of disease?

Tank spoke up. His voice was gravelly. "Tank go get supply for journey. Rope. Lots o' rope."

Wakan was taken back by surprise. He could tell everyone else was as well. He had never heard anyone speak like that before. Wakan thought this guy could be trouble and wondered why Memphis recruited him.

Tank took off south towards the village center to buy supplies.

"Wow," said Copper. "What have I gotten myself into? To the inhospitable blazing dunes if I know what to bring. Maybe some hiking sticks? A good pair of shoes?"

"Come on," said Wakan. "This is serious." He knew Copper was just trying to lighten up the mood.

Copper patted Wakan on his shoulder. His big smile was slowly receding. "Sorry."

A few moments passed and Wakan saw an idea pop into Copper's head. "Hey, I know what," said Copper. "I'll go get some crab nets and equipment. You never know if we will come across a water bed on the way, where some crabs will be hiding." Copper headed southeast towards the beach to gather his equipment.

Wakan figured this was the obvious thing for Copper to bring. He was happy that his friend came up with the idea on his own. He would have been embarrassed if the other people were around and had come up with the idea for him.

Five minutes had passed until Christine exited the spaceship and headed down the ramp. Wakan noticed she was carrying a book. He handed her the bag.

"Sorry for the wait," she apologized. "I had to get my medical journal from the nurse's office." She looked around. "Where is everyone?"

"They went to gather supplies for our journey," said Wakan. "Can you think of anything else that we might need?"

Christine thought about it. "No, I'm sure the boys have thought of everything. There's only six of us. We don't need much for a journey that takes fifteen changes of the sun."

"Come walk with me then," said Wakan. "We are meeting them by the hill over there." He pointed west. They began walking together. "So, what's your story, Christine?"

"Well, where to begin." Christine blushed. "When I was very young, I loved picking flowers. My parents were both crabbers but they could see that I cared about people at a young age. They figured I had the potential to be a nurse or even a doctor one day. They had me apprentice under Ms. Loretta for a few years, starting on my sixteenth birthday and then I started training under Memphis after that. A decade later and I'm one of the top healers in Dunestone."

"Impressive," said Wakan.

"Everyone loves your stories," she said. "What motivates you to get up there and speak every day?"

"The way I see it, stories are magical," said Wakan with a sparkle in his eyes. "There are the tall tales, the myths, the legends, the true accounts, and the notes left behind; all of these make up our history. I think it is important to remind all of us about our past and present to prepare us for the future."

"Huh, I never really thought about it that way," said Christine.

Wakan continued. "I also do it for the reactions on peoples faces fill me with joy. All those big smiles from comedies, the frightened faces from adventures, and the tears from inspirational stories keep bringing me back every day because I know I have moved them in ways they can't find anywhere else."

Wakan had to stop. He leaned up against the rock and rubbed his bad leg. Christine stopped with him. They were almost to the hill.

Wakan became overwhelmed with emotion. There was one thing on his mind. His eyes became moist. He knew Christine caught on to his change in mood because she looked at him with sad eyes.

"My wife," said Wakan. He took a deep breath. "My wife was a great storyteller; the best. When Star was just a baby, Sapphire would cradle her every night before bed and tell her wonderful stories. After a while, I joined in. Then when Triss and Zato were born, we made story time a daily habit. The kids loved it. They would jump around and act out the scenes."

At the thought of this, Wakan broke down in tears. Christine hugged him and rubbed his back. Wakan took a finger and rubbed the tears off his cheeks. "Thank you," said Wakan. Christine let go.

Christine walked with Wakan to the meeting point and waited for the others.

Pai was walking by when she spotted them.

"Hello," said Pai, running up to them. "I heard what's going on. Take me with you."

"Pai…" hesitated Wakan.

"Hold on," said Pai. "Before you come up with any bright ideas to prevent me from going, I have already spoken to that mysterious man, Bruce. He's packing enough supplies for one more person. I ran right home and gathered some of my stuff. I'm prepared and ready to help out."

This brought a smile to Wakan's face. "Ok. Thanks Pai. Good to have you with us." He would have said, "No," but her enthusiasm changed his mind. It was always good to have someone like Pai, when facing a dangerous path.

They waited ten minutes until everyone finally showed up. All their packs were full; they were all ready to head out. Wakan, Christine, Copper, Rufus, Bruce, Tank, and Pai started up the hill, as the journey to the top of Mount Crimson was about to begin.

The sun was still hiding and wouldn't show itself for another seven hours. Stars twinkled in the sky.

The group quietly walked up the hill. It was easy to tell who was comfortable around whom.

Occasionally, Wakan sparked up a conversation with Rufus and Copper. They never discussed the purpose of their journey or anything to do about their family.

Wakan had noticed Bruce and Tank had side conversations by themselves. He couldn't quite hear what they were saying because they were pretty far up in front.

Bruce was eating dunelope, a small orange watery fruit with an outer shell, and spitting out the seeds on the ground.

Staying closely behind Wakan were the two women. Although Christine and Pai weren't well acquainted, they made the effort to get to know each other. Christine mostly talked about how she became a nurse. To Christine's surprise, Pai told her that she also wanted to be a nurse. She was specifically interested in the healing forces of the universe. Pai was still young enough to train to become one.

On their first resting break, Wakan looked up at the stars shining brightly in the night sky as he laid on the ground to rest his sore leg. They had already made it a good distance away from Dunestone. Wakan noticed a difference in the sky. The space seemed darker and the stars and planets shined brighter than usual. He wondered why that was.

"What a spectacle to see," Wakan blurted out in pure awe. "Look at them." He pointed upwards.

Everyone except for Tank looked up at the night sky. Tank was too busy going to the bathroom around a cluster of stalagmites.

Rufus was so amazed he stood up slowly, almost as if the heavens lifted him up towards the cosmos. "Wow," said Rufus.

"You never get used to it," said Bruce. "I always look forward to traveling out of Dunestone because of this amazing sight. I never look up at the night sky back in the village anymore because it's not nearly as beautiful."

"That cluster of stars right there," said Christine, pointing at several stars clustered together.

"Those ones right there?" asked Copper. "Those ones that make a big round oval?"

"Yeah," said Christine. "It looks like my brother."

They all laughed. Bruce had an annoying laugh.

Tank coughed and grunted loudly, still going to the bathroom.

Pai took out a journal that was hidden away in her bag. She looked back and forth from her journal and the cluster of stars they were laughing at. "That's actually the Aureole constellation."

Wakan looked at her quizzically.

"I have all the known constellations here in my journal," said Pai.

Wakan was impressed. "How many are there?"

"Only twenty-one so far," said Pai. "About a hundred years ago we only had four or five but since then, we have broken them up into even smaller constellations to help us navigate better."

Pai pointed towards a group of stars that was human shaped. It was hanging in the sky right above Dunestone. "That constellation right there is called The Venerable Spirit. It's named after the spirit that helped us get here. If you look closer at its left hand, you might be able to see a blue glow, which is another planet."

Wakan gazed up at The Venerable Spirit. He hoped one day soon he would get to meet the spirits of old. He couldn't see the blue planet. He must have lost some of his sight due to old age.

Tank appeared from behind the stalagmites. He scratched his butt. "Don't come."

"On that note, let's continue on," said Bruce.

The group was still busy looking up at the stars.

"I would hurry," said Bruce." Tank is notorious for his horrendous smelling…"

Everyone understood what he was getting at and leapt up simultaneously.

"Shit!" yelled Copper, grabbing his belongings and ran away from the group. "Get me outta here!"

Everyone grabbed their bags off the ground and quickly continued up the hill.

There was about an hour before the sun peeked its scorching rays over the horizon. Some light appeared in the sky behind them and Wakan could slightly feel a slight change in temperature.

"Listen up people," Bruce spoke up. "A little farther up this hill is the base of Mount Midoriyama. There is a tunnel there, so we can continue to travel upwards. From here to the peak of Mount Crimson, there are strategically placed tunnels to travel during the night while the sun is up. About halfway up on the outside of Mount Midoriyama, a small flamerod bridge leads to Mount Crimson. We need to cross it during the day, while the sun is away. No exceptions."

"Is there no other way across?" asked Wakan.

"Well, there is," said Bruce.

Wakan detected hesitation in his voice.

"But it's treacherous." Bruce's face had a hint of horror on it. "Why do you ask?"

"If we make it to the bridge when the sun is out, we don't have enough time to delay," said Wakan.

"No. No, that would be a bad idea," said Bruce. "You see, there is a steep jagged drop off on the near side of the cliff. If you were lucky enough to get down safely there is a steep slope leading up to Mount Crimson, which leads right near the opposite end of the flamerod bridge. But judging by your bum leg, Wakan, that will be impossible."

Wakan took offense to that.

"You'd be surprised what Wakan can do," said Copper defensively.

Tank stepped in between Bruce and Copper, his hand on Copper's chest.

"No need to get hostile," said Bruce, sneering. "We don't have time for a hostile environment. The clock is ticking, as the saying goes."

"Let's just get to the tunnel before the sun comes up," said Wakan. "Some of us deserve a rest."

Bruce continued to lead the group up the hill.

Wakan slowly started to sweat as the temperature gradually increased.

Wakan could finally see the tunnel. There was a mound of dirt at the base of the mountain. There was an opening about two humans tall and there were lights flickering on the inside.

Rufus must have spotted the tunnel too because he started running towards it. Wakan didn't realize why everyone started running until they all left him in the dust. He realized they weren't running because they longed for a long rest. Wakan noticed a long shadow forming and extending out in front of him. The sun!

"Run, Wakan!" yelled Rufus. "Run!"

The sun's tip had already passed the horizon. Wakan quickly forgot about the pain in his leg as he ran for his life. He ran as fast as he could towards the tunnel entrance. Wakan was the only one out in the open. He was closing in on the tunnel. The group were waving at him, encouraging him to run faster.

Wakan was fifty feet away when he felt the back of his neck start to burn and blister.

Copper left the safety of the tunnel and ran to help him out. Copper ducked and grabbed onto Wakan's arm and quickly pulled him inside.

Wakan and Copper gasped for breath. "Everything is ok," Wakan whispered to himself. "Everything's fine."

Wakan turned to Copper and hugged him. "Thank you, my friend."

Copper smiled back at him.

Bruce was leaning against the wall. "We definitely deserve this break," he said. "I will wake everyone up in seven hours. Get a good days rest."

7. ALONE

It was dark in the two-story building. Too dark for the eyes to adjust. There was an inescapable musky, rotten, and decaying smell. On the second floor, Brant crawled along the ground and held his breath. He heard gentle footsteps coming from the stack of barrels just shy of ten feet away. Suddenly, they stopped. Brant turned his ear towards the sound. He put his hands on the ground and lifted himself up to his feet. He was crouched now as he grabbed for his daggers. Brant put his hood up, slithered his way around the wall, and made his way to the barrels. He made sure he didn't brush up against them.

Noise was Brant's worst enemy. He froze as he heard the footsteps begin again. They were headed back to the spot he had just left. Brant took a step towards the entity as it took a step so his footsteps would be disguised. Brant must have been taking larger steps because he was already closing in on to the entity. He prepared himself and raised his daggers. Brant lunged at the victim as he slashed its throat with one dagger and stabbed its back with the other.

"What the fuck?" the victim whispered. It was a man's voice.

"Shhh," hushed Brant. "You know the rules."

Brant felt the man roll over onto his back. "Brant, is that you?" asked the man.

Brant chuckled.

"God dammit. Why is it always you? How many do you have now?"

Brant patted the man on his head. "You're my eighth, Ulysses," bragged Brant.

"Going for the school record again?" said Ulysses. "Not if I can stop it."

Brant knew what Ulysses was about to do and quickly took his foam dagger, bashing it upside Ulysses' head.

"Brant's over here!" yelled Ulysses in pain, as Brant hit him on the head again, knocking him unconscious. Always the sore loser.

Brant crouched low to the ground as he made his way to the opposite side of the room, away from the stairs.

This was a schooling exercise, named Sneak, that happened twice a week. There were two teams of thirty students. The different age groups were thirteen to fifteen, sixteen to twenty, and twenty-one to twenty-five. If you were good enough to qualify, there was an advanced game with students ages twenty-six to thirty. This was the group Brant has been in for the past three years. Sneak was an exercise to teach students how to stealthily move around and protect themselves in the Outside. Sneak had been Brant's other hobby, besides tinkering with his tech. Ever since he was old enough to play, he was one of the best players since the game which started nearly seventy years ago. It was his sole purpose for seeking out Master Alexis, as she too had been one of the best.

Brant hit the wall with his hand. He turned around to lean against it. He closed his eyes to calm himself down as he realized he was breathing heavily.

There were multiple footsteps rushing up the stairs. Their mistake; now was his chance. Brant quietly made his way to the stairs. There was a crate to the right of the railings and he hid behind it.

"Which way did he go?" Brant could tell it was Patches. "Well?" There was a hard kick followed by Ulysses moaning.

"Southeast corner boss," replied a waking Ulysses. "Or was it southwest?"

Brant stuck his middle finger out from behind the crate. He's supposed to be dead, why is he talking?

"Fan out," ordered Patches. "We're all that's left. Faruk, stay by the stairs. Peebles and Carpenter go south. Hanks you're with me."

So there was five left. Thanks for the info Patchy.

The footsteps came around the stone crate and disappeared off into the distance. Brant waited a couple minutes until he had fully calmed down. He had an idea of the general location where Faruk was standing guard. They couldn't have picked an easier guy for the job. Brant knew Faruk had never broken the rules and gets distracted easily.

Brant took out a piece of string and tied it to a little slab of metal he found on the ground earlier. He swung it around and launched it towards the wall in front of Faruk. It made a light clanging sound so only he could hear it.

"Shit, what was that?" said Faruk.

"Don't be fooled," said Ulysses.

"If I hear you speak up one more time, you will regret it," said Faruk.

Faruk tiptoed towards the wall and Brant was soon behind him. Brant reached around Faruk and jabbed his foam daggers into his opponent's stomach. Faruk put up his hands in surrender and laid on the ground. Brant patted him on his head. That's *nine*.

Brant heard more footsteps come up the stairwell. He heard someone whisper, "Brant, you there?" It was his teammate Alexander.

"Ain't I always?" he whispered, arrogantly.

"Good, how many do you have so far?" asked Alexander.

"Nine," said Brant proudly.

"That's more than double what the entire team has total," said a girl, impressed. It was Elise. "Always glad you're on our side."

Brant walked closer to his teammates. "Two took off south and the wise guy and his lackey headed east. Are we all that's left?"

"As far as I know," answered Elise.

"You two head east," said Brant. "I'll take out the other two and meet up with you after." His teammates knew he liked going solo. "Don't strike before I get there." Patches was the one he wanted, badly.

"Gotcha," whispered Alexander. "Let's move."

The air blew against Brant's face as he lightly crept eastward. He wanted to go fast because he thought Patches and Hanks were too much for his teammates to handle and he wanted to make it back to them in time.

Suddenly, Brant heard two whispering gangsters. Peebles and Carpenter were just up ahead. Brant came to a halt. They must have given up because they were just milling around. Perfect. Now was his chance.

Brant slithered between them. Judging by the sound of their breathing, he determined where they were standing. He took both of his foam daggers, jammed them into each of their sides, and then swung at their heads. *Ten. Eleven.*

Peebles immediately fell noisily to the ground and groaned. Brant could tell he was frustrated as he pat him on the head.

As for Carpenter, he gave Brant his famous right hook but missed his jaw completely and clipped his ear instead. Brant charged at him, aiming for his legs. He tackled him to the ground and punched him in the gut. Carpenter cried out, "Ok. Ok. I surrender."

Brant pat Carpenter on the head. "Good boy."

Alexander and Elise must have been getting close to Patches and Hanks. Brant calmly headed east along the wall.

As he made his way closer, Brant heard his teammates talking to the opponents. He climbed up on top of a container and listened in.

They were in mid-conversation. "What will you do for us in return?" asked Alexander.

"Name anything," said Patches. "I will find a way to give it to you."

There was a pause. Alexander must have been thinking it over. "Deal. Let's discuss this later tonight. I need to consult with my teammates first."

Patches and Hanks laughed. "Well then, let's seal the deal."

Brant heard someone get hit by a foam dagger followed by a second. Two bodies hit the ground. "Now, where is that loser," said Patches.

Brant stood still on top of the container. What had just happened? Did Alexander and Elise just sell him out?

Fueled with rage, Brant leaped into the air. With one dagger aimed forward with the other back by his right ear, he darted through the air towards Patches and Hanks. Brant struck an immoveable object first. It must have been Hanks. The foam dagger ricocheted off of Hanks' jiggling belly and flew to the ground. Brant lifted up his other foam dagger and smashed Hanks' head.

"Boss, he's here," said Hanks.

"Timber!" cried Brant as Hanks fell to the ground with a thud.

Brant launched himself towards Patches. "You're mine!" Brant dropped his other foam dagger and put Patches in a headlock. "What were you just planning to do, Patchy boy?"

"Get off!" yelled Patches. "This is against the game rules!" Brant squeezed tighter like an anaconda forcing the life out of its prey. Patches clawed at Brant's arms.

"Your team breaks the game rules constantly," Brant said as he squeezed tighter. "Did you let the wolfwraiths into the city?" asked Brant.

"What?" squeaked Patches. "Is this what this is all about? You've got to be kidding me."

Brant squeezed even tighter. "Someone must have let them in. There were no signs of forced entry." Patches was gasping for breath.

Unexpectedly, a foam dagger hit Brant in the back of his head. Angered, he turned around while still holding on to Patches. Brant let out a bloodcurdling scream.

"I thought you were the last one!" Brant shouted at Patches.

By the sound of the voice, Brant could tell it was Tarjeel, the newest member of the Greasy Gangsters. Tarjeel laughed like a hyena and said, "Finally got what was coming to you Brant."

"What do you mean?" asked Brant.

Brant could hear Tarjeel walk up to him and get in his face. "We finally came up with a plan to knock you down a few pegs. First we had to lure you in, then blindside you with a change in allegiances to get you confused. To make you think it was only Patches and Hanks left. Then, once you were off guard...well you know the rest." Tarjeel laughed again with Patches and Hanks. "We were all in on the plan. Even your teammates."

Brant squeezed even tighter around Patches' neck. "I'll kill you. I'll kill all of you!" He assumed the position to break Patches' neck. Patches cried out in fear.

Suddenly, the lights came on in the room. Brant covered his eyes with his free hand. People rushed over to Brant and wrestled him, forcing him to let go of his enemy.

Tarjeel was standing in front of Brant. He had a tattoo of a crescent moon etched into his forehead and had purple eye shadow around his sunken eyes.

Hanks, Alexander, and Elise all made it to their feet and looked on in horror.

Alexander had green spiked hair with shaved sides. He wore a nose ring and a neon green black cloak with chain links.

Elise had long brown hair that was pushed to one side and shaved on the other. She wore a blue hoop earring and neon blue and black robes.

Brant struggled with the guards.

"What is wrong with you?" one of the muscle-bound guards asked.

Patches answered for him with a sore voice. "His fake parents were torn apart last night from the wolfwraith attack. Instead of protecting them, Brant was away, fucking that old witch. He thinks I let them in. This dude is crazy. He almost killed me."

Adrenaline was surging through Brant's body. He stood alone, his heart pounding out of his chest.

Two guards picked up a shocked Patches and carried him away.

Brant turned to Alexander and Elise. "You were conspiring with the enemy. Why?" They both had a look of regret on their faces. Before either of them could answer, Brant felt hands on his arms and they violently tugged him away. "How dare you!"

"Better luck next time, Brant," snorted Tarjeel. "If there is a next time."

Brant was being manhandled out of the Sneak Arena when he heard a familiar voice. "Leave him to me." It was Alexis.

The guards let go of Brant and pushed him towards her. "Walk with me," she said.

Alexis lead him down a flight of stairs and outside of the building. She escorted him into the building next-door.

Inside were stacks of monitors playing back the game of Sneak Brant had just finished. The playback was in night vision and full color. Brant could see how close everyone was in relation to each other. In all of the years playing Sneak, he had never stepped inside this room.

Alexis pulled up a chair for him. "Sit down," she demanded to Brant. "Please. And take off that damn hood."

Brant did as he was told. A video was playing back the part where Brant was choking out Patches.

"What the darkzone is this?" asked Alexis.

Brant stared on in disbelief. He was having an outer-body experience. He grabbed onto his silver necklace. "I don't know what has gotten into me." Brant shook his head and stood up.

Alexis shoved him back in his seat. For an old woman she was surprisingly strong. She put her hand on his head and made him lean close to the monitor. "Look at yourself, Brant. Do you want to be a cold blooded murderer one day? Because that's how you become a murderer."

In the video, Brant was squeezing Patches until his face turned purple.

"Despite popular belief, this is not how Assassins behave," she said. "You know that right? If not, this is the last time you will ever see me."

Many thoughts went through Brant's head. He took something out of his pocket and stuck it in a port on the side of the monitor without Alexis noticing. Brant put his head in his hands. "Master…"

"You can forget about your payment from yesterdays kills," she announced.

Before Brant could spit out any words, Alexis interjected. The tone in her voice changed from anger to sympathy. "Do you know why I took you under my wing?"

Brant looked at her, expecting her to continue, but she didn't. So he answered, "No."

"It's not because you are phenomenal at Sneak," she said. "Don't get me wrong, you are one of the best I have ever seen, and I have been there from the start." Alexis played back the video from the beginning showing off his stealth and attack skills. "How many did you get today?"

Brant didn't even have to think about this. He immediately answered with, "Thirteen," and added, "If you count Patches. It could have been fourteen if not for that damn Tarjeel."

Alexis shook her head disapprovingly. "No, I didn't make you my apprentice because of your skills. It's not because I felt sorry for you for being an outcast either. It's not because of your ruthlessness or your temper. Your attitude is something you should definitely work on. Listen very closely because what I am about to tell you is very important."

Brant twisted around in the chair and leaned in close to his Master.

"I made you my apprentice because no matter how good you are, I still see a lot of potential in you. Your strategies are unlike any I have ever encountered. You pay close attention to even the smallest of details. You could be a great detective one day. Your technological innovations are the best I have ever seen. And I have been around for a long time. This is why I made you my apprentice."

"I don't know what to say Master Alexis," said Brant.

"I'm only looking for one word," said Alexis.

Brant looked at her. "Sorry."

Alexis smiled. "There it is."

"I promise to think before I act from now on," said Brant. "I will also try not to go on any meaningless rampages anymore. I was foolish to attack Patches. I didn't know what I was doing. Of course he didn't let the wolfwraiths in. No one would have done that."

"Good," said Alexis. She motioned for him to get up. "Now get on out of here. If I were you I would run back home." She turned her back to Brant. "Where are you staying now?"

"Some place warm and welcoming," said Brant. A small smile started to form at the corner of his lips. With his master's back turned, he grabbed the item from the monitor and stuck it back into his pocket. He then walked towards the exit. "See you tomorrow?"

"As you wish," said his Master.

Brant put on his hood and exited out into the dark streets. He stopped to grab his belongings from the drop off point. Brant kept his head down, watching his feet for most of his journey. He continued walking as he came up to his house. Brant couldn't build up the courage to look at it. He walked past it and didn't look back.

Brant headed northeast towards Alexis' house. To his right he could hear construction going on. The higher ups must have started the excavation of the spaceship earlier today. He heard Lizbeth chanting something in the distance, most likely trying to shut down the construction.

Brant took a left. He came upon a house with shiny ornaments hanging from the roof. They twisted and turned, catching the light from the streets every few seconds. He walked up to the porch and knocked on the door. A thin beautiful woman with short brown hair, light green eyes, and jewelry covering her ears opened the door. She was wearing a neon teal and black robe.

"Hello, Persephone," said Brant. "Thank you so much for letting me stay here again." He shook her hand.

"You can stay as long as you wish, Brant," said Persephone. "We *are* destined to be together you know."

Brant laughed.

Brant and Persephone were paired together at a young age. The pairing process analyzes multiple factors and accurately matches you up with someone of like mind. The one thing Brant and Persephone had in common was they both were orphaned at a young age. Sometimes, Brant thought that this was the only thing they had in common.

Before yesterday, it had been years since they had spent quality time together, usually only seeing each other at gatherings.

Persephone pulled up a chair for Brant and had him set his belongings down.

A cute black cat rubbed against Brant's legs. "Greetings Pandora," Brant chuckled.

Pandora purred.

"I hope you don't mind, but I would like some alone time," said Brant to Persephone. "It has been a long couple days. Too long if you ask me."

"I'm sure it has," said Persephone as she walked over to him and hugged him. "Be my guest. Just make sure to clean up after yourself tonight. The counter was a mess this morning."

"Gotcha," said Brant. "No more stress eating," he noted to himself. Brant grabbed his belongings and walked into his new bedroom. He knew Persephone had cleaned up because the bed was made and the floor and desks had been dusted. He breathed in through his nose and out his mouth. Clean fresh air for the first time in a long time. "I could get used to this," he said.

"What was that?" asked Persephone. She was standing in the living room.

"Oh, nothing," answered Brant. He took his first step inside as Pandora ran through his legs. "Gah! Watch where you're going, little one."

Pandora's tail was sticking straight up in the air with the tip arced to the side. She jumped up on the desk and rubbed her head on his cloak.

Brant smiled. He picked her up and started scratching her furry neck. "It seems I have found a new roommate," said Brant just loud enough for Persephone to hear. "She may have already found a way into my heart too."

He heard Persephone's cute laugh. "I thought you wanted to be alone," said Persephone.

Brant pet Pandora's head. "I can be alone with my thoughts around her. She doesn't talk back and doesn't judge me. People could learn a thing or two from cats."

"You can say that again," said Persephone. "I'm headed into town to get some food. Need anything?"

"No thanks," he said.

"See you later, Brant. Enjoy your quiet time, okay?" He heard the door to the house close.

Brant set down Pandora. "Peace at last." He took out his Virtuvisor and DigiPens from the drawer. He lay down on his new bed and put on the Virtuvisor. Pandora jumped up and curled up on his chest. He saw the green lettering appear before his eyes: *WELCOME BACK USER.*

Brant picked up his DigiPens and selected a model that was currently in development from the main menu. It was human shaped and had the build of an adult male.

Brant moved the DigiPens through the air, sculpting the face to look more like Tarjeel, the man who beat him today. After he was finished he pressed a button labeled 'Action' in the virtual world.

He typed in the code:

```
/reaction.caa (fight_flight)
    < command = [stab] , [punch] , [kick] ,
    [defend] , [run] >
/input – "run until successful"
/execute: IRL-Drive
```

Brant took off the Virtuvisor and set it down. He set the Projectocube onto the desk. He reached into his pocket and took out the IRL-Drive. Earlier, Brant used this to download the entire video of the game of Sneak from the monitor in the Sneak Arena command room, right underneath his Master's nose. He stuck the IRL-Drive into the Projectocube.

111

"Initiate holo 32-B," commanded Brant.

The Projectocube glowed and then hovered in the air. Pandora hissed and ran out of the bedroom. There was an image of Brant choking out Patches in the middle of the room. Brant walked up to the projection of himself and fit into his mold. The projection of himself disappeared. Brant put his arm around the neck of the projection of Patches. "We meet again, enemy of mine."

"Play holo," said Brant.

There was a hum in the air as the projections started to flicker. Brant counted the seconds as he squeezed Patches like he did earlier that day. At thirteen seconds, he turned around and countered Tarjeel's blow with his holo foam dagger.

"Not today!" said Brant. "You will never sneak up on me ever again, Tarjeel. Let that be known."

Brant dueled against Tarjeel again and again until he was exhausted. To be honest, Brant couldn't remember if he won the first time. He ran the same simulation countless times during the night. Brant couldn't even remember if Persephone came back home. He was in the zone and enjoying himself. It was just how he liked it. Alone.

8. DARK DAY

Jaylin stood in the auditorium, hovering above her chair in complete disbelief. Principal Edison had just announced the two names for Student Ambassador and neither of them were hers. Jaylin turned to Akeer who was also standing up. Akeer gave her a hug as he walked passed her. *What just happened?* Jaylin saw a student giving Akeer a handshake as everyone in the auditorium clapped and cheered.

"Who are the Student Ambassadors again?" Jaylin asked the girl next to her who was whistling.

"Arabella Huang," the girl said as Jaylin tuned out the rest of what she had said.

Arabella Huang was a girl's name. But that wasn't *her* name. How was this possible? How did she not win? Jaylin's hearing came back.

"You must be so proud," the girl continued.

"Why?" asked Jaylin, in complete disarray.

"They called your brother up too. Akeer Robins," the girl explained. "Your brother is our male Student Ambassador."

Jaylin looked up at the stage and saw a nerdy looking girl with Akeer standing next to her. They were holding each others hand in the air.

"Seriously?" she said. "Those two?" Jaylin was enraged. She lost control of her actions as she pushed away people in her aisle. Jaylin stormed out of the auditorium leaving the cheers behind her. Three of the moons filled the sky as she made her way to her family's house.

Jaylin opened the door. Her mom, Lydia, was tan, had light brown eyes, braided hair, and muscles. Her dad, Denna, was scrawny and pale. He wore glasses and had a rat tail haircut. Her little sister, Arkadia, was tall for her age and looked a lot like her mother.

The Ambassadors from her parents age groups must have already been picked. Arkadia was twelve and the cutoff age to be an Ambassador was fourteen. She stayed at a daycare during the day. Someone must have picked her up already.

Lydia was the first to notice that something was wrong with Jaylin. "Let me guess," her mother said. "Your worst fears have come true?"

Jaylin opened the door to her bedroom, which was filled with dozens of trophies. "Even worse than that," she said as she slammed the door. Her trophies on the far wall shook.

Inside, she lay on her bed and looked up at the ceiling. She heard a knock at the door. "Go away," she said. They didn't heed her warning as her mother gently opened the door.

Footsteps came closer to her bedside. Her mother peered down at her with a concerned look on her face. "Wanna talk about it?" she asked her daughter.

Jaylin flipped herself over, punched the pillow, and laid on her stomach. She grumbled.

"You didn't get elected as Ambassador, I take it?" said Lydia, rubbing her back. "I'm so sorry honey."

The floor creaked. Jaylin imagined her father standing at the door looking at his wife for answers.

"It's not fair," whined Jaylin. "I've been training since I was born. I am much better and more skilled than anyone here my age. Why does he get to go over me?" she wailed. She rolled back over to face her parents. Jaylin could tell both were confused.

"He?" her father asked. "Wait, did you get elected or not?"

"No, dad, I didn't get elected," said Jaylin. "Some girl named Arabella Huang was elected instead of me. But for the male Ambassador," Jaylin hesitated, "The male Student Ambassador is Akeer."

Jaylin's mother and father seemed to get even more confused. Almost as confused as she was. Their expressions quickly changed once they realized that their son had been elected. Their grins on their faces were as big as they could be and Lydia jumped up in the air and cheered. A trophy of a woman holding a spear fell and cracked on the ground. After a few moments, her parents stood there acting like nothing happened. Jaylin knew that they did their best to hide their emotions because they both knew that she was extremely disappointed.

Her father spoke up. "You should be happy for your brother."

"How can I be happy for him when he didn't even want to be Student Ambassador?" said Jaylin. "I have only ever wanted one thing in my life and it was just taken away from me in just a few seconds. What do those two have that I don't?" After a long silence, she angrily asked impatiently, "Well?" Her parents didn't have an answer for her.

Arkadia peeked her head inside the bedroom. Her father escorted her out and didn't come back. Her mother still stood there with her hand on Jaylin's forearm. This calmed her down a little.

"I am positive that I aced that exam, mother," said Jaylin. "There wasn't one question that I didn't know."

There was silence. "I came in first place in the endurance test," she continued. "For the life of me, I *cannot* think of any possible reason for someone else to beat me." She laid there thinking hard to herself. Who was this Arabella Huang?

"I mean," she continued, "clearly they didn't choose the best of the best. Akeer was fast in the endurance test, but let's face it. He isn't that fast. He also isn't that smart. He was going so slow during the exam, I'm surprised he finished on time. You know how he always second guesses himself."

"You always compare your brother to yourself," said Lydia. "Sometimes I think you forget he is your twin. Akeer has the same potential as you do, Jaylin. He just doesn't reveal his full potential in front of you because he is afraid how you will react."

Jaylin sat up and stared out the window. She wasn't fully convinced her brother could be as good as her, but she felt sad for the way she was acting. Her parents were completely right. She should be happy for him. Something inside her soul prevented her from showing it. She was still furious at Arabella too.

"One of these days, you will see I am right," said mother.

Jaylin got out of bed and kicked the broken trophy under her bed. She grabbed her backpack off her desk. She put her aqua-breather in the backpack and slid her force spear through the strap. "I'm going to catch some dinner," said Jaylin. "I'll be home late." She exited her bedroom and walked into the living room. "Goodbye," she said to her family. Jaylin opened the door and stepped outside.

Akeer was walking towards her. She didn't hold the door open for him as he smiled at her. She turned her head away and continued walking toward the docks.

Outside the auditorium was packed with hundreds of people. Most of the Ambassadors were announced for each age group. Jaylin concluded the only ones left must be for the older people. These people must be their families gathering outside the auditorium.

Jaylin's grandparents all died within the past three years. They had lived with her family her entire life and she missed them. She walked faster before any memories of her grandparents came flooding back. She didn't want to think anymore sad thoughts right now.

The air smelled fishy as Jaylin walked down the pier. There were four moons out now. The big purple moon touching the horizon was Franz. The gray moon that peeked over the ocean to the south was Stonewall. The blue moon overhead was Jezebel. Jaylin could see the crescent of the small orange moon, Miss Ippi, which was hiding behind Jezebel. She could have sworn she could feel their cosmic pull of the ocean.

In the light blue sky, she saw a dark planet she had never seen before hovering in space. "There must be millions of planets out there," she said to herself. "I wish I could go." She looked up sadly at the dark planet. "I am not giving up," she promised herself. "It is my dream."

The docks were empty. Jaylin never noticed how long they were. There had always been people lined up all along the docks and now with no one on them, they seemed to spread out far into the horizon and beyond.

There was still a large scar along the dock where a portion of Hydronia once expanded out across the ocean. Eighty years ago, a big storm shook Hydronia and the city split in half. That portion of the city as well as the estimated one hundred and fifty citizens drifted away. No one had heard or seen them since. Dozens of search parties were sent out to find and rescue any potential survivors. All evidence suggest there were none and the city sank. Jaylin believed they were still out there somewhere.

Jaylin walked to the farthest dock, which was where the good fishing grounds were. She put on her aqua-breather, grabbed her force spear, and jumped in feet first.

Jaylin started swimming out, away from Hydronia. She wanted to be alone. Her muscles ached from the endurance test. She didn't care. Jaylin dove under water. As deep as her muscles could take her. Out here, the ocean floor was farther down. The pressure of the water on top of Jaylin was intense. It made her feel weak. She pushed herself to reach the bottom. Her feet touched the sandy ground.

Armored fish startled Jaylin as they swam past her. She did not have her force spear ready in time to attempt to stun one. Jaylin had the setting on the force spear set to stun because the armored fish tasted better fresh. If she stunned the fish, she could easily bring them back to the surface alive before they regained consciousness.

The other setting on the spear was pierce, which narrows the beam of force so much that it pierces the armor of the fish, wounding it at the very least.

The spawning grounds must have been in the direction the armored fish were headed. Jaylin took off in that direction. She tried hard not to think about her day, but her plan to be out in the silence backfired. All she could think about was Arabella and Akeer becoming Student Ambassadors. Was there a way she could convince the teachers that she should be the one instead? Maybe she should campaign against Arabella and Akeer and prove to the teachers she was the better decision.

Jaylin drifted over a ridge and saw a school of armored fish swimming back and forth. She held her force spear tight to her chest. Jaylin hugged the ground, trying to blend in with her surroundings as she inched closer to them.

Once Jaylin was underneath the armored fish, she slowly aimed her force spear towards them. She held down the button to build up the pressure within the shaft. Jaylin released the button as she lunged forward with the force spear. A sharp shockwave pierced through the water and Jaylin saw it enter the school of armored fish. She held down the button again as she saw the shockwave hit an armored fish on its side.

The armored fish turned sideways as Jaylin lunged and released the button a second time. The sharp shockwave ripped through the water and landed on another armored fish.

Two armored fish fell to the ocean floor. This didn't satisfy Jaylin. The other armored fish started swimming erratically. Jaylin knew at the speed they were going, the stun wasn't going to have much impact so she switched the setting on the spear to pierce. She held down the button.

Jaylin felt the pressure build up within the shaft again, but this time it built up even more pressure. The button below her thumb started pressing back against her. She released the button and a sharp thin shockwave pierced through the water towards the school of armored fish. Jaylin saw the shockwave pierce through their armored scales of several fish, killing them instantly.

Four more fish fell. Scales piled up on the ocean floor. Still not satisfied. She wanted to bring home a feast for her family. She also wanted to impress everyone she would walk by on her way home.

"Let's do this one more time." Jaylin held down the button on the spear for as long as she could. She aimed it towards the armored fish, which were now huddled by a large boulder. The pressure on the inside of the shaft was so great, Jaylin was hugging the spear and holding down the button with both of her hands. She lined the spear up perfectly with the center of the group of fish. Suddenly, she was thrown backwards off the spear, as the spear itself zoomed off behind her. She watched as the shockwave rammed into the school of armored fish, killing half a dozen more.

A loud crackle filled the water as Jaylin witnessed the enormous boulder on the edge split in half and fall into the trench. She looked back and could not see where her force spear had landed.

Jaylin swam up to the stunned and dead armored fish and filled up her backpack with a dozen. She swam over to see where her force spear went. It had completely vanished. How was she going to explain this to her parents and her instructors?

As she started to swim back up to the surface, she noticed the ocean floor starting to shake. A loud noise came from the direction where the heavy boulder had disappeared. It must have fallen far into the trenches and caused the whole area to shake. Pretty cool. She was powerful enough to make the planet quake.

Jaylin broke through the surface of the water and pulled herself up onto the docks. Some people had started coming out for a late afternoon dip or hunt. Her backpack hung low as she walked past them.

Should she start campaigning now? This was a good enough audience as any. She knew some of the families walking along the docks.

"Good afternoon," Jaylin greeted them. She knew one of them was one of the instructors that had a say in choosing the Student Ambassadors of her age group. Jaylin decided she wanted to prove a point to her.

"Whoa," Jaylin started. "My backpack is *so* full of fresh fish I can barely hold it up. I bet the new Student Ambassadors couldn't do what *I* just did." She made sure to speak louder during the last sentence. "I know the two eighteen year old Student Ambassadors. One reads books all day and doesn't provide for our community," she lied about Arabella, "and the other didn't even want to be elected. What a shame."

The teacher peeked at Jaylin to see who was bad-mouthing her decision.

Jaylin continued down the docks. She noticed another teacher who was specifically designated to the eighteen year olds. "If I were elected instead, I would have done *so* much more for our community," said Jaylin. "I just caught twelve armored fish for my family. I could have been one of the ones to unite the human race and lead us into a better future."

Heads turned one by one to see who was talking. She noticed they recognized who she was.

A little girl said, "Hey, that's Jaylin," to her parents.

Another person in her thirties stopped and gave her a high five as she passed. "Jaylin, keep up the good work," encouraged the lady.

"If I *had* become the Student Ambassador instead, I could have improved our way of life," said Jaylin. "I am the best at everything I do and could have led our people to greatness."

Ms. Britta ran up to her. She looked irritated. "I totally believe you could have, Jaylin. You were in the top five in our discussion but Arabella slightly took the lead based on her performances on the exam and endurance test."

"What do you mean?" said Jaylin. "I know I beat her in both trials."

"That may be," said Ms. Britta. "But her answers were clever and her performance was slightly better."

Jaylin stood there shocked. She thought getting the highest score and beating everyone else would have convinced the teachers she was worthy of the title. She never thought *how* she did these things were just as important.

"As for your twin brother," Ms. Britta continued, "Akeer wasn't even in our discussions until he worked wonders on the exam and made all of us think twice after he finished the endurance test. We couldn't help but factor him into our decision."

"Could he really have been holding back all of these years, just like mother told her?" she thought to herself. "Was he really as good as her? Maybe even better?" She didn't believe it was possible.

If he had been holding back, that would mean he was lying to her this entire time. Lying about his true potential. Lying to his own twin. And if he waited until this moment to prove himself, that means he had also been lying to her about wanting to become the Student Ambassador. Just another reason for her to be angry about.

"I fought for you as much as I could," said Ms. Britta. "But I am only one person. If you plan on campaigning against them, it could possibly work to your favor, but I fear it is too late. You should have done that beforehand."

"I didn't think I needed to," said Jaylin. "I prove myself every single day. I didn't think I had to do anything else. Apparently I am just not good enough."

"There are two weeks left, Jaylin," said Britta. "As of right now, only two of each age group are allowed to go and I know for a fact the rule will not change. If you really want to go and change their decisions, you must prove you are worthy in more ways than just *being the best at everything*."

Jaylin nodded her head. "Prove I am worthy in more ways," thought Jaylin out loud. "I can do that."

"I must get going now," said Ms. Britta. "My family is getting hungry." She waved at her and strolled down the dock.

Jaylin tightened the straps on her backpack so it was better placed on her back. The armored fish were getting heavy.

She made it to the end of the docks and walked along the pier. She was in deep thought about the conversation she just had. "How can I prove myself in such little time?"

A large object flew past her at lightning speed. Whatever it was clanged against the building behind her. Jaylin looked at the hole in the wall. A loud booming noise echoed in the distance. She looked around to see what the noise was.

Black smoke filled the air in the east. There were people in panic running from that direction, followed by another loud explosion. There was an orange glow shining underneath the black smoke. Something must have caught fire.

Jaylin ran in the direction of the explosion. People ran past her in the opposite direction. She ran for two whole minutes until she noticed which building was on fire. It was the School of Building. Akeer spent most of his time here since he wanted to become a master builder.

Jaylin continued to run closer to the fiery mass. People were running out of the building. Jaylin stood there as she pondered her best course of action.

A fireball burst out of a third story window. Jaylin could see there were still people trapped inside.

She ran into the burning tower without hesitation. She took the flight of stairs to the left and ran as fast as she could to the third floor.

A group of men in hardhats were stuck inside an office room. Jaylin saw them through the window on the door. She went to open it but the doorknob was burning hot. She kicked the door over and over again. To her relief, the door finally flew open. The men thanked her. She heard a woman scream in the room above her. The men ran down the stairs while Jaylin ran up.

She thought about what Ms. Britta said. She needed to be a hero for these people. This motivated her to push forward, even if she wasn't being herself.

The woman was paralyzed with fear in the corner of her office. Jaylin ran up to her and took her hand. What would a hero say? "Come with me if you want to live," she said. Jaylin brought her to the stairwell. "You're doing great, miss. What's your name?"

The woman replied with one word, "Janette."

"Okay, Janette," said Jaylin. "Can you take a step onto the stairs for me?"

Janette lifted her wobbly right leg and placed her foot on the first step.

"Good," said Jaylin. "Great job. Now can you keep on going down?"

Jaylin and Janette walked down to the first floor. Jaylin could tell she was still scared for her life. Another woman was helping rescue people and Jaylin had Janette follow her outside.

It was starting to get hard to see inside the building. The black smoke appeared everywhere and made her eyes water. The heat started getting to her.

Ms. Britta's conversation played on repeat in her head. *I must prove myself.* She was motivated to save people, but for the wrong reasons.

She crouched down so she was below the smoke. She ran into the hallway where she heard someone yell, "We're trapped!"

Jaylin came around the corner and saw a man and woman helping them out already. She moved closer until she recognized the man. It looked a lot like him at least. *Akeer?* What was he doing here? Did he come to help like I did or was he already in the building when the fire broke out? The woman looked familiar too. Jaylin just stood there and watched as Akeer helped lift a piece of plywood out of the doorway just enough for the group of people to escape.

Suddenly, there was another explosion from up above and it sent the ceiling down on top of everyone.

Jaylin laid on the ground covered in ash. She coughed as she got back on all fours. She looked in the direction where Akeer and the group were.

Akeer was screaming in pain. The group of people were helping him up. The woman grasped his hand but couldn't break him free of the rubble.

Jaylin didn't know what to do. She was scared. A cloud of smoke filled the room. Jaylin couldn't see anything anymore. She left her brother behind. She crawled back to the entrance and made her way outside.

She found Janette and the men in hardhats huddled up with a group of people outside. She joined her and looked up at the building, gasping for breath. The building began to lean as the fires burned through the upper floors.

Jaylin didn't know exactly why, but she turned away and ran as fast as she could towards home. Was it because she didn't want to see the building fall and possibly kill her brother still trapped inside? Was she simply running away from herself? Did she think she caused this catastrophe simply by wishing her brother away for lying to her? Did she think she caused whatever happened with her force spear and the large boulder? Or maybe it was all of them combined? Jaylin couldn't quite figure it out.

Jaylin huffed and puffed until she made it home. She knocked on the door until her parents opened it and she continued knocking on thin air. She collapsed in her parents arms as tears streamed down her face.

Behind her, the sky was black and lightning filled the air. A front moved in and brought a big rain cloud to wash out the fire on Hydronia. Jaylin watched as the orange glow dissipated.

In the distance Jaylin heard people crying. All of Hydronia was in mourning.

9. RENDEZVOUS

The cave was loud and smelled of sweat from the miners hard at work. Torches lined the cave walls, providing light for everyone. The flashing lights of the melters lit up the tunnels a light shade of blue. It has been two weeks since the news broke out they would all be leaving Quaketown.

"It has been a great day lads!" Christopherson exclaimed as he took a rag out of his trousers and wiped underneath his armpits. "It looks like we have increased our daily payload by at least twenty percent. Keep up the good work." Selene heard his jolly laugh. "Before we're done, we'll have enough fuel to power dozens of ships. Finish up with the section you're currently working on and then go home to get some rest so you can come back bright and early tomorrow. I'm headed out to give the good news to the old man." Selene knew he meant Akira.

Selene powered up her melter and blasted it around the chunk of blue and white kyanite, which was used for jewelry. Quaketown already had a stockpile of kyanite but miners were instructed to mine through everything and anything to gather all the resources they could find.

After breaking the kyanite out of the stone, Selene walked to the supply drop-off and traded in her melter. The tradeswoman removed the blue laser crystal from the melter and carefully set it down in a bin labeled 'used.' Later, a tester would come to see if the used laser crystals still had enough juice to power the laser in a melter. If so, it would be put into the 'power' bin. If not, it would be recycled and used in the stage projector. The tradeswoman gave Selene a shovel and a pan in return.

Selene went back to her pile and shoveled the kyanite into her pan. She gazed into the sparkly blue kyanite and wondered why her mother never wore jewelry. She certainly had enough to trade for it since it was cheap. It dawned on her that she herself had never worn jewelry before. It must have been because she never saw her mother wear any. Maybe that's the same reason her mother didn't wear it either…

Lost in thought, Selene worked her way to the mineral drop-off. Today, Isadora was working. She was a woman in her thirties who always wore hooped earrings and a stylish green dress that floated around her ankles. She could tell Isadora loved working here and interacting with the miners.

"That's a pretty blue," Isadora the jeweler said, looking at the kyanite under a magnifying glass.

"Isn't it?" Selene replied. "It reminds me of the crystal clear water east of Quaketown." Once a week, a special unit of hunters traveled east to gather fresh water for the whole village. Selene's friend, Farhad, brought back the blue water and showed it to her before it was taken into the water purification room.

"Hey, why don't I make you a nice cat's eye ring out of it?" insisted Isadora. "I heard you have recently been assigned a Chosen."

Selene blushed, rolled her eyes, and wondered who told her that. It was probably Christopherson; he couldn't keep his mouth shut.

"Thank you, but I'll have to decline. I don't wear rings," said Selene.

"Well then I'll make a beautiful necklace for you as a gift," said Isadora. "I insist. Our storage spaces are filling up so quickly we need to make room for the important stuff."

"Alright, Isadora. A necklace sounds great," said Selene. Why give it away if they had no need for it? "Thanks a bunch." Selene handed her the rest of the sparkly crystals. "I'll see you later. Have a good day."

Isadora waved at her as she left.

It took Selene a good twenty minutes to reach the exit of the mines. She waited in the inspection line. Security officers patted her down to make sure she wasn't bringing anything she wasn't supposed to have outside of the mines, like a melter or a laser crystal. If someone brought a melter into the cavehomes, it was usually with the intention of harming someone. The officers only inspect you coming out of the mines. Going in wasn't a problem; lasers were allowed.

While standing in line she overheard a group of concerned citizens talking behind her.

"Why should we have to leave?" one man asked. "We have lived our entire lives here. I've had zero problems."

"We are safe here too. What if we leave and are attacked?" another man said. "What if our ship has a leak in it and we all die before we make it to the space station? My wife and I are freaking out over this. How can Akira expect us to just pack everything we know and love and leave everything behind?"

A woman butted into their conversation. "I hated how Stefano broke it to us too. He was too scared to tell it to us himself so he used that poor girl to break the news to us. That bastard."

Selene moved up in line. Her stomach dropped. Mr. Bradham is a good man. He wouldn't do that to her. It just happened to be her day to perform.

The second man who spoke said, "I am not looking forward to meeting those dang Jambos and Sirfates either. They should stay on their own planets and mind their own business. We don't need their help."

Another woman spoke up. "We can't live here forever." Her voice sounded familiar. It was Kelly. What was she doing in the mines? Selene turned around but remained hidden from the group who were complaining.

"Bullshit," the first woman spat. Selene noticed that it was the other Selene. She was four years older than her and had a sour attitude. Her hair had several knots in it and her clothes were always splattered with dirt. Selene never liked her because she reminded her of an angry step sister from the fairy tales.

Kelly continued with her side of the argument. "We will eventually run out of food if we stay here. Edible plants are growing thin the more we populate. At this rate, jennybobs will all be gone because we hadn't taken into account how much we were consuming. We also use plants we eat for medication. It could be disastrous if we run out."

The group didn't want to acknowledge this.

"We are running out of meat too," Kelly continued. "Every single day that goes by, the hunters are bringing back less and less meat. The native animals are being hunted to extinction. Most of our resources are running out."

The men and women looked at their feet. Other people listened in.

"If we don't leave now to find a more suitable planet for us to live on, it could be the end of our people within the next sixty years or so," explained Kelly. "We have to do this for ourselves. Think of the children…"

By now the entire line, including the security officers were listening in. They held on to every word she said.

"We need help to find a new planet too," said Kelly. "These *people* you speak of in distasteful terms are *human beings*. We all came from Earth. The human race needs to work together to find a new version of Earth."

Selene cut in line and had the distracted security officer pat her down. He did so without taking his eyes off of Kelly.

"You may pass, Selene," the officer said.

Selene took a final look at Kelly and the crowd. Most of the onlookers seemed convinced of her side of the argument. Maybe it should have been Kelly to perform that show instead of her. She could have convinced them immediately.

Selene made her way to her cavehome. She opened the door. Mona and Aqib were standing just inside. Aqib was cooking up three bosa burgers. Bosa were little furry creatures with a fluffy tail. Elias told her they actually were squirrels, which were animals from Earth that found their way onto their spaceship before it took off. She had no choice but to believe him since no one in Quaketown could possibly know if this was the truth.

"Hey, honey," her mother greeted her. "How was your day?"

"Busy." Selene was rushing around the room. She reached inside her pack and took out a wooden brush. She started to brush her hair. She loved her wooden brush because it didn't make her hair static.

Aqib slapped the bosa burger in between two jennybobs. "You seem to be in a hurry," he said interested in her plans. "Where might you be headed?"

"I told Miles that I'd meet him at his cavehome this afternoon," said Selene. "I want to get to know him a little more."

Mona and Aqib gave each other curious glances. "It's nice you have calmed down since the Chosen Ceremony," said her mother. "You did a good job at hiding your distaste of the outcome. I give you a lot of credit for giving Miles a chance. He's a good kid."

Aqib nodded in approval. He handed her a bosa burger. It was still sizzling. "You may think you're the only one in this situation, but in reality, over two-thirds of the Chosens start off exactly the same way; complete strangers. You will grow to love that boy, Selene."

Selene munched on her bosa burger, refraining from making the slightest eye contact with her them. She crumbled some vegetables on top of her burger. "Yeah," she sighed. "I suppose you're right."

There was a long awkward pause. Selene decided to change the subject. "I saw Kelly on my way home."

"How is she holding up?" asked her mother. "Is she making any progress?"

"I don't really know. I didn't get a chance to talk to her," said Selene with her mouth full. "I just overheard her defending the decision to leave the planet. Is it true we are running low on supplies?"

"Unfortunately," father answered. His happy-go-lucky attitude changed into a serious tone.

Mona gave him a dirty look almost as if she didn't want Selene to know.

"We were lucky enough to land next to this cave system two hundred years ago," he said. "If we landed out in the open jungle, we wouldn't have had the safety and protection the cave provides for us. Who knows, the scabites might have destroyed us instantly with the limited weapons that we had back then."

Selene shivered. Finished eating her bosa burger, she went to her closet. She only had four changes of clothes. She pulled out her only dress and wondered why she hadn't worn it for her Chosen Ceremony. It was pink with purple polka dots. Selene walked into the changing closet. She changed out of her mining clothes and into her dress while her father was still talking.

"We are lucky we haven't run out of food yet," he said. "Good thing we landed where there was a large population of native animals. Our forefathers scared them out of the cave during the first weeks here. Hunters have traveled in every direction and the farther they went out, the fewer animals there were. We are lucky the fresh water pond is nearby too. The animals are attracted to it and we have an unlimited water source."

"Okay, okay, that's enough for today Aqib," Mona interjected.

Aqib smirked at his wife. "What? You don't enjoy my history lessons?"

"Your history lessons are too depressing," joked her mother.

Aqib filled the room with a great big laugh from the depths of his belly.

They heard a neighbor yell, "Quiet!"

The three of them laughed even more.

Selene grabbed her pack and headed towards the door. "Thanks for the bosa burger, dad. I should be home before you two go to bed."

"Alright, young one. Have fun!" her mother exclaimed with joy.

"Be safe," added her father.

Selene opened the creaky door and shut it tight behind her. She put her face in her hands. It was one of the only times she had lied to her parents and she felt really guilty. Selene hoped that she wasn't going to get used to it.

Selene did not head deeper into the cavehomes where Miles lived, but instead went in the opposite direction. Selene was going outside the cave to meet Sarva.

Thwang! Thwang! Thwang! Three arrows hit the painted red bullseye hanging on the tree, making a perfect triangle. Selene stood behind Sarva while he nocked another arrow and pulled back the bowstring against his right cheek. With his dominant right eye, he looked across the field at the same target.

Sarva then looked at the rectangular device that was strapped near the center the bow. The device read '16 YARDS' in green lettering towards the top. Right underneath it was a screen that had a green dot in the center. He clicked a button on the back of the device with his left pointer finger, which centered the green dot onto the target. The green dot turned into crosshairs. A red arrow pointing upwards and a little to the right flashed on the device's screen. Selene knew the new wind detector was working. Sarva lifted the bow up and to the right while continually holding down the button. The crosshairs lit up and the word 'READY' displayed above the screen.

"Watch this," said a female voice. Ciri stood next to Selene. Her muscles were toned and she had a lot of freckles on her face. "He gets it every time." The three of them were the only ones at the practice range.

Sarva inhaled. Then, on his exhale, he paused. With a steady hand, Sarva released the bow string and the arrow went flying. It soared up high. The wind blew the arrow to the left and gravity pulled it to the ground. Its arc was beautiful.

Thwang!

Selene was in awe. The arrow was perfectly lodged into the center of the bullseye, right between the arrows that he shot mere moments ago.

Selene and Ciri clapped their hands. "Wow, that was awesome," said Selene.

Sarva smiled. "You ain't seen nothing yet." He waved his hand towards them. "You're going to want to step back for this one."

Selene and Ciri both took a few steps back. The girl placed her hands on Selene's shoulders and leaned into her. She was overly excited, she could feel her jumping up and down, up and down.

Sarva took three practice arrows from his quiver. He stuck two in the mud in front of him. He knelt down, nocked the first arrow, and drew it back. He aimed at a different target and centered it with the crosshairs. Then, he bent backwards, aiming sixty-five degrees into the air. He released it and in the same movement, quickly grabbed the second arrow. He locked onto the end of the arrow that was currently flying through the air. Nock, draw, release. With the targeting device still locked on to the first arrow, Sarva grabbed the third arrow. He drew the arrow back and aimed at his target. The second the screen read 'READY', Sarva released.

Selene watched as the second arrow split the first arrow in mid-air, horizontally, down the middle. The arrowhead prevented the two pieces from separating. The broken arrow rocketed down towards the original target. Selene could see it wasn't going hit the target because the trajectory was skewed after it was hit by the second arrow. It was going to be a few feet short, headed to the ground feet in front of the target. She followed it down and right when it was nearly level with the target, the third arrow came whizzing in. It hit the split arrow, splitting it again, but vertically.

The arrow struck with so much force the arrowhead jolted off and stuck into the ground. The third arrow hit directly in the center of the target.

Selene and Ciri stood there, eyes wide open in awe. All of this happened in a matter of seconds.

"Come. Follow me." Sarva took their hands and walked them down the path towards the target. The arrow that was shot last was through the target and stuck nearly a foot into the evergreen. Selene looked at the ground just underneath the target and the arrow that was shot first was in five perfect pieces. Two wooden halves from the front, two wooden halves from the rear with the fletching still attached to each one, and the stone arrowhead separate from the four pieces.

Sarva then put his hand to his ear. "Do you hear that?"

Selene strained her ear towards the jungle. She heard soft chirping just across the ridge.

Sarva ran ahead. Ciri suddenly pulled Selene aside and whispered, "Leave while you still can. Stay away from him." She sounded serious. Ciri ran up to Sarva.

Selene was puzzled. What did Ciri mean by this? Was this a threat? Was it jealousy? She didn't know what to do with this odd information.

Selene decided not to listen to Ciri and hiked up to see what they were looking at. Right on top on the ridge was a cute little bosa. There, lodged in its side was the second arrow.

"Poor little bosa." Selene whimpered. "She was in the wrong place at the wrong time."

Sarva had a big grin on his face.

Ciri turned to her and said, "You idiot. He was planning on hitting it this entire time, weren't you Sarva?" Ciri placed her hand on Sarva's abs.

"Of course," he said.

Selene slowly walked over to the bosa. She grabbed it and snapped its neck, putting it out of its misery. "Poor thing. How could you?" She turned and faced Sarva.

"It's my dinner," he said. "Want some?"

"No, I just had a bosa burger at home," she said.

"Your loss." Sarva picked it up and started skinning it.

It was past midnight. Selene and Sarva waved goodbye to Ciri as she left the jungle. During their conversations, Selene found out that Ciri was a hunter in training. Something seemed off with her.

Selene and Sarva sat down next the fire they made. Sarva finished his meal and cleared his throat. Minutes went by as they sat there in total silence except for the wood crackling in the fire pit.

Selene decided to break the silence. "This is so serene." Selene scooted closer to Sarva. "There's no place I would rather be."

Selene looked up into that vast sky. Selontris was out tonight. So were the stars and planets. Selene laid on the ground with her hands supporting her head.

Sarva stopped dragging a stick around in the dirt and joined her. Their shoulders met. Selene pointed up at an interesting looking red planet, which must have been far far away.

"What do you think is out there?" she wondered, pointing to the red planet and other stars one by one.

"Can't be much," he replied. "Humans have been around for thousands of years. We have yet to come in contact with any other intelligent beings, even after journeying into space."

"The native animals here are pretty intelligent," she pointed out.

"Have you even seen one?" said Sarva, looking at her questioningly.

Selene only knew what a scabite looked like because of the 2-D images from the shows. The only real creatures she has seen with her own eyes were bosas and there weren't many.

"No," she answered. "But they must have some intelligence."

"Believe me, they don't. I hear all the animals on Earth were much smarter than the scabites," Sarva chuckled. "I've never seen them communicate with each other. Never seen them use strategy. There is a reason we use the same traps over and over again. They keep on falling for it. They definitely don't have a memory. I wouldn't be surprised if they didn't have a brain in that tiny skull of theirs."

Selene continued looking at the stars. "Huh, I guess you're right." She reached out to the red planet, attempting to grasp it, wondering if there was anyone living there looking back at them.

A few minutes went by until Selene interrupted the silence again. "What do you think the other humans are doing right now?" she asked.

"You mean the ones on the other planets?" he asked.

"Yeah," she replied.

Sarva took some time thinking about it. Selene could practically see thoughts racing in his head.

"Well if they are still alive, they're probably doing the same as us," said Sarva. "Fighting for survival and preparing to head to the space station. Why do you ask?"

"I was just wondering," said Selene. "What if we didn't land on this planet? What if our people landed on a totally different planet, one that the other humans landed on? Our lives would be so different."

"Yes they would be," he said.

Selene wondered if she would have met Sarva if they did land on a different planet. She hoped so.

"Sarva?" Selene turned her head towards him. He looked at her. "I have one last question."

"Shoot," he said.

Selene thought it over. She thought she was finally ready. She gathered all the confidence that she could muster, more than she thought she was capable of, and whispered to Sarva, "May I kiss you?"

A little smile started to form on Sarva's face. "Of course you can, Selene."

Selene looked deeply into his dark eyes as he nodded. Her heart starting pumping. She moved in closer. Inches away, she closed her eyes and prepared for her first kiss.

Sarva lightly set his hand on her jawline, his fingers lay gently on her cheek. Then, their lips met. Selene now knew why the princesses in the fairy tales kissed all the time. It was the most wonderful sensation that she had ever felt. Selene slowly moved her head away as she opened her eyes.

"Wow, I better not be dreaming," she said.

They both laughed. They continued to kiss each other, for what felt like an eternity in the best way possible. She rolled over on top of him and straddled him. Selene held his wrists to the ground and she bent over for what must have been the twentieth kiss. She had him all to herself.

Sarva suddenly put his finger on her mouth and hushed her. "Did you hear that?"

Selene shook her head. A dozen bad thoughts instantly ran through her. She feared for her life. She prayed to the Five Ancients the scabites weren't about to attack. She definitely didn't want to die the day of her first kiss!

While still straddling Sarva, she saw him slowly open his mouth. He raised his hand and pointed behind her. Selene slowly turned her head around and saw what he was pointing at.

A face with piercing emerald eyes stared at her menacingly. It was her mother.

Chapter 10

10. MEMORIES

Wakan woke up to sharp pains running through his leg. He jerked up from the hard rocky ground and stroked his leg, wincing in pain. It was like someone was driving dirty nails into his leg one by one. Wakan took a deep breath in and slowly let it all out. He did this a couple more times to try to calm down and wondered if he could continue on this journey up the mountain. He thought about his three children and knew he had to do *anything* to save them, no matter the cost.

After a while, the pain died down. Wakan laid back down on his back. He figured he had an hour left to rest. He rolled over and Rufus was facing him, four feet away. His eyes were open. Rufus must have been watching him rub his leg. Wakan became embarrassed and turned over. He didn't want people to think of him as a hindrance. They were all on this journey because of *him*, after all.

Wakan couldn't see the exit of the tunnel but he could see the sunlight shining through. The heat inside the tunnel wasn't too bad. They were insulated just like the caves back in Dunestone.

Wakan's neck became itchy. He scratched it and he felt something flaky on his neck. He peeled it off slowly and brought it in front of his face. It was dead skin. He must have been badly burned from the sun's rays. Come to think of it, his neck was one fire. He never wanted to experience that feeling again. Lost in thought, Wakan swiftly fell back to sleep.

After what felt like only ten minutes, Wakan was woken up by a tap on his shoulder. It was Bruce.

"What a night," Wakan yawned and stretched.

Everyone was already up and walking around. It looked like Bruce and Tank were ready to go.

"We leave in fifteen," said Bruce. "If I were you, I would eat something and stretch before we head out. Here." Bruce handed Wakan a yellow sparkfruit. This was Wakan's favorite fruit. He was very thirsty and sparkfruit would quench one's thirst no matter how thirsty they were. It's also a little sour and provides a lot of energy. He bit into it and he could almost hear his tongue squeal with happiness.

Wakan stood up and grabbed his bag that was sitting beside him. "I'm ready whenever you are."

Bruce circled a finger in the air, signaling it was time to leave. "The sooner we leave, the sooner we arrive at the end of the tunnel and we'll have more time to rest until the sun goes down. Everyone ready?"

"Is everyone feeling okay?" Christine chimed in. She looked around at her companions, assessing the condition everyone was in. Christine came to the conclusion everyone was healthy and ready to head out. They grabbed their bags and started through the tunnel.

Today, Wakan noticed everyone was still in their own groups. The two journeymen, Bruce and Tank, remained up front followed by the best friends, him, Copper, and Rufus, with the caretakers, Christine and Pai, bringing up the rear.

A few miles in the tunnel, Rufus walked alongside Wakan. "I apologize if I freaked you out when we were sleeping," said Rufus. "I couldn't help but hear you in pain. How is your leg?"

"Hanging in there," said Wakan. "I'm not going to lie, the pain has been coming more frequently. It used to be once a week but now it's at least a few times a day. Walking up a giant mountain in this heat isn't helping either."

"I bet," said Rufus.

"I just know I have to keep on going because time isn't in our favor." Wakan could tell Rufus was deep in thought. Rufus began walking slower and Wakan slowed down to his pace.

"Hey," said Rufus. "If…I mean *when* we make it back to Dunestone I think I can make something to help better support your leg before we get on the spaceship. All it will take is some simple parts."

"Really, Rufus? That would be great." Wakan knew he could count on his friend.

"No problem, old pal," said Rufus. "When I see someone in pain, I always wonder how I can help."

Wakan remembered something. "What were you working on yesterday? It seemed like you had a breakthrough."

"Ah," said Rufus. "I have been meaning to tell you and Copper this."

Copper listened up.

"I created this device that separates the water from all of the silt and scum."

"No shit!" exclaimed Copper. "Really? How does the device work?"

This was the most interested Wakan had seen Copper in years. Copper had been waiting for a long time for something to make crabbing easier.

"Well, it's a twelve foot by ten foot rectangular box with no top or bottom. It can be raised or lowered depending on the depth of the water. The bottom edges dig just beneath the silt to create a sealed barrier. The box sends out pulses into the water that separates the particles in the water and sends them to the top. The top edges shake the particles out of the box leaving the water inside the box clear. I have already tested it and it works perfectly."

"We will be able to see the crabs now under the silt," said Copper with excitement. "We might not even need to lug around those big nets anymore, we can go back to using the spears. That's so great, you're a genius, Rufus!"

"That's not all," Rufus continued.

Wakan knew Rufus liked to show off his brilliant mind. "What else did you cook up?"

Rufus reached into his bag and pulled out some capsules.

Wakan knew this is what he saw Rufus dropping into the test tube yesterday. Upon closer examination, the capsule was pill shaped and had a fuzzy outer shell with something green glowing on the inside. What was this? Could it be…?

"This, my friends, is a water purifier capsule," Rufus announced proudly.

This grabbed everyone's attention. Bruce turned around immediately and Tank followed suit.

Wakan heard an audible gasp of excitement come from Christine behind him. Christine and Pai ran up to Rufus.

They all stopped and gathered around him.

Rufus held up the capsule to the light from the tan illuminating mushrooms. "Behold! This little baby can purify hundreds of gallons of water."

Wakan was impressed.

"We won't have to boil our water anymore," said Bruce.

"Purified water will make the crops grow bigger," said Pai. "Fruits and vegetables will taste better and be healthier."

Christine unknowingly held on to Copper's arm. "This will greatly improve our vaccination process," said Christine. "You don't know how much dirty water we go through each day just to make one simple vaccine."

"This sounds just like your purifying box," said Copper.

"Yes, that is where I got the idea from," replied Rufus.

"Little pill make Tank feel stronger?" said Tank. He reached for the capsule.

Christine and Copper prevented Tank from taking a capsule by each grabbing onto one of his huge arms. It took all of their body weight to stop him.

"No, Tank," said Rufus, swatting at his hands. "There's no telling what swallowing a capsule will do and I'd rather not find out." Rufus put the water purifying capsules back into his bag.

The group continued through the tunnel. Wakan noticed that the once divided group was now closer together. He could reach out and touch Tank on the shoulder, not that he would want to. He couldn't even guess what the consequences would be.

"Anything else you want to boast about?" asked Wakan jokingly.

"I always have more," said Rufus. "I have been secretively holding on to this one." He captured the ears of the entire group, now at the center of attention.

"What I am about to tell you, I have yet to build, but I have plans for a self-propelled boat."

Wakan was unsurprised when Copper spoke up first. "Are you kidding me?!" shouted Copper. He jumped in the air with joy. "That would be so awesome! I have always wondered if there are any other creatures besides crabs living in the lake. I bet everything I own there are more creatures out there. Man, I can't wait for this."

"You can use them for relaxation too," said Pai. "Imagine laying down in a boat far away from land and looking up at the stars."

Wakan pictured this in his head. "Beautiful."

Everyone must have been picturing this in their head because it quickly grew quiet.

After a while, Rufus came up close to Wakan.

"Come to think of it," said Rufus to Wakan, "I was working on an invention of mine many ages ago." Rufus paused for a moment. "In hindsight, this might have come in handy. It could have gotten us to the peak of Mount Crimson much faster. It's only meant for one person though. But sadly, it's unfinished and I forgot about it until just now…"

"What is it?" said Wakan.

"You know what? Forget I told you that." Rufus shook his head. "It doesn't matter. It can't help us now."

Wakan was interested in what Rufus was going to tell him, but he wasn't going to press him for more information because he knew it was pointless. Rufus never talked about his unfinished inventions.

They ventured through the tunnel. Wakan told them two stories along the way.

The first was about the five great spirits who blessed their planet with life. The five were loosely based on the five spirits from *The New Frontier*. The Verdurous Spirit blessed the soil for them allowing crops to grow. The Venerable Spirit provided the crabs for food. The Vivacious Spirit gave them the knowledge to build inventions out of the scraps from the spaceship. The Virtuous Spirit gave peace to everyone so they all would get along. The Virile Spirit gave them all the strength to get through all the tough times.

The second story was about the many voyages of Stifu, an early explorer who mapped the surrounding lakes. He was a jolly fellow who made up songs on his voyages.

One of his songs, titled *Hidden Frogs*, went something like this:

Today on the lake, I was a family's guide.
They asked me if I was crossin' to the other side.
"I cross these green lakes e'ry day," I replied.
The family boarded, then sat down and sighed.

We were just about halfway across the tide,
When one of the children sat up and cried.
In the lake, something green slipped and slide.
"Don't you worry, they're just frogs," I lied.

The father spoke up and said, "The frogs died."
The mother said, "I thought they went to hide?"
"The frogs are very much alive," I denied.
"Up on the mountain, is where the frogs reside."

Up on the mountain, is where the family eyed.
I looked around the boat, hoping it wasn't inside.
I steered to the shore, which concluded our ride.
"Thank you," they said. I was happy to provide.

They finally made it to the end of the tunnel. The sun was still in the sky but was almost touching the horizon. They had another hour before the sun fully set. This was their opportunity to rest.

The moon and the stars shone brightly as the group walked up the path along the mountainside. Wakan pushed himself to keep on going. Whenever his body and his mind strayed from his goal of reaching the summit, he would just think about his wife and kids.

Everything Wakan had learned from his wife, Sapphire, made him push forward; her passion for life, for stories, for adventure, for love. All of the traits she had possessed, Wakan had inherited after she passed away.

To further push himself, Wakan pictured the future.

He saw Star and a gray-haired Rufus working together as equals on a faraway planet, giving each other tips on improving their inventions. He pictured her with tools in hand, working on something massive for the survival of the human race.

Wakan pictured Triss apprenticing with Memphis and Christine. One day she would far surpass both of them and become a well-respected nurse that would treat the human race with not only top level medical prowess, but with her mother's kindness as well.

As for Zato, Wakan knew he loved helping the crabbers catch the crabs but he didn't think there would be a future for crabbers if they were to live on a new planet. Chances were slim there would be any crabs or any underwater creatures to hunt. The crabbers would have to discover their own talents other than crabbing. Wakan thought hard and figured Zato would be a good explorer. He loved to wander off by himself, digging in the sand and collecting his finds. Wakan once found him on top of the spaceship. To this day, Wakan never discovered how he got up there in the first place. But up there, Zato found the antennae that would power the irrigation systems timer. Wakan pictured Zato in a spacesuit leading an expedition to a new world.

Bruce was crunching and spitting out dunelope seeds when suddenly he halted. There were eleven marked graves just off the edge of the path. Wakan walked closer so he could read what they said.

"This is Memorial Hill," said Bruce. "Let's pay our respects."

The grave on the far left read: *Here lies Tommy Sokko. His flag was the first.* Wakan knew this name. Tommy was the first one to reach the peak of Mount Crimson. His first step off the peak was his last. Eyewitnesses reported that he flew down the mountain.

The next grave read: *Rayyan Almasi. Father to us all.* Wakan thought he knew all the stories, but that name didn't ring any bells. "Who was this man?" he asked the group.

"Rayyan Almasi," said Rufus. "He led the science division here a hundred and fifty years ago. The science community called him the father of science. Rayyan was the first one to recommend taking the parts out of the spaceship and shape them into things that would benefit us. Before that, we were just farmers and crabbers. He allowed us to use our minds."

"I'll have to remember that one," said Wakan.

"I never knew what happened to him," said Rufus. "I guess he died on this mountain."

Pai was kneeling down at the third grave. Wakan couldn't read what the gravestone said. Tears rolled down her cheeks, down her chin, and dripped onto her knees. A puddle formed on the sandy ground. "My grandmother," whispered Pai. "She was a guide here many years ago."

Wakan set his hand on her shoulder. She stood up and hugged him.

"I miss her so much," she said. "She taught me everything I know. All I have left of her is this journal and the memories we shared." Her hand was grasping her bag.

"Chiyo Ito," said Wakan.

"You knew my grandmother?" Pai wiped away her tears.

"In many ways she was my teacher," he said.

Pai gasped. "What?" She held Wakan's face and looked into his eyes.

"Yes. When I was little she would take me around Dunestone," he said. "She was pretty young too, in her early twenties. She held my hand dragging me around the village telling me the history of everything we passed. In many ways, I got my love of history from her."

Pai was silent.

"I remember when she took me to the Grand Dune just over the hills of the village center," said Wakan. "Chiyo kept on building it up like it was some sort of monument. When we finally reached our destination on top of the hill, I looked over the many dunes covering the landscape. I couldn't figure out what was so special about it, I could have just stayed inside the village to look at dunes. Chiyo must have seen the look on my face because she laughed. I started to get angry so she calmed me down and told me to turn around. So I did and I saw the most beautiful sight I have ever laid my eyes on, even to this day. What I saw," Wakan paused, "was Dunestone in all of its glory. The village shone in the bright lights under the moon and stars. The spaceship lit up like a beacon. I gazed down onto the village at all our people bustling around and busy at work. We have come together as a community to rebuild civilization. It was that day when I realized how special we all were. All thanks to your grandmother, Pai."

Pai gave him another hug.

"Chiyo also introduced me to my wife," said Wakan. "I owe her so much. I'm sorry for what happened to her. My condolences."

"Thank you, Wakan," said Pai.

They paid their respects to Chiyo Ito together.

The fourth grave read: *Pakku Shiffron.* Before Wakan could read more, Christine interrupted.

"Pakku was one of the elite healers of the Healing Corps, when it was formed around twenty-five years ago," said Christine. "Memphis told me a lot about him. He traveled to this mountain with the Healing Corps because there was an earthquake that rumbled Dunestone and we believed it came from the direction of Mount Crimson. There was a team of explorers on the mountain at the time. When the Corps reached the explorers, they found a massive fissure in the middle of the mountain."

"That's the earthquake that split Mount Crimson in two," said Bruce. "The lower mountain that was formed was called Mount Midoriyama, this mountain we are on right now. That fissure is why they built the flamerod bridge."

"Correct," said Christine. "Anyways, Pakku was helping out the explorers at the bottom of the fissure when a giant boulder came down and crushed him. He saved many lives and was the only casualty that day. When the Healing Corps brought the survivors home, they disbanded the Corps in honor of Pakku."

Wakan noticed Copper was standing alone over by the edge looking down the mountainside while they looked at the graves. Wakan decided to join him.

"Something wrong, Copper?" asked Wakan.

"No," said Copper. "It's nothing."

"Well, if something is, you can always come to me," said Wakan.

Wakan turned away and was about to head back to Memorial Hill until he felt a hand touch his back. Wakan turned back to Copper. Copper nodded at the last seven graves and then looked at the ground.

Wakan looked at the last seven graves and realized why Copper was acting this way. Each of the gravestones had the name of the person followed by *Taken away from us too soon by The Burstfly Epidemic.*

The Burstfly Epidemic. Everyone remembered this fateful day. The Burstfly Epidemic stormed through Dunestone nine years ago. It was the darkest time in the history of Dunestone. It happened during one of the hottest summers in recorded history. The burstfly population was booming. While the sun was out and the people were resting in their caves, a loud explosion woke everyone up. They thought it was a volcano eruption, and it very well could have been, but they never found any evidence. The burstflies came in from the west by the mountains. They invaded homes and infected people. People grabbed on to anything they could get their hands on to swat away the burstflies. Finally, they dispersed into the desert. Supplies were limited and nearly a quarter of the population was infected. In the end, one third of the population fell victim to the disease. Wakan knew Copper's parents and fiancé died that day.

These seven graves must have been the team of explorers that was overrun by the burstflies nine years ago.

Wakan turned back to Copper who was still looking at the ground. "Copper. Buddy," said Wakan. He saw tears forming in Copper's eyes. He went in for a hug.

Everyone else, except Tank, who was taking a nap on the ground, came over to Wakan and Copper. They huddled in a circle with their arms around each other. Everyone had lost someone during The Burstfly Epidemic. They put their heads down together and Wakan led a prayer.

After a moment of silence, Bruce went over to Tank to wake him up. They all grabbed their bags and continued up the path.

Shortly after, they came upon a tunnel, the sky still shining bright.

Bruce looked up and around and calculated the hours remaining. He turned to the group with a concerned look on his face.

"What is it?" asked Wakan.

"Well, the good news is we made it to the tunnel safely with plenty of time to spare."

"And the bad news?" asked Copper.

"The bad news is," hesitated Bruce, "by the time we reach the end of the tunnel, the sun will be out. Meaning we might just have to go out in the sun to make it to the cure to be back in time for your departure."

An uneasy feeling bubbled up in the pit of Wakan's stomach. The burn on his neck still ached. "I must do what it takes to save my children."

11. THE SEARCH

Brant woke up to a wet face. He had been lying face down in a pool of his own drool. It smelled like bad dry mouth. He realized his back hurt; he had fallen asleep on the hard floor. Persephone must have put a blanket over him in the middle of the night. She was really sweet. He sat up, hugged his legs, and looked around.

The Projectocube was still turned on, humming in mid-air. His Virtuvisor was upside down next to him. It was wet too. He must have fallen asleep while still wearing it.

Pandora stealthily crept up on Brant, but he heard her coming. He put his tattooed arms around her. "Where's Mommy?" he cooed.

"Mommy is studying," said Persephone. Brant looked out the bedroom door and she was sitting at a desk in the living room.

Brant took off the blanket and walked into the living room. "When did you get home?"

"Late," said Persephone. "If I were you I would avoid the excavation site right down the road. There are a lot of people gathered there, either working on the excavation of the spaceship or rebelling against it."

Brant could tell she was annoyed.

"Why can't they just leave them alone? They don't have to leave if they don't want to," she said.

"Are you going?" asked Brant curiously.

"Yeah, I'm currently reading through the manuals that were left behind," said Persephone. "I will be able to make sure the spaceship functions properly, like a mechanic." She turned the page. "But I really just want a seat on the spaceship so I can find something else to do. I'm bored out of my mind here, being confined to the city my whole life isn't fulfilling to me. I'm sure there will be a lot more professions that will open up once we find out what's going on." Persephone turned another page. "Are you going?" she asked casually.

"At first, I hated the idea of leaving," started Brant, "But I really don't have much left for me here. Alexis invited me to be her apprentice and protect her wherever we end up. Speaking of Alexis, I was supposed to meet her this morning."

"There's some food over there," said Persephone, pointing at the counter. "Help yourself before you leave."

Brant shut the door and changed out of his shirt and pants. He then put on his usual cloak and put up his hood. Brant opened the bedroom door after putting his tech in a pouch.

Persephone was still reading the manual of the spaceship as he picked up a potato. "Sorry to run on such short notice," he said.

"Hey, you gotta do what you gotta do," she said. "Good luck and have fun. See you later."

Brant left Persephone's house. She was right. There were a lot of people gathered around the excavation site down the street. Brant wondered if it would be faster to go straight through or to go around. If he were to go around, he might run into the Greasy Gangsters. Brant walked straight ahead munching on the potato.

Brant could hear the sound of shovels hitting the dirt as he moved closer to the construction. There were hundreds of people excavating the tip of the spaceship. Brant looked up and saw people standing on top of the largest structure he had seen inside "The Eye." They were sawing an opening for the spaceship to launch out of the glass dome. A latch was being installed.

Continuing down the street, Brant heard the Pretty Pranksters shouting at the workers. He was watching the people at the top of the dome when he accidentally bumped into someone.

"Watch where you're going," the woman said. "Brant?" It was Lizbeth. "Long time no see."

"Good morning, Lizbeth," said Brant. "I hear you have been up to no good." He motioned her to walk with him.

"That must be a different Lizbeth," she said. "I have been doing nothing but good honest work."

"Is that why you call your group the Pretty Pranksters?" Brant laughed.

"Oh, so maybe I am that Lizbeth," she smirked.

"There are cooler things you could have named your group," said Brant. "Something that actually makes sense instead of rhyming it with the worst group of people."

"Name one," she said.

"Well, if you wanted to keep the same ideas you could have named it the Pretty Poisons. Since you are poisoning the community."

"Fuck off," said Lizbeth. She punched him on his bicep. She laughed out loud. "You know what? That does sound better."

"Glad to be of service," he said.

"Where are you off to, looking so mysterious?" asked Lizbeth.

"Did no one tell you?" said Brant. "I am Master Alexis' new apprentice."

"No fucking way," Lizbeth said punching him in the same spot.

Brant winced in pain but only for a second.

"Congratulations!" she said. "Well I'll let you go then. We should catch up sometime."

"Don't get in too much trouble now, Lizbeth." Brant waved goodbye.

"You know me," she waved back.

Brant had to push his way through the tough looking women who were most likely with Lizbeth. They all wore neon pink outfits.

Finally, he made it out of the crowd and was a few streets away from Alexis' house. Brant wondered what she had in store for him today. He hoped she wouldn't go hard on him to make up for his outburst the previous day.

The alleyway he went down was pitch black. He realized he had never traveled this way before. Brant felt around to memorize his surroundings for the next time. There was a heating pipe he had to duck under and a pair of vents he had to step on to make it across a gap. He made it to the other side and the creepy house was right in front of him. Brant thought it was strange how he had never seen this alleyway before.

Brant walked up the steps onto the porch and knocked on the door three times. He heard the creaks of Alexis' footsteps coming to greet him. The door squeaked open as he saw her wrinkly hand reach out, expecting him to hold on. He did as he had always done and grabbed her hand. Alexis lead him inside and the lights flickered on.

"Always meditating, I see," said Brant. "What's on the agenda for today?"

Alexis was already packing her handbag. It was a bigger bag than normal. She put in a bottle of water, some vegetables, and a raw slab of raw meat that was encased in a clear bag. She put her daggers in the sheathes around her waist. Alexis also grabbed a silver-plated sword that was hanging above the doorway. Brant smiled because he knew he was going to see some action today.

"Rescue mission," said Alexis. "A young couple ventured off into the Outside yesterday and never returned. They were hunting with a group ,of scavengers when it happened. My guess is they wanted some alone time and wandered off. The group they were with reported the missing couple's spool of yarn was severed and they couldn't find their way back. Luckily, I know there is a cave system near where they were reported missing. That's where we will be going. If you ask me, something seems suspicious."

"Yeah, to me it sounds like someone in the group was jealous of the young couple," said Brant. "Yarn doesn't just get cut in the middle of nowhere."

"So there *is* a brain under that hood," said Alexis. "My thoughts exactly. Our mission is to find the couple first. When we come back, we can question the group to see if there should be any suspects. Keep your eyes open for anything out of the ordinary."

Brant grabbed his pouch and slung it around his shoulder. "Sounds like a plan," he said. He sheathed his daggers under his cloak. "Do I get a sword too?"

Alexis pulled a silver sword out from under the arm of a chair and held it out for him.

He looked at the other furniture. "Geez, do you keep weapons everywhere?" Brant chuckled.

Alexis sighed. "Are you ready to go? Do you have everything you need?"

"As long as you have everything, I am ready to go," he said.

Alexis opened the door to the Outside. She picked up her spool of yarn and tied the end of it to the stake. She put the spool inside the box at her waist.

"You seem a bit more cheery today," she said. "Does that have anything to do with Persephone?"

"How did you find out?" he asked.

"I have my ways," she said.

Brant *was* feeling happier today. It had been years since the last time he'd felt like this. He didn't think about it until Alexis brought it up. *Was it because of Persephone?* He had barely even seen her last night and this morning. Maybe it was because of Pandora? Or maybe because he didn't have to deal with the Greasy Gangster?

162

His mind wandered and he thought of Elijah and Phoebe. *Elijah and Phoebe*...He missed them so much.

Alexis could sense his good mood start to die down. "Touchy subject?"

They both turned on their illuminating objects. "No," he said. "Just thought of my adoptive parents." He started following Alexis. "Has it really only been two days? It seems so much longer than that."

"What you have been through and how you dealt with it, I'm sure it feels like a lifetime ago," said Alexis.

Brant nodded.

They walked in silence through the darkness and dense fog. The only sound that could be heard was the yarn lightly unspooling.

There was a weird smell in the air. Brant couldn't tell exactly what it was. He felt a tap on his shoulder. That meant she was changing directions. He followed.

While looking down, he saw a pair of footprints in the dirt. He alerted Alexis and pointed down at them.

"Good eye," she whispered. "Yesterday's group was definitely out this way, so it's a good chance these are their footsteps."

Alexis and Brant followed the footprints. There were some spots of blood and specterling prints as well. Brant felt a chill go up his spine. Where there was blood, wolfwraiths weren't too far behind. Brant's heart rate increased.

They followed the footsteps for a half hour. They had already passed the footprints that lead back to "The Eye." They reached a point where the footprints were scattered and were going around in circles.

There were no signs of hunting or an attack. This is where the group must have taken a break. Somewhere around here will be two pairs of footprints leading off into the unknown.

They could tell a fire had been put out. Specterling fur was on the ground near the ashes. Brant concluded the blood from earlier came from the specterlings the scavengers hunted.

"Let's break off here," whispered Alexis. "If you find the couples' tracks, just tap your daggers lightly together until I find you. I'll do the same."

Brant nodded. He knelt down to look at the footprints more closely. There were three pairs of footprints with soles and one pair of footprints that were made with bare feet. The soled footprints went off to the right while the barefoot tracks went forward.

Brant decided to follow the barefoot tracks first. Just before the footprints turned around, he found a piece of yarn that had been cut. Brant picked up the yarn. By the way it was frayed, Brant concluded it had been cut with a dull blade. Who would have done this? Brant looked up and saw two pairs of footprints leading away from the cut yarn. Brant unsheathed his daggers and started tapping them together. After a few moments, Alexis showed up.

"Look," he whispered pointing at the yarn and footprints. "I think I'm on to something." He showed Alexis the frayed yarn. "Let's keep searching," he said as they narrowed in on the tracks.

They followed the footsteps down a winding path. "This is definitely the way to the cave," said Alexis. "If the couple was experienced out here, they would know where to seek shelter."

Brant held on to his silver necklace and was in deep thought. "Do they have kids?"

"Who? The couple?" asked Alexis.

Brant nodded.

"I'm not sure, why do you ask?" she said.

Brant stopped in his tracks. "Have you heard of the stories about me?"

"What do you mean?" she asked.

"What I am about to tell you happened a long time ago," said Brant. "I am too young to remember what happened but I have heard stories from different people and they are all the same, so I have no choice but to believe them."

"My father, Beck was a young handsome man, younger than I am now, and my mother Kat was even younger. I don't know much about my father except he had a bad temper. As for my mother, she was an adventurer and liked pushing the boundaries of the Outside. I don't remember what they looked like but I remember the distinct smell they had. The same musky smell the Sneak Arena has."

Alexis looked at Brant with a straight face. Brant then noticed a slight smile start to form in the corner of her lips. Had she known them?

"One night, Beck and Kat spent the night in the Outside. What they were doing out there, no one has a clear answer. Some say they had to do it because of their faith, which I don't understand. They told their parents they had an important meeting they had to attend in the Outside. Why would there be a meeting out here? Witnesses saw them leave through the southernmost gate. That night, my mother and father never came back. It's all shrouded in mystery."

"A team of assassins led a search party to look for them," continued his story about his parents. "For three days, they looked for them with no luck. On the third night, an assassin made a great discovery. She found a baby curled up in a basket filled with blankets. This assassin thought the baby was dead because it wasn't crying. To her relief, when she picked up the baby, it smiled and reached out for her with its tiny arms. She brought the baby home to her husband and they adopted it the very next day. The assassin's name was Phoebe."

"And you were the child?" Alexis finished his story.

"I was indeed," said Brant. He grasped his silver necklace and showed it to Alexis. "The only thing my parents left behind was this necklace. It keeps me close to them, even though I have no memory of them. A part of me dies when I hear someone has gone missing, but the other part of me wants to help them, to find them, to make sure they can be safely returned to a loving family."

The silver daggers on his necklace glowed in the darkness. It was reflecting the light from Brant's Projectocube.

Alexis held on to his hand. "I knew you had a heart in there." She tapped Brant's chest.

Brant smiled. "At least someone recognizes that."

They continued following the tracks until Brant spotted blood sprayed across the ground. "Uh oh, this doesn't look good."

"Stay close to me," said Alexis. "We are out too far. If something were to attack, we could be done for. Take out your daggers and stay vigilant."

Brant did as he was told.

They huddled together as they kept the pair of footprints in their eyesight. Brant listened to his surroundings, trying to detect movement from any bloodthirsty predators.

Suddenly, Brant saw something big out of the corner of his eye. It had grey matted fur. He turned to see the wolfwraith charging at him with fangs bared and claws protracted, ready to pounce. It moved so fast but made little noise.

"Move!" yelled Brant as he pushed Alexis to the side.

The wolfwraith leapt over Brant. This was the first time Brant had actually seen a wolfwraith up close. It was just as big as him, but must have weighed much more. The wolfwraith had big, glowing, piercing yellow eyes. Its snout and jaw were long and the two sets of fangs were the length of Brant's forearm. The fur on its body was mostly grey with black stripes that seemed to have no pattern. Its front legs were bound in muscle as it used its front legs to propel itself forward.

These features were what made Brant so fearful of running into these monsters. But it is what was beyond those features that surprised, and now scared, him even more. The wolfwraith's torso was not covered in fur at all. It had a rough scaly texture. From the torso down, there were no back legs, but instead there was a long thick muscular tail. This must be how they could move so fast and quietly around in the Outside.

Brant looked on in shock as the tail soared past his face and whipped him on his cheek, drawing blood.

Alexis rolled on the ground away from the attack. Once she stopped, she immediately jumped to her feet so she could stand her ground.

Brant saw the look on her face when she saw the tail and knew she had never encountered a wolfwraith either.

"The fuck is that?" said Alexis, her eyes wide.

The wolfwraith arched its back and pointed its head skyward. It howled into the night sky calling for its pack.

The hair on the back of Brant's neck stood up and scraped against the inside of his hood.

"Get out of here!" yelled Alexis. "Now!"

"There's no way I'm leaving you to face them alone," said Brant as he readied his daggers. "They're much faster than us. We need to kill this one before the others get here or else we will be outnumbered."

Alexis nodded. "Make every movement count."

The wolfwraith averted its attention towards Alexis. Brant ran towards it while it leapt towards her.

The wolfwraith's claws on its right paw dug into Alexis' left arm.

Brant saw her arm being pulled away with the claws still deep within her skin as he tackled the beast. She was thrown to the ground as Brant stabbed the wolfwraith several times in its side hoping to strike a lethal blow to an artery. "Take this, you bastard!" The wolfwraith squirmed and kicked its front legs. It cried out in agony. Blood covered Brant's arms.

As Alexis fell to the ground, her daggers flew out of her grasp and landed on the ground out of sight. She was lying on the ground trying to pry the claws out from her arm.

Brant noticed the wolfwraith's paw was missing a toe. It must have been the same wolfwraith that killed Elijah and Phoebe. This must be the leader.

He swung his daggers at the paw that wouldn't let go of his Master's arm. Once. Twice. It took three slashes until he hacked the paw off.

The wolfwraith leaped up on one leg and howled in pain. It slithered into the fog leaving a trail of blood behind.

Blood poured out of Alexis' arm as she sat up. "I can't pull these out," she said referring to the claws that were still imbedded in her arm. "Or else I will bleed out. I need to make a tourniquet fast. Come help."

Brant fell to his knees. "What do you need me to do?"

"Cut off your hood and wrap it tightly around my arm," she said. "As tight as you can. It will prevent the flow of blood into my arm."

"My hood...?" asked Brant. He loved his hood. But he also loved his Master. Brant took his dagger and sawed off his hood. He took it and wrapped it tightly around her arm.

"Very good," she said. "Now pull it tight and tie a knot." She held on to the paw to make sure it didn't slip loose. She could bleed out if she took it out.

Brant did as he was told. "Now what do we do?"

Alexis took his head in her hands to look at him straight into his eyes. "You need to defend us. You dealt with that one quickly. You should have no problem fighting the others. Once you are done, we will have to follow the yarn back to seek professional help to save my arm. Then, you will need the help of

169

other assassins to come help search for the couple. We have yet to find definitive proof that they are dead or alive. But I still have hope."

Brant put his arm on her shoulder. "I'll do my best." He smiled to lighten the seriousness of the situation.

Three wolfwraiths came out of the fog into the light. Brant noticed that neither of them were the one he had just fought off. Brant reached behind him and pulled out the silver sword Alexis gave him.

"Stay behind me," he ordered Alexis.

Brant grabbed his Projectocube and tossed it in front of him. "Initiate holo 18-J." The Projectocube glowed even brighter and hovered in the air. It started humming.

The wolfwraiths lurked closer as the Projectocube projected eight different holograms of Brant onto the fog. The wolfwraiths looked around in confusion. One of them even attacked a holoBrant to no effect. Brant's plan to distract them was working.

Brant turned around to Alexis. "Come on, let's sneak out of here." He grabbed on to her good arm and tried helping her up, until he heard a loud shatter behind him. Pieces of the Projectocube slid past him and he looked up in horror.

The wolfwraiths growled behind him. Brant turned around and raised his silver sword. He slashed it out in front of him. The wolfwraiths were unafraid. They slithered even closer.

Brant could smell their breath, reminding him of how his house reeked two nights ago: fresh blood, raw meat, and death. Brant wanted to puke. He kept on slashing at the wolfwraiths.

Brant suddenly realized the wolfwraiths had somehow moved him out of position so they were between him and Alexis. Two of them turned to face her as the middle one stood its ground against Brant.

"No!" yelled Brant as he instinctively held out his hand to Alexis. Brant closed his eyes and lunged forward, slicing his silver sword through the air. The sword hit the ground with a thud. He thought he had missed, until he opened up his eyes. The wolfwraiths head was decapitated from its body and laid on the ground. He gasped.

The other two wolfwraiths were dragging Alexis off into the fog in the same direction the first wolfwraith went.

"Master Alexis!" yelled Brant. He ran after them but the wolfwraiths were much faster. "Hold on, Alexis! I'm coming for you!"

Brant heard Alexis yelling back at him in the distance. "All is lost! Save yourself!"

Out in the fog, he saw two pairs of yellow eyes staring back at him. How many more were there? What was he supposed to do?

Brant held on to his silver sword as tight as possible. He knew his life depended on it.

12. TOTAL DEVASTATION

The sky was pitch black and orange flames were all around. Jaylin looked out into the horizon. All seven moons were present. She was standing on top of a tall building. She walked forward as she closed her eyes, spread her arms, and dove off of the skyscraper. The flames engulfed her as she sped past people screaming in the windows. On each floor that went by, the people catching fire turned into Akeer. Faster and faster she fell farther into the flames. She was about to hit the ground when suddenly she was shaken awake.

"Jaylin," said her mother as she continued shaking her. "You're having a nightmare. Snap out of it."

Jaylin opened her eyes slowly. "I'm up. I'm up."

Lydia stopped shaking her.

Jaylin saw that she was concerned. Not about her nightmare but about something else. "What's wrong?"

"Akeer," said Lydia. "Have you seen Akeer at all? He didn't come home last night. Your father and I fell asleep early and didn't put two and two together."

Jaylin processed this information. "No," she lied through her teeth. "I haven't seen Akeer since I left home yesterday." She couldn't let her mother know she saw him at the School of Building last night. If her mother knew she had run away after seeing Akeer helpless and in pain, she would disown her.

Lydia's eyes were wide and mouth agape. "Akeer went to study shortly after you left," she said. "I fear he went to the school that burned down and collapsed. He didn't tell me where he was going. You would think if he was with someone, they would let us know immediately."

The thought of her brother being dead crept across her mind. The last time she saw her brother, he was pinned down by debris and people were trying to help him. Then fire and smoke filled the room and she lost sight of him. She knew he was in pain.

"I'm sure Akeer is okay," Jaylin lied again as she hugged her mother. "Let me get dressed and I'll come with you to search for him." She didn't know what else to say.

Her mother started to cry as she left Jaylin's bedroom.

Jaylin put on fresh clothing and faced the mirror. She looked like she hadn't slept in a week; dark bags sagged under her eyes. "I'm sure he's okay," she tried to convince herself. She brushed her hair and splashed her face with cold water from the hydropond to wake her up. Her muscles ached.

Yesterday felt like a blur to Jaylin. She went to pick up her force spear until she saw the empty corner and remembered she lost it when she shot the large boulder.

Her backpack was in her room. Jaylin knelt down and opened it up. The backpack was still filled to the rim with dead armored fish. It smelled awful. She gagged as she closed it back up.

Her stomach growled. She realized her family didn't eat dinner last night; too shocked by the events that had taken place. She picked up her backpack and left her bedroom.

Denna, Lydia, and Arkadia were in the living room, sitting in silence. Mother already had her sandals on.

Jaylin dumped her entire catch down the garbage shoot. Her father looked impressed but didn't say anything.

She rinsed out her backpack and motioned to her mother that she was ready. Jaylin grabbed her aqua-breather and set it in her backpack. She waved goodbye to her father and sister.

"Where should we start our search?" asked Jaylin.

"The infirmary," her mother answered.

Jaylin thought this was the perfect place to start. She knew at the very least he was injured so of course he would be there. Her mother was on the right track.

"Let's go to Jersey General Hospital first," said Jaylin. "If he *was* in the school last night, that infirmary is the closest."

Mother and daughter held hands as they journeyed to Jersey General Hospital. There was a dispatch crew working on salvaging the remains of the School of Building. It looked like all the injured had been taken to the infirmary. The night crew had already disposed of the dead bodies in the ocean. Luckily, not many people were inside at the time of the fire since most people were out celebrating the elected Ambassadors. It could have been *much* worse.

Lydia held the front door of the hospital open for Jaylin. They walked swiftly up to the young chubby receptionist who had the bluest eyes and curliest brown hair, so curly it seemed to be in knots.

"I'm looking for my son," said Lydia. "He might have been in the school last night and we need to know if he's alright."

The receptionist asked, "What's your son's name and what does he look like?"

Jaylin took control. "His name is Akeer Robbins," she said, "…and he looks a lot like me." She looked at the receptionist to see if she could put two and two together. The receptionist looked at her with a blank face. "I'm his twin." *Duh*.

"Ah yes, Akeer," said the receptionist. "I heard our Ambassador just woke up and is doing well." Jaylin flinched at the mention of these words.

With this great news, Lydia gave Jaylin the biggest hug she had ever received.

"He saved countless lives last night," said the receptionist. "Your son is a hero. You should be extremely proud."

Both mother and daughter laughed and cried at the same time. Relief washed over them.

"Well, where is he?" asked Lydia. "May we go see him?"

"Akeer is down the hall to your right," said the receptionist. "Go up one flight of stairs and he should be in the room straight ahead." She looked at her papers. "Room 089."

"Thank you very much," said Lydia.

Jaylin and her mother sprinted to Room 089. They entered the room and there was a doctor in front of Akeer but they could see he was awake and smiling.

"Akeer!" screamed Lydia. "I was so scared when you didn't come home. I'm *so* glad you're okay." She went in for a hug but suddenly stopped short. Jaylin wondered why.

"Hi mom," he coughed. "Hey sis." He coughed again.

Jaylin stepped further into the room. The doctor moved aside. Akeer was waving at her. But it wasn't his human arm waving, it was a robotic limb. She averted her eyes, unable to look at him.

"What happened?" asked a curious Lydia.

The doctor answered for him. "When he was in the burning building, the ceiling collapsed on him, bringing down support beams and plywood," she said. "His arm was trapped underneath the rubble. Luckily, the workers who Akeer rescued lifted the beam off him and brought him here. They saved his life. His right arm was badly injured. We had to amputate it just under the shoulder. We replaced it with the brand new model of bionic limb, the arm04. As you can see, Akeer also has minor lung damage from the smoke. That should heal with time."

"Thank you so much, doctor…" said Lydia.

"Dr. Petra Tsoukalos," she introduced herself as she extended her hand. She had a certain glow to her, very pretty and gentle.

"Lydia Robbins," Lydia responded as she shook Petra's hand. "Nice to meet you. You are our hero." She looked at her son. "When can he come home?"

"Give it a couple of days," said Petra. "He just needs some time to rest and get used to his new appendage. I'm about to give him some physical therapy now."

"I will go get your father and sister," said Lydia. "They are so worried. I'll be right back. I love you." She kissed Akeer on his forehead.

Jaylin followed her mother out of the room.

"Are you coming with me?" asked Lydia.

Jaylin must have had a certain look on her face because of what her mother asked next.

"You're going to have some alone time, aren't you?"

Her mother knew her too well. She hugged her mother and nodded.

They left Jersey General Hospital and said their goodbyes. Lydia headed towards their home and Jaylin went in the opposite direction, towards Spear Temple. She wanted to get a new force spear so she could go back to the docks to catch fresh armored fish to eat. She was starving.

On her way to Spear Temple, she couldn't help but think what happened to Akeer was all her fault. She didn't know how the fire was started inside the school. She thought maybe the mini quake she had caused with the large boulder that fell into the trench knocked something loose in the school and set off the explosions. Jaylin also thought she could have saved Akeer's arm if only she had helped him save the group of people. She was still bitter though because she thought he had lied to her.

Two moons were in the sky as Jaylin made it to Spear Temple. She walked inside.

Ms. Britta was at the counter. She had straight dark hair that was always wet and she was in great shape. For some reason, she always seemed to be in a rush. "Jaylin! It's nice to see you again and so soon. What brings you in here today?"

Jaylin walked around looking at the different spears. "Yesterday, before we bumped into each other, I lost my spear while hunting armored fish."

"Lost your spear, huh? That's very unlike you, Jaylin," said Ms. Britta. "That's a bad omen. How the foreboding forbidden trench did you lose it?"

"I don't want to talk about it," said Jaylin. She didn't want her to know the details. Jaylin picked up a heavy spear that was taller than her. She decided it was way too big for her and placed it back on the shelf. She wandered around, viewing each spear as she passed.

"Are you busy?" asked Ms. Britta.

"Not currently," said Jaylin. "Why?"

"We just got in this new machine," said Ms. Britta. "It's like a weapon and a vehicle all rolled up in one. I haven't tested it out yet. Would you like to join me?"

"Are you kidding?" asked Jaylin. "I would love to!" Anything to take her mind off of the events from the past couple days.

Ms. Britta locked the front door and led Jaylin around back. There was a pool in the middle of the room with a ten-foot long boat in the water. There were force spears mounted on the sides, facing in opposite directions. There were windows on the front and the back of the boat. Jaylin was impressed by this new machine.

Ms. Britta laid down a plank to walk to the boat. "I call it the Lean Mean Spear Machine 7000. Why? I have no idea."

Jaylin laughed. "You're crazy."

Ms. Britta held out her hand. "Join me on this adventure."

Jaylin took her hand and boarded the boat. The door automatically closed behind her.

"This baby fits four people and has enough oxygen for three hours of travel," said Ms. Britta. "It goes up to 65 kilometers per hour. The front spears are offensive. They can clear away boulders and make new paths for us to search. The back spears are defensive, for protecting us from big fish." She put one hand on the ignition and one on the steering wheel. "Are you ready?"

"Oh fin yeah!" Jaylin nodded her head and pumped her fists in the air. "Of course I am."

Ms. Britta started up the boat. She flipped a lever and they began to sink under the water. Jaylin looked through the windows. She couldn't believe how clear the water was. She could see far in the distance. She didn't realize until now how much vision you lose with your eyes open while under water. There were schools of fish all around.

"To test this machine, there is a wreckage over by the trench," said Ms. Britta. "I will fire the spears at half power to clear it away." The wreckage had been thought to be broken off the part of Hydronia that was lost.

On the way down to the trench, Jaylin was looking at and touching every instrument on board, wondering what each controlled.

"I tried my best this morning to persuade the other teachers to overturn their decision," said Ms. Britta. "To just tell Arabella this was all a big misunderstanding and elect you in her place."

Jaylin blushed. "I tried taking your advice," said Jaylin. "It worked for a while until it counted the most. I failed."

"What happened?" asked Ms. Britta.

"My brother was in the burning school last night," she said. "I could have rescued him." She paused. "Now he lost his arm and it's all because of me."

"Don't be so hard on yourself," said Ms. Britta. "Everything happens for a reason."

"Yeah, and that reason was because I wished I was Student Ambassador instead of him," said Jaylin. "I wished him away and now he is suffering because of it." A single tear ran down her face.

Ms. Britta anchored the machine and faced the wreckage in silence. She held down a button on the control panel with her thumb. The spears built up pressure and released as soon as she let go. The wide shockwave from both side spears blasted the rusted wreckage off into the trench.

Jaylin winced at the sound it made.

It was a success. Ms. Britta turned the machine around.

Jaylin still had tears in her eyes.

"I'm not supposed to tell this to you," started Ms. Britta. "But I think it might make you feel a little better."

Jaylin looked up at her, desperate for good news; anything. She wiped her tears away.

"There is one major reason the teachers didn't elect you as Student Ambassador," said Ms. Britta. "They felt your skills would be better utilized here. You are a great asset to our people. You will provide for us and protect us."

Jaylin was surprised by this news. She didn't know what to say.

"I asked if any of them ever had a dream," said Ms. Britta. "I told them it had been your one goal in life to become Student Ambassador and every single one of those teachers would be destroying your dream if they chose someone else. That was the main point I wanted to get across. You have the drive and the passion for the role."

They began to rise through the water towards the surface.

"The teachers, especially Principal Edison, are questioning the safety of the journey to *The New Frontier*. The spaceship is all rusted. They fear it might not make it. That is why they didn't want our greatest students to go."

This flattered Jaylin but she quickly realized what this meant. "So they decided to send my brother on a potential suicide mission instead? That's utterly ridiculous! We need to warn the people! Have the journey delayed!"

"We cannot let anyone know," said Ms. Britta.

The machine broke the surface and they were now back in Spear Temple. She opened the door and stepped out onto the plank.

"We can't cause any panic during a time like this. The spaceship will leave automatically anyways, whether there are people aboard or not. We need

Ambassadors on the spaceship to unite with the other humans so we can start a new world *together*. We wouldn't be part of that if we didn't send anyone. Because of our concern and the size of the spaceship, we had decided to only send two Ambassadors from each age group, fourteen and up, even though this was against the Sleepers decisions. They wanted us to send a quarter of our people. We just could not agree with what they had planned for us, no matter how great they are."

Jaylin didn't know what to do with this information. She stepped outside the vehicle and Ms. Britta led her back into the shop.

Ms. Britta unlocked the front door and tossed Jaylin a force spear that was similar to her old one. She caught it with one hand.

"Take it," said Ms. Britta. "It's on me. Just please don't tell anyone about this conversation."

Jaylin looked down at the force spear and then back at Ms. Britta. Jaylin left Spear Temple without a word. She slung the force spear through the strap on her backpack and decided to head back to Jersey General Hospital.

Even after what Ms. Britta had just told her, her dream was still to become Student Ambassador. Somehow, some way.

Ever since she was a young girl, she wanted to be a leader. It was too late for her to change her goals in life, right? She didn't care if she might die on the journey to another world either. If there was a chance to leave and venture into the stars to meet the rest of the human race, she wouldn't stop until she reached her goal.

Jaylin tried to think of a way she could possibly sneak onto the spaceship before it embarked. She needed a plan, fast.

Jaylin neared the hospital. She was deep in thought when she heard people yelling behind her. Suddenly, people started screaming and running past her. This startled Jaylin and she snapped out of her daydream.

Alarms all around Hydronia sounded, warning the people of an incoming tsunami.

Jaylin turned around and saw a massive wave, taller than any skyscraper, looming on the horizon. Her eyes widened at this beautiful and yet terrifying image. This tsunami will cause massive, possibly irreversible damage.

The blaring alarm rung throughout Hydronia. Jaylin needed to act fast or she would be swept out into the ocean. She heard a loud splash as Hydronia's large anchors dropped into the ocean, stabilizing the massive floating city. Jaylin needed to get to the nearest water bunker and fast. A water bunker was a steel room in the shape of a bubble which laid just below the surface of the ocean; they could be closed off from any outside threats, were impenetrable, and stored their own oxygen supply.

"Where was the closest water bunker?" Jaylin frantically asked herself. "Of course, there are multiple bunkers underneath the hospital. How else would they get the sick and injured to safety?"

Jaylin ran as fast as she could to Jersey General Hospital. Her force spear knocked against her back with each stride. A large shadow loomed over her. The wave was about to hit.

Jaylin finally made it to the hospital. Since there were steps leading up to the entrance, she would have to go down three sub-levels before she made it to the water bunkers.

The streets of Hydronia were desolate. Jaylin was the only one out in the open. She threw open the door and hurried inside the hospital.

Jaylin remembered from her last visit there were stairs to her right. She ran to them and started heading down. She was knocked to the side and hit her shoulder on the wall. The tsunami must have made impact with the city. Jaylin got back up and made it to the first sub-level.

Jaylin had to open the doors and go across the hall to get to the second flight of stairs. On her way down, she was knocked over again as the building shook violently. She hit her head on the railing, giving her a headache. The tsunami must have just crashed into the Hospital. Jaylin rubbed her head as she struggled to stand back up.

Water came rushing into the stairwell. Jaylin knew she had to be careful going down the steps. Rushing water was very powerful and it was enough to sweep her off her feet.

Jaylin opened the doors to the second sub-level. Again, she had to make it across the hallway to reach the stairs. She sloshed her feet through the running water. The water level rose rapidly; it was already up to her hips. A desk floated past her. Finally, she made it to the doors. She had to pry them open.

To her surprise, the stairwell was completely submerged under water already. How was she going to make it to the third sub-level?

Luckily, Jaylin remembered she had put her aqua-breather in her backpack this morning. She took off her backpack and pulled out the device, which now doubled as a life-saver. She put it on and dove into the stairwell.

There were all sorts of furniture and mechanical equipment floating around her. She used them to propel herself forward. She made it down the flight of stairs and came upon the doors. She tried to budge the door open but it looked like it was sealed off from the inside. She panicked. Now what was she to do?

The hilt of the force spear knocked against her head. This reminded her of when she blasted the large boulder. *Of course!*

She grabbed the force spear Ms. Britta had just given her. She set the setting to pierce and held down the button. Like last time, she forced herself to hold on until the pressure was too great. She aimed the spear in the middle of the two doors until she was thrown backwards. Instead of blasting the doors down, the force pierced a hole in the center, which was big enough for Jaylin to swim through. This time the spear floated down back to her since there was nowhere else for it to go.

Finally, Jaylin was on the third sub-level. She just needed to find the entrance to the water bunkers. She swam all over the room. Maybe there weren't any water bunkers down here. She was a goner.

She noticed a hole in the ceiling. She must have just made the hole with her force spear. She looked upwards to see if it was safe to go underneath. There were large support beams leaning downwards. She had no choice but to swim under them.

When Jaylin was halfway across the gaping hole, she heard a scraping sound. She turned around to see if it was a water bunker opening up. It wasn't. One of the large support beams gave way and landed in front of her with a heavy thud. More started falling down on top of her, clouding her vision with bubbles.

Jaylin curled up in a ball, making herself smaller in an attempt to avoid being hit. She kicked with her feet to propel herself forward. She was getting knocked side to side by waves as heavy pieces fell on top of her. She used all of her strength to stay afloat.

Another much larger support beam was coming down just above her. Bubbles rapidly came out of her aqua-breather. Jaylin was scared. There was nowhere to swim to get away from the oncoming threat. Her body ached from the pain. She closed her eyes, ready for whatever was about to happen next.

Jaylin felt something hard move underneath her. An arm wrapped around her waist. Whoever it was pushed her to the ground and stood over her. Jaylin saw that it was her brother.

Akeer picked up two small support beams and held one in each hand. He wedged each end into the ground and crossed them. The larger support beam that was falling towards them fell on the center of the crossed support beams Akeer was standing under as he held them up with his new bionic arm04. His metallic arm whirred from the weight. He let go and grabbed Jaylin as the two side supports held the larger beam up like a teepee.

Jaylin was amazed. Akeer had just become a human Achilles Heel, just like the answer to the question she had trouble with on the exam.

Akeer bent over and lifted up the hatch door. The water bunker had been below her the entire time. What were the chances her family were in the one directly below her?

Akeer pushed Jaylin in. Their mother and father closed the door behind them. Akeer pulled a lever that drained the water from the pressure hull.

Jaylin looked up at her brother and said, "Thank you, Akeer."

She passed out.

13. LIES, LIES, LIES

The night before, Selene's rendezvous with Sarva had been interrupted by her parents, Lem, and a few other worried citizens. Mona stamped her feet like the scabite do before they attack as she made her way to prevent Selene and Sarva's intimate session from escalating. Aqib wasn't too far behind her. He yanked Selene off Sarva. Sarva remained on the ground, backed up against a tree with a horrified look on his face. Mona and Aqib gave Sarva looks of disgust. Selene's father grabbed her arm so hard it left a red mark on her bicep. The group escorted her back to Quaketown while Sarva was left there all by himself.

The only thing Selene remembered about the trip home was the string of unknown faces staring at her and the constant stream of profanity coming out of her father's mouth. This was the first time she had heard her father swear in public.

When they arrived at their cavehome, her parents reassured her she would get an earful in the morning. Since it was past midnight and they spent a good portion of their night searching for their daughter, they were too tired to discuss their distaste with her decisions. As Selene lay in bed, she thought maybe her parents just wanted to stall until morning to formulate what they were going to say.

It was morning now and Selene was pretending to be asleep in her bed. She could hear her parents' footsteps moving around in the room she was in. She smelled jennybob and pogo fruit salad, which they made her for breakfast. They were tempting her with her favorite breakfast salad. *How dare they.* Selene wondered if she could stay completely still until they left.

After staying still for a while, she thought her parents were never going to leave. They would probably stay there waiting for her to wake up until they were packed on the spaceship, leaving the planet, thinking she had died from shock. They would never pass up the chance to catch their only daughter in her first lie.

Selene's stomach gurgled, wanting some of the salad. *Not now. Bad timing.* She heard her parents stop moving around. Selene let out a small sigh. She rolled over toward her parents.

"Good morning, daughter" her father said with an unwelcoming attitude.

"Here's your breakfast," snapped her mother as she slammed a plate of pogo salad in front of her.

Filled with guilt about lying to her parents, all she could say was, "Sorry." She looked each of them in the eyes as she said it. "Sorry, mom. Sorry, dad." Then looked down at her plate; her breakfast salad looked unappetizing.

"Sorry is not going to cut it," said her father. "It's about time we disciplined you."

"Discipline me for what?" spat Selene. "Following my heart?"

"For disobeying our orders and lying to us!" her mother answered, audibly hurt.

Selene became frustrated and thoughts raced through her head. "But…But…I…" She then felt the most painful heartache. She felt bad she lied directly to her parents and made bad decisions they would never forgive her for; she began to weep.

Feeling too confronting, Mona sat beside her daughter and put her arm around her shoulder. Aqib sat down in his chair and put his face in his hands. Selene realized her tears had defeated them. Maybe she *would* be a great actress one day…

Selene watched through wet eyes as her mother composed herself.

"My little Selene," said mother. "I didn't want to tell you," she paused. Mona took a deep breath before continuing. "The real reason why we didn't want you hanging out with Sarva is because of his family's history."

Selene was taken back. History? What was her mother talking about? She looked at her with interest. Aqib took his hands away from his face and leaned forward with bad posture.

"You see," Mona continued. "Sarva's parents were some of the most ruthless people to ever live in Quaketown."

Selene's mouth dropped open. She had so many questions she knew were about to be answered, so she patiently waited.

"Their names were Malcolm and Darcie. Your father and I knew them a long time ago. Malcolm was a handsome young man but had a mean streak. I remember he would burst out into arguments over nothing in the middle of town."

"Sarva takes after his mother, Darcie. She was feral looking. They have similar facial features. She was completely insane. I saw her cut people with her sharp fingernails and laugh hysterically." Mona lifted up her shirt to show three scratches on her abdomen.

"It is said on the day Malcolm and Darcie met, it was during the most disastrous rainstorm we have encountered. They both were being held in detention for the night when the guard had to let them go to help bail out water from the mines. Malcolm and Darcie escaped Quaketown that night. Your father swears he saw them on top of Antilles Peak, right across from the spaceship, holding each others hands and laughing maniacally."

Aqib stared into space and nodded his head up and down. He seemed to be haunted by what his wife was saying.

"Six years later, Malcolm and Darcie returned to Quaketown, seeking revenge. We never sent out search parties to find them. We left them out there in the wild alone to rot. It wasn't worth risking anyone's lives. During the night, Darcie snuck to the entrance of Quaketown. Somehow, she had captured three scabites and used a metal rod to lure them inside Quaketown. She let them loose and the scabites ran rampant in our cavehomes."

Selene interrupted. "How did the guards not notice this?"

"We didn't have guards stationed at the entrance back then," said mother.

"Where was Malcolm?" asked Selene.

"Malcolm was on the top of the Quaketown entrance, where he pushed multiple giant boulders off the ledge, blocking our way out. That night, the scabites terrorized Quaketown. Dozens of people were killed by the three scabites and infected even more. It was horrible to watch them deteriorate, knowing there was nothing we could do. We weren't prepared for an inside attack. It took just over an hour to put down all three scabites. A young Fortuna and her apprentices eased the pain of the infected, until they too passed away."

"I remember the sickly souls screaming in pain," her father added. "I felt myself slowly lose my mind. It was like a nightmare. Our neighbors were dying and we were ready to protect you with our lives."

Selene let out an audible gasp. Of course she was alive during this. However, she had been too young to remember any of it. She wondered why no one ever brought up this horror story.

Mona continued the story, "When morning came, every able-bodied person helped clear the boulders and debris away from the entrance. Akira led a small army of people, including Christopherson, Gratius, Mr. Bradham, and your father into the jungle to find Malcolm and Darcie."

Mona sat down and let her husband finish the story. She looked exhausted.

Aqib sat as far back in his chair as it would go. He cleared his throat. "Akira tracked their footprints to a clearing near one of the safe havens. On the other side of the clearing, there was a small cave. We drew our weapons as we crept up to the cave. They must have known we were coming for them. Darcie took out some of our hunters with a makeshift bow and wounded me with an arrow." He lifted up his shirt to reveal an "x" shaped scar on his stomach.

"Gratius shot Darcie with an arrow right through the center of her forehead. She lashed around frantically until she finally fell to the muddy ground. I thought she was possessed. Holding my stomach, I ran over to the cave and saw a shadow of someone on the cave wall. I weakly drew back my bow and dove into the opening, releasing my arrow as I fell to the ground. The arrow went straight through Malcolm's heart."

Selene was currently trying really hard not to cry. Hearing her father murdered her boyfriend's father was enough to bring her tears over the threshold. She sought comfort in her mother's arms.

"After we protected ourselves from the two maniacs, we rested to catch our breath," her father continued. "To our shock, we saw a timid little boy hiding behind a chest, staring at his father's dead body."

Aqib stopped talking and looked at the ground. Selene knew who the little boy was.

"His parents were protecting him, Selene. Just like we are trying to protect you," Mona whispered gently. "We know of his troubled past and he reminds us so much of his parents. Every time I look at him, it reminds me of what happened. Every time I see the scratches and scars on your father and my skin, I can't help but think of them, as well as their son."

Selene and her parents sat there in silence.

Selene spoke up. "But that doesn't mean Sarva is bad."

"Well, over the years we have heard the son of Malcolm and Darcie had been up to no good," said her father. "I don't blame him, having to go from family to family, searching for love and acceptance, but never finding either."

"Like what?" demanded Selene. "Tell me one bad thing he has done."

Mona looked at Aqib for help.

"You're lying to me," said Selene. "He hasn't done anything wrong. You're just judging him based on his parents' actions."

"When he does, you will be sorry you ever met him," said her father. That was a low blow. "Now eat your pogo salad and head to the mines. They need all the help they can get. Before you come back home, I want you to break it off with Sarva and set up a date with Miles."

"Yes, dad," said Selene under her breath, fuming. She was lying again, but this time it was just a tiny bit easier.

———————————

Selene let out a great big cough. Then she heard everyone else around her coughing loudly, drowning out the usual clinks and clanks of the mines. Her lungs were filled with dust and debris from a cave-in. Luckily she was on the right side of it.

Selene heard Christopherson's loud footsteps before she saw him lunge into the area she was working in. "Everyone listen up," he yelled with his hands over his mouth so everyone could hear over the coughing. "All experienced miners, please grab your melters and follow me. Everyone else, go home and get some rest. Excellent work today." He ran past Selene as he headed towards to cave-in.

Selene made it through the dust and arrived at the supply drop-off. She recognized the man at the counter.

"Lee, wasn't it?" Selene asked him.

"Hey, Selene." It was Lee, the handsome guard who escorted her to her Chosen Ceremony. "How are things these days?"

Selene handed him her melter and Lee flexed his muscles as he put it in the 'used' bin. Selene didn't know if he realized he was flexing in front of her or not. "I'm hanging in there."

"Not going too well with Miles, huh?" he asked.

Selene left the supply drop-off without answering him. She didn't want to talk about her situation with Lee. It was a good thing the line behind her was growing because she didn't want him to think she blew him off.

The noise inside the mines grew louder from all the coughing. Selene could hardly hear her own thoughts. She was on her way to the exit when someone tapped her on her shoulder. It was Isadora. She mouthed something to her but she couldn't hear her. Isadora reached into her shirt pocket and lifted out a beautiful necklace. The silver sparkled in the torchlight and the blue cat's eye stone in the center was the bluest blue Selene had ever laid eyes on. Isadora waved her hands, signaling her to follow.

They both worked their way into a little hideout hole where miners took breaks. It was much quieter there.

"How do you like it?" asked Isadora.

"Oh, it's the most beautiful thing I have ever seen," said Selene. "Thank you so much, Isadora." Selene looked at it again and decided to put it on.

"Here, allow me," said Isadora. "Turn around."

Selene did as she was told and Isadora placed the necklace around her neck and hooked the two ends together.

"It looks lovely on you," she said. "Your mother is going to jump up and down with joy when she sees you wearing it."

Selene's cheeks turned pink, which accented her birthmark on her face. Her right foot stood on tiptoe as she twisted her foot around in circles. "Thanks. I really appreciate it." She looked down at the necklace and thought she could get used to wearing it. "I better get going before the line gets too long. I'll see you later." Selene waved to Isadora as she headed for the line.

"Take care, Selene."

To her surprise, the line wasn't as long as she thought it was going to be. The miners must not have wanted to go home early.

The security officers patted her down. Selene walked through the cavehomes. She made sure her parents weren't in or around their cavehome. She didn't want them knowing she left the mines early. Luckily, they weren't there. They must have been at a meeting with the Council. They had their own office in a side tunnel, next to the stage, where no one else was allowed.

Towards the back of the stage seating, Kelly was at her cavehome working on her important tasks. This time she was too far in her own world to notice Selene. She could tell her friend was having the time of her life. Her ponytail was tighter than normal.

Selene crossed the stage seating and made her way to the Quaketown exit. She greeted the guards as she passed into the jungle.

The trees blew around in the gentle breeze as Selene skipped down the path to the training grounds. She could smell the pogo trees upwind.

Selene arrived at the training grounds. She walked up the stone flight of stairs leading to an overlook with stadium seating. She looked out of a hole in the stone wall. She searched the field for Sarva, thinking it would be easy to spot a man with wild hair. To her dismay, she had a hard time locating him.

She saw Hazel in the middle, training younger hunters, most likely giving them safety instructions on how to handle a bow. Hazel was pointing at different parts of the bow and waving her pointer finger back and forth. Sarva wouldn't be there.

Selene's friend Farhad was on the left side at a wooden table with a group of hunters. Farhad was a tall, dark, strong man Selene's age. Her other friends thought she was crazy for not having a crush on him. She always thought he was a great friend, but never had any romantic feelings for him. They just had a lot in common. They had been friends ever since she could remember. Sarva couldn't have been with this group either. Farhad was tampering with the device on his bow. They must be heading east to gather fresh water soon.

Selene scanned the field and thought she saw dark ratty hair on the right side. She continued looking around in that direction. There were a group of hunter girls hanging around wooden targets. Selene saw them laughing together. One of the girl's heads leaned back far enough that Selene caught a glimpse of Sarva in the middle of the group.

Selene leaned through the wall's opening to get a better look. They were still far away and she could barely make out what they were doing.

One of the girls in the group was Ciri, the girl with freckles she met yesterday. Sarva was pointing at the target. The girls looked impressed. Then, Sarva took Ciri, dipped her, and kissed her on the lips. How could he? After everything that they shared last night? Selene's blood began to boil. She was more jealous than angry. She threw her hands up in the air. "What the scabbie? I hope he gets scabitus."

It looked like Ciri was enjoying it. She must have told her to stay away because she wanted him herself.

Selene didn't want to confront Sarva or embarrass herself in front of everyone, especially the hunter girls. She calmed herself down the best she could and ran all the way home.

The security officers at the entrance quickly patted her down because they could tell there was something upsetting her.

Selene ran into her cavehome and her parents were there. She broke down and tears began streaming down her cheeks onto her mining shirt. Her father leapt up from his chair and pulled her close to him. Her mother dropped what she was doing and joined the hug.

"What happened, sweetheart?" asked Aqib.

"Are you okay? We heard there was a collapse in the mines," said Mona.

Selene felt comfort in her parents' arms. She thought of what to say before she spoke. "I'm okay. I wasn't hurt in the collapse. Since I got out early, I decided to go break up with Sarva at the training grounds." She winced as she lied to them. She had really planned on going to hang out with him. "But when I got there, he was kissing all the hunter girls." She continued to cry.

"I guess you didn't have to break up with him after all," said her father. "Actions speak louder than words. I told you so."

Mona gave him a dirty look. "Why are you crying, if to dump him was your plan all along?" said her mother.

Selene halted her tears. She stopped hugging them and looked at her mother. "What do you mean?" Was her mother on to her? Could she tell when she was lying now?

"You went to Sarva to break up with him, did you not?" asked her father. "Seeing him kiss other girls would certainly make it more easy on you. Why are you really crying?" Her father raised an eyebrow.

Selene felt trapped. She had just lied to her parents for a second time. While it was getting easier for her to lie, it was getting harder for her to get away with it. She realized her parents saw through everything and decided to tell the truth.

Selene averted her eyes. "Okay, I was going to hang out with him. He was going to give me acting tips on my facial expressions. While helping me, I was going to watch him practice with his bow. But once I saw him with the girls, I felt betrayed and cheated on."

Her mother butted in, "Don't you think that's how Miles feels? You are out there behind his back with another man."

Selene didn't think of it this way. Surely Miles didn't feel the same way she does now? He barely knew her. "Maybe." Selene held her head low.

"There's no *maybe* about it young lady," her mother said sternly. "He felt special when the Five Ancients chose him for you. Now, his wife-to-be is in love with another man. How would you feel? Did you even give him a chance? No. Do you even know what he does around here?"

Selene thought about it for a moment. She knew absolutely nothing about Miles.

Her mother continued, "Let's make a deal. Forget about Sarva for the time being. Start going out with Miles. Get to know him. If you don't fall in love with him before we leave the planet, you can call the wedding off and do whatever you want."

Selene was intrigued. What had she got to lose? She walked over to the changing room to take off her mining clothes.

"I'll meet up with Miles tomorrow and give it a shot," she said. She didn't really like the idea but figured it would kill time until they left and take her mind off things. She had no idea what was waiting for her out in space. Maybe she could find someone even better looking than Sarva. All the rules were going to change anyway once they leave. She might as well do what her parents thought was best in the meantime.

Selene laughed at a joke Miles told her. They were in The Elias Library of Quaketown. Hundreds of handwritten books lined the shelves. It had a sort of peaceful smell inside. Most importantly, it was quiet.

There was a week and a half left before they had to leave the planet; it was almost time to leave Quaketown for good.

Selene was actually enjoying her time with Miles, but she still didn't feel attracted to him. Selene was wearing her new necklace and she noticed Miles kept on looking at it while he talked to her. He was definitely the nervous type. He kept on sneaking peeks at her breasts too and quickly averting his gaze, which unnerved her to no end.

The last time she saw Sarva was a week ago. They were no longer on speaking terms. Word got out Selene saw him kissing Ciri. Sarva wasn't seeing Ciri either, or other girls for that matter. In fact, no one had seen Ciri since that day, which was suspicious. Did she run away because she was embarrassed or was she in trouble? Hunters were sent out on a rescue mission.

Selene learned many things about Miles over the past month. She found out he was a miner, which shocked her because she had never seen him in the mines. He was shy; they hadn't kissed yet.

Miles also enjoyed spending most of his time in the library reading about the history of the village and their ancestors. He wasn't smart but he wasn't dumb either. Miles also liked sculpting objects out of clay. This skill seemed useless to her.

Elias had just finished reading to Selene and Miles about the time he and Fortuna spent the night at a safe haven. He wrote it himself. Elias was a great writer. She found out he was the one to write most of the scripts for the shows. Elias even wrote the script for her first show, the last show that everyone would remember on the planet.

"Okay kiddos, I have to go meet with Akira to inspect how the dig is coming along," said Elias.

Selene knew the dig referred to digging out the spaceship. "Say hi to Kelly for me," she said.

"I will. Take care." Elias left the library. It was just the two of them now.

"What do you want to do now?" asked Miles.

Selene thought about what she wanted to do. She looked around the library at the different journals and notebooks. "How about reading me one of your favorite stories?"

Miles looked at her, star-struck. She could have sworn his pupils turned into hearts.

"Sounds like a plan. Wait right here, I know the perfect one," he said excitedly as he stumbled over his words. Miles took off his backsack and set it on the counter. He ran off to the far side of the library.

Selene was waiting for him. A minute passed as she watched him go up and down the rows of bookcases.

"I know it's around here somewhere," he said. Every time Miles bent down, Selene could see the crack of his ass. Selene was slightly disgusted and averted her gaze.

Selene heard something behind her. It was the door. Sarva was walking towards her with a sly grin.

"What the scab are you doing here?" she angrily whispered to him. She quickly stood up from her chair and led him outside.

She peeked her head inside the library. Selene yelled to Miles, "I'll be right back, I have to go to the bathroom," to Miles.

She turned back to Sarva. "Explain yourself," she demanded.

"Hi, Selene," said Sarva. Selene wanted to punch the grin off his face.

She looked at him with disgust, while also secretly thanking him. Her patience was growing thin at the library.

"I have a plan," said Sarva, looking at her mysteriously.

"Wait, wait, wait," she interrupted. "I have a couple questions first. Why were you kissing Ciri? I thought she was just your friend?"

Sarva laughed "Ciri isn't just my friend, Selene. Ciri is my cousin. I kissed her because she is family. She beat me at a game we were playing. She is pretty impressive with that bow of hers."

Selene felt a little relieved. "You kiss your cousin on the lips?

"What? No way," he exclaimed and waved his arms. "I kissed her on her cheek."

She *was* far away. She could have misinterpreted.

"Then why were you avoiding me this whole time?" she asked. "You could have said something."

"I heard rumors going around that you were going to kill me, so I decided to let you cool off." His face told her that he was telling the truth. "Do you forgive me?"

Selene decided to wait to give him her answer. She didn't want to seem too desperate. Ever since that night, she wished she could just be with Sarva again. She felt she had given Miles enough of a chance. She wanted to feel the things she felt during the night of her first kiss again and Miles was giving her nothing.

"Yes, I forgive you," she said. "Do you know where Ciri is? I think she is missing."

"No, I have no idea where she is," he said. He looked troubled. "Nor do I care. Right now, I only care about you." He put his hand on her shoulder. "Now hear me out. Do you want to stay in Quaketown with me? Let everyone leave so it will just be you and me on this entire planet," he said.

Selene was in complete shock, "What?" She didn't believe what he said.

"You heard me," he said tapping his foot.

Selene didn't know what to say. He must be in love with me if he is willing to leave everyone behind to be with me and me alone.

Selene thought of the fairy tales her mother told her when she was little. Specifically the ones about princesses. At the end of every story, the princess and the prince left everything behind to live happily ever after. This is what she had wanted for a very long time. A love like this. But at what cost?

Selene would be leaving behind everyone important to her. Her parents would never forgive her. She would never see Kelly again. Fortuna, Akira, Mr. Bradham, Farhad, Christopherson, Isadora, Miles, Aunt Luci, Uncle Tobe, Elias. Everyone. They would be in safe hands, wouldn't they? She weighed the positives and negatives.

"Fine, I don't need an answer just yet," said Sarva. "Just let me know within the next couple of days. I have a plan all set and I will be executing it with or without you."

Sarva left Selene to her thoughts. The last sentence seared into her brain. He was going to stay on the planet with or without her.

Selene almost forgot Miles was waiting for her in the library. She walked back in.

Miles was still by the bookcases. He picked up a book from the shelf. It was titled, *The Great Big Book of Great Big Adventures*. "I finally found it," said Miles with glee. "I hope you will enjoy it."

Selene didn't think she was going to enjoy anything for the rest of the day. All she could think about as Miles read her his favorite short stories from the book was the conversation she just had with Sarva. Selene was disappointed and frustrated with how quickly it took her to reach her final decision. She had already made up her mind and feared she would regret her decision once again.

14. BETRAYAL

It had been four changes of the sun since the morose band left the comfort of their homes in Dunestone. Just over two-thirds of their journey was still ahead of them if they were to be successful.

Wakan was looking down at his feet calculating how many changes of the sun were left until he could return back to his family, until an intense light caught his eye. He tried to look up, but the sun's rays were blinding. Right before he turned away, he noticed there was a bend at the end of the tunnel. That must be the way out. Wakan sat down and put his face into his hands.

"That there is the greatest threat we face," said Bruce. "As you already know, Wakan."

Rubbing the sore spot on his neck, Wakan wasn't looking forward to meeting the burning touch of Incinerus, the name of their sun, again.

Christine reached into her pouch where she kept a vial of healing ointment. She squirted some cream about the size of a pebble into her youthful hands.

Wakan winced as the cold ointment hit his burn mark. "Thanks a bunch," he said.

Meanwhile, Tank set down his bag in the corner. It looked like he was frantically sorting through the bag. Copper, Rufus, and Pai sat against the sandy wall and closed their eyes. Bruce reached into his bag of dunelope seeds and chomped down.

Copper then spoke up, "Okay, so how are we going to trudge out there again? Or were you just joking?" Copper chuckled to himself. No one else did. "You *were* joking right?"

"I'm afraid not," said Bruce.

"How can we possibly do it?" asked Pai.

Bruce put his hand on the wall next to Pai. "On very rare occasions, adventurers had no choice but to travel out into the heat. If one was severely injured and they didn't have the medical supplies to treat the injuries, if there was any possibility they could be saved, they would have to be rushed back to the village." He looked nervous.

Wakan could read Bruce's face and knew he was hiding something. "You have never traveled outside in the daylight before, have you?" asked Wakan.

Bruce looked at the ground.

Wakan could tell everyone was scared.

Bruce spit out the dunelope seed he was munching on. "Fortunately, we have obtained important supplies from storage," said Bruce as he pointed at Tank who was still rummaging through his bag.

"Wait a second," said Wakan as he slowly got to his feet. "When we split up to get our supplies, you and Tank left the spaceship. You didn't go below to storage."

Bruce grinned. "There are other storages in Dunestone you know," he said politely. He laughed and looked at Tank.

Wakan had been around Dunestone many times. He had seen many faces and met many villagers. When he first laid his eyes on Bruce and Tank, he didn't recognize them. It had been years since he had seen new people. He couldn't quite figure out why he hadn't seen them before as they both had memorable features. "Who exactly are you two?"

"Do you want to reach the peak or not?" asked Bruce. "Tank, give them their supplies. They will need 'em."

Wakan saw Tank lift his hands out of the bag. He was tying something together. Whatever it was, Tank launched it in the air towards Wakan. It knocked him to the ground.

This angered the group.

Sore, Wakan looked it over. To his surprise, it was a dark cloak with an oversized hood. Tied to his was a translucent face mask with a plastic lens covering it. Wakan pinched the material and some sort of liquid swished around inside.

Tank threw one to each member. "Tank give charity. Expect payment later."

"These," said Bruce, "are your survival cloaks."

Audible gasps filled the tunnel. "Whoa," said Rufus. "How have I not heard of these before?"

"It's a trade secret," said Bruce. "All of you have a lot to learn."

"How does," started Rufus before he was cut off.

"There is liquid coolant between the layers of the cloak," said Bruce.

Rufus was annoyed that he was interrupted.

"Once you put it on and activate the reaction, the coolant will keep your body temperature at a reasonable average," he said. "The hood blocks out and deflects all UV rays. Wakan, that mask you are holding is made with material that doesn't fog over with moisture when you breathe. It also has coolant flowing inside of it."

Rufus waited five seconds to make sure Bruce was done explaining. "How is this possible? How come I have never seen this gear? I have seen many inventions but this one has evaded me. This is so ingenious, how are these cloaks not being handed out to everyone? This has a lot of practical uses for our community. Think of the possibilities that we can do while the sun is up."

"Shut up," said Bruce. He massaged his temples.

"Don't tell me to…" Rufus bolted up and raised his fists. Before he could throw a punch, Tank grabbed onto his forearm and yanked it down. Rufus cried out in pain.

"We have provided you protection," said Bruce raising his voice, "…and now we must leave right this instant to stay on schedule."

"To the inhospitable blazing dunes with the schedule!" cried Copper. "Let go of my friend you mean, ugly bastard." Copper threw two punches into Tanks side, who didn't flinch.

"Men," said Christine to Pai.

Pai was empowered with courage as she lifted herself off the ground. "Hey! Will you guys stop it?" Tank was still holding Rufus' arm as Rufus and Copper kept on punching him. "Stop!"

"The whole village is counting on Wakan to be with them on the spaceship," said Christine. "That's why we are all here, isn't it? We are risking everything on this journey, just so you can make it back before they take off."

Copper and Rufus were barely paying attention.

"Listen to her," said Bruce to Tank. "People really do view him as our leader," he said sarcastically.

Bruce turned to Wakan. "Tell them you only came on this journey to prove to them how spirit-like you are. Putting their lives in your hands just for you and you let them come on this dangerous journey without any hesitation. You're so selfish."

Tank was choking Rufus. "He doesn't need to prove anything," said Copper as he punched Tank again. "We believe in what he stands for."

With a shit-eating grin on his face, Bruce glared at Wakan. "We need to keep going. You *do* want to make it back in time before the spaceship launches, don't you Wakan?"

Looking defeated, Wakan struggled to his feet. Everyone was watching him. All of a sudden his knee couldn't support him anymore and he collapsed. He immediately attempted to stand back up and this time he succeeded. He leaned on the wall. "Please stop this fighting," he pleaded. "Please."

Hearing their old friend, Copper and Rufus calmed down and stopped the failed assault on Tank.

"I knew it," said Bruce.

"No, no you don't," said Wakan. "You know nothing. Do you have children?" He could tell he didn't. "Well then you don't understand. I could care less if we made it back in time. All that matters is that we find the rosena petals and get back home. Star. Triss. Zato. They are all counting on me."

Everyone looked guiltily at Wakan as a tear ran down his cheek. "Now please," said Wakan, "Let's get this over with."

Silence filled the tunnel. Bruce helped each of them put the cloaks on to make sure they were completely covered. Starting with Wakan, he roughly zipped up Wakan's suit trying to irritate him.

When everyone was ready, they walked towards the light at the end of the tunnel. They ripped off the tab connected to their cloak to release the chemicals which activated the coolant. The lens on their face masks slowly darkened, blocking out the bright light. Wakan watched as the coolant poured into his mask from the crown of his hood.

The group stepped into the open. Wakan peered out and saw what lay before them, the flamerod bridge.

Unlike the paths and tunnels where they had been venturing, the flamerod bridge had no name. It was simply just there.

Through his face mask, Wakan stared at the bridge. On both ends of the bridge, there was a large boulder strategically placed to act as a counterweight. Underneath the boulders were flamerod wood planks that stretched out to the boulder on the opposite side. To Wakan's disappointment, the bridge had no supports or railings. He looked up at the mountain on the other side. On top lied his final destination.

As Wakan limped closer, the flamerod bridge looked older than it actually was. There was wear and tear on more than half the flamerod planks. A few were even missing. To get onto the bridge, one would have to hug the boulder and shimmy along the edge to step onto the planks.

Speaking of the edge, Wakan looked down at the craggy wasteland below, which was cast in shadow. It was exactly as Bruce had explained it to him. The side closest to him was comprised of jagged steeples that could impale anyone who fell. That would not be a fun way to die. Across the way was a steep drop off. There was no safe way anyone could climb back up.

"Holy crab," said Copper.

The others stared off in wonderment as they contemplated what they were tasked to do.

"Alright, everyone listen to me," said Bruce. "Since he is obviously handicapped, Wakan will go first. We will all go at his pace. Next will be me, followed by Pai, Rufus, Christine, Copper, and bringing up the rear will be Tank."

"Rear, ha," said Tank.

"We will all go across at the same time. The bridge can support all our weight."

Wakan looked at him skeptically.

"Let's move," said Bruce.

They all formed a line around the boulder. Wakan put his back to the boulder and leaned against it. He slowly worked his way along until he reached the first flamerod plank. He tapped his foot on it to make sure it was sturdy. To his amazement, it was. The bridge was around four feet wide and the planks were tied together with rope. The rope had some substance on it to prevent it from burning in the hot sun. Wakan inched out, making sure not to step on his cloak floating around his feet. He heard Bruce behind him. The bridge creaked as Bruce stepped onto it. He continued to inch along.

"What have I done with my life that has lead me here?" Copper asked to himself out loud.

Christine laughed. "I was wondering the same thing."

Wakan pushed himself forward slowly but surely. He felt the planks bow underneath him and suddenly felt a rumble. It must have been Tank finally stepping onto the bridge.

Wakan was nearly halfway across. He kept his eyes ahead, not wanting to look below. The farther he went, the more scared he became. He started to breath heavily. With each breath he heard himself wheeze.

Suddenly, he felt a hand on his shoulder. It was Bruce. "You might want to start picking up your pace, Wakan."

One by one, Wakan heard gasps behind him. Pai screeched. "We're all doomed," said Rufus.

Wakan looked around to see what the commotion was all about. He couldn't see anything out of the ordinary. Bruce started pushing him forward. "Move!"

Wakan spotted something in the distance. He realized the wheezing noise wasn't from his breathing; it was coming from a cloud on the horizon.

"Burstflies!" someone yelled out in a high-pitched voice. It definitely wasn't Pai or Christine though.

Wakan hurried as fast as he could go along the bridge but the cloud was coming closer and closer. Wakan felt Bruce's hands pushing him along.

Two-thirds across.

"Come on, you old man, get out of the way!" screamed Bruce as he aggressively pushed Wakan to the side.

"Watch it!" yelled Wakan. "You almost tossed me off!"

"Don't rock the bridge," said Christine.

"What in the inhospitable blazing dunes are you doing up there?" asked Copper.

"They're coming!" exclaimed Pai.

Bruce knocked into Wakan's bad leg, attempting to push him off the side. Wakan fell to his knees and started slipping off. He grasped at the edge of the planks as Bruce tried to pass him.

Pai grabbed Bruce by the back of the hood and pulled him towards her. "You asshole," she growled.

Wakan climbed back up and started heading towards the end of the bridge.

Bruce was lying sideways preventing anyone else from passing him.

"You're going to be the death of us!" Rufus yelled at Bruce.

"No, those are going to be the death of us if we don't hurry back," said Christine, frantically pointing towards the burstflies. "Turn back, we're not going to make it."

"But we are closer to the other side," said Rufus.

"Obviously Bruce has bad intentions," said Pai as Bruce grabbed on to her ankle. "He's not going to let us pass."

"Knock his ass over the edge," said Copper. "Come on!"

Tank, Copper, and Christine headed back.

Rufus took something out of his bag and used it to slice off a piece of the plank. He picked it up and whacked Bruce's hand. He let go of Pai. Rufus extended his hand to her. They ran as fast as they could to the opposite end.

Wakan finally made it to the other side. He hugged the boulder and went around it. He looked on as his friends ran in the opposite direction across the bridge.

Wakan could see individual burstflies now. They were red in color and each as big as his fist. They had huge suckers as a mouth. Their wings were twice the length of their bodies.

"Wakan," said Bruce. "Look at me."

Wakan did as he was told and looked at Bruce angrily. "What is it you want?"

"Wakan. You have failed," said Bruce.

"What do you mean?" asked Wakan.

"You were never meant to make it back to Dunestone alive," Bruce explained. "You are on a wild goose chase."

"What?" said Wakan.

"There aren't any rosena flowers at the top of Mount Crimson anymore," said Bruce. "The last ones shriveled up months ago. That's the real reason why we haven't traveled up there recently."

"You're lying," said Wakan. "Why are you lying?"

The burstflies arrived and started circling the bridge. Wakan heard his friends screaming.

"Am I?" asked Bruce. "You strut around the village acting like you know everything. Well, guess what? You know very little. You think the people

215

back in Dunestone love you, but in reality, we are all sick of you."

Wakan felt his stomach drop. There's no way this was true. He forced out a laugh. "Sick of me?"

"To be honest, we have been trying to get rid of you for a while. We couldn't have someone like you leading us into the future. We need someone strong and powerful, not someone weak and waiting to die."

"Who is we?" asked Wakan.

"We have been having secret meetings during the night while you are sleeping in your hole. We call ourselves the Forgotten. We put this whole plan into motion."

It took a few seconds for Wakan to understand the entirety of what Bruce was saying. He remembered that man with a hood who stared at him in the crowd and the woman who disappeared from the group he instructed to go help the crabbers. Had they been a part of the Forgotten? Had there really been a group that formed under his nose that saw him as a threat? Did they have something to do with his children falling ill?

"Wait," said Wakan. "Don't tell me that you...?"

Bruce laughed maniacally as the burstflies surrounded him. "I injected your children with the burstfly disease."

Wakan became furious. He wanted to step back onto the bridge and strangle Bruce to death but he knew it was too late for him anyways.

Bruce took out a knife from his bag and started cutting the string holding the planks together. "But you will never guess who gave me the orders," said Bruce.

Snap!

Bruce's knife cut through the rope and the planks started to detach. Wakan watched as Bruce held on tight to a couple planks.

At the other side, Wakan could see that the group had not made it across yet as the burstflies continued their onslaught.

The planks underneath the boulder gave way and broke under pressure. The bridge swung down with three planks still attached at the upper end. Tank was near the top. He climbed up onto the cliff's edge and reached down to rescue Copper. Wakan was surprised at Tank's actions.

Christine was climbing up the planks, while guiding Rufus up as he clasped to her legs. Pai was staying still as she hung on. Bruce was catching up to her.

"You can do it, Pai," said Wakan. He didn't care if she couldn't hear him over the buzzing. "Please make it, they need you."

Tank lifted up Christine, followed by Rufus. Pai started to climb up. Wakan saw Copper and Christine jumping up and yelling something. Probably cheering her on. Rufus was frantically searching through his bag. Tank laid on his stomach reaching down the ledge towards Pai. Her little hands reached up for help as Bruce was a foot below her. Tank reached as far down as he could and grasped her outstretched arm. He picked her up and set her on the ground. Tank went back down to help Bruce. Copper and Christine angrily raised their hands in the air.

Wakan watched as Rufus pulled different jars out of his bag. He unscrewed the lids and he started to launch the powder into the air. After unloading the seventh jar, the burstflies dispersed. They seemed to hate whatever the powder was. Shortly after, Wakan could hear his friends' voices again.

"That man deserves to die," said Christine as she pointed at Bruce.

Bruce grasped onto Tanks outstretched hand just as the planks below him snapped and fell to the bottom of the pit.

Bruce let out a victorious yodel. "Tank, my friend. I owe you dessert when we get back home."

Wakan then heard something. It shocked him more than anything that has happened on this journey. Tank spoke using full sentences and a different tone of voice. "Oh, you think I'm saving you Brucey? Guess again."

"What's going on?" asked Copper in disbelief. "What the fuck is going on?"

"I grabbed on to your arm," Tank said to Bruce, "To make sure I have a hand in your death."

"Tank? What is going on?" asked Bruce. "You sly bastard."

"It appears my agenda differs from your own." Tank shook his arm trying to break Bruce from his grasp. "I never did like you since the day Memphis partnered me up with you."

Questions quickly ran through Wakan's head. Was Memphis part of the Forgotten? Why would he have wanted him dead? Or did Memphis order Tank to protect me? Memphis spoke to him and Christine before they left, did he give her orders too?

Tank reached down, grabbed onto Bruce's hood, and yanked it off.

Incinterus' rays instantly fried Bruce's flesh. Bruce let out a deathly scream. He began to wither as his skin quickly dehydrated, shrinking off the bone.

"Scum," spat Tank as he let go. The skeletal remains of Bruce crashed to the ground below. Tank stood up and turned around. "Is everyone okay?"

Christine was looking around at everyone and noticed the rips in their cloaks. "Let's head back in the tunnel, I need to get everyone checked out." She shooed the group into the tunnel where the light couldn't touch them. "Wakan, we'll be right back."

Confused and out of breath, Wakan laid down near the bridge. He looked down and contemplated how he was going to make it back across once he had found the rosena petals. *If* there were any left. What if Bruce was right and he was on a pointless journey?

Twenty minutes passed by the time Christine and Tank emerged from the tunnel. Both were carrying bags in their hands.

"The three of them aren't looking too good," said Christine. "Their adrenaline must have ran out, they look a lot worse now than they did a minute ago. The burstflies have gotten to Rufus' skin. He was burned as well. Pai and Copper are bruised and burned. I don't have enough medical supplies for everyone so we will have to turn back now." Christine paused for a moment. "Any way we can change your mind and come back with us?"

"I'm going all the way," said Wakan. "Especially now, since Rufus needs the cure too."

"Didn't think so," said Christine.

Wakan heard Rufus cry out in pain back in the tunnel.

Christine set down the bags in front of her. "I suppose I'll leave my brother to fill you in while I go check back on them." Christine walked away leaving Tank to a very confused Wakan.

"My apologies, Wakan," said a elegant Tank. "For everything that has happened. I have plenty to say but with very little time. Allow me to introduce myself. My name is Tobias Fetterman. Yes, Christine is my sister. I have been working undercover for Memphis for a decade, trying to bring an end to the Forgotten."

"So the Forgotten is real then?" asked a sullen Wakan.

"What you heard from Bruce is true," answered Tobias. "The Forgotten has been around since before Dunstone was founded. There is a lot of secrecy surrounding them. Memphis and I formed a counter terrorist organization to thwart all plans linked to them. I have been working as a double agent for many years, infiltrating their land over the hills of Dunstone by the volcanoes."

Wakan looked on in astonishment. The world now appeared bigger to him than it ever had been. Larger than the time Chiyo showed him Dunestone on the hill, and more expanse than the universe. He thought their journey into the stars was going to be a time of happiness but now he thought there were more danger out there than he would have once thought. A story is a story even if it didn't have a happy ending.

"So everything he said was true?" asked Wakan.

"Not everything. I can't confirm that the rosena flower has shriveled up," said Tobias. "Only you can discover the truth. It's up to you and only you to save your family, Wakan."

Tobias tossed him over the bags one at a time. They landed right next to Wakan. "You are lucky you have very generous friends. They wished for you to have these items for the rest of your journey. Copper's crabbing nets, Rufus' purification pills, Christine's medical journal, Pai's stargazing journal, and I tossed in some rope for you. There is also some food and Bruce's dunelope seeds in there."

"Thank you, Tank. I mean Tobias," corrected Wakan. "Take care of my friends. Lead them back home safely."

"I will try my best, Wakan," said Tobias. "We wish you the best of luck out there. Here's hoping we meet again." Tobias saluted and then headed back into the tunnel.

There were three more changes of the sun ahead of Wakan until he would reach the peak of Mount Crimson. Then another long seven changes of the sun until he would return home. Could he make it back fast enough to save his children and depart on the spaceship? Wakan prayed to the spirits that he would. He just knew time was running out.

15. THE RESCUE

Brant stared into the fog at the wolfwraiths. The piercing yellow eyes were staring right back. There were two wolfwraiths waiting for him out in the darkness, hungry for their next meal.

Brant had a gash on his shoulder from the previous skirmish, making it difficult to fully lift his silver sword.

Glistening blood covered the ground in front of him; the blood of both Alexis and the wolfwraith's decapitated corpse.

Brant looked three-hundred-and-sixty degrees around him to make sure there weren't any more wolfwraiths hiding in the fog. From what he could see, it was only the two left.

"Come on!" he said. "I'm right here! Come get me! Come on!" The silver sword reverberated as Brant tapped the tip of it on the ground, calling attention to himself. As he yelled at the wolfwraiths, he studied them. Since their eyes are glowing bright, they must have great eyesight in the darkness. Their long fangs allowed them to rip the flesh out of their prey which must be specterlings...and humans. Could there be other monsters out here too? The wolfwraiths had a long snout and long whiskers giving them even greater awareness through the fog. Brant looked at their bodies. The front half was thick in fur with legs bound in muscle. The paws had long retractable claws that could pierce through armor. The back half had leathery scales covering a long thick tail that could kill. Brant took in all of this information, calculating the best way to bring one down.

The two wolfwraiths began circling Brant, inching closer with each pass. Brant had never realized how intelligent these creatures were. They were working together to get their next meal. These creatures should be studied. Maybe they could be trained or domesticated. "Focus, Brant. Focus," he said to himself.

Brant heard a rustle behind him and instantly knew one of the wolfwraiths had made its decision to strike first. He readied his silver sword and faced the demonic creature.

Suddenly, the second wolfwraith tackled him from behind. This took him off guard, reminding him of Tarjeel's attack which made him angry. Brant fell to the ground with the entire weight of the wolfwraith crushing down on him with such a powerful force, it knocked the wind out of him. After gasping for breath, he used all his strength to push the creature off of him.

Jumping back onto his feet, Brant aimed his silver sword at the enemy. He went into his stance; one leg slightly in front of the other, ready to defend or attack.

The bigger wolfwraith ferociously lunged at him. Brant jammed his silver sword sideways into the jaws of the creature. It howled in pain as Brant slashed the sword away from him. He decided to attack the face of his enemy because it contained the sources of its highly sensitive senses; vision, smell, taste, touch.

The wolfwraith jumped backwards and growled at him. Dark blood dribbled from its muzzle. It let out a haunting howl, signaling its brother.

From behind, the smaller wolfwraith clawed Brant's back. He winced. It felt like his back was on fire.

Brant was out of breath as the wolfwraiths played with their meal. His body was so sore, he was sure he wouldn't make it out of there alive.

He had finally found a worthy opponent to match his skills. Brant fought back with the best of his ability, slashing and swinging his silver sword with as much force as his body would allow him to. The wolfwraith's hides were just too strong to do any real damage to them.

Suddenly, the sky opened up above him. The wolfwraiths retreated for a moment. Brant stood there in shock.

A fiery red chunk of rock flew through the sky, making a clear trail behind it, dispersing the clouds and fog.

It was the first time that he had seen the open sky. There were bright sparkles in the sky and a green planet glowing way up high. Is this where we came from? Or is that where we are going? The flaming red rock finally went over the horizon. It was followed by a loud noise.

Most of the fog Brant had lived with his entire life disappeared and he could see the landscape around him. The lights from the sky lit up his surroundings. It was flat as far as the eye could see. He turned around and saw "The Eye" in the distance. *Wow*. There was a cave a little farther north. That must be where Alexis was taken. Between him and the cave stood the two wolfwraiths.

Brant felt a jolt of energy run through him, the second wind he had been waiting for. He was about to charge at the wolfwraiths with his final burst of energy until he noticed something peculiar.

His silver sword was shining so bright it hurt his eyes. Something else was shining bright as well. He looked down at his chest and saw the silver necklace that his parents had given him was glowing. He looked up at the sky again. "Thanks, mom and dad."

Brant lifted the shining silver sword and charged at the two wolfwraiths as they ran full speed towards him. They finally met each other and with every hack and slash Brant dished out, he yelled out with anger. "This is for my mother, Kat. This is for my father, Beck. This is for Phoebe, for Elijah, for everyone else your kind has murdered."

After minutes of a heated battle, the lone survivor laid on his back in a pool of blood. Brant looked up at the twinkling stars, breathing heavily. Almost there. He struggled to his feet and looked around.

His Projectocube laid there in pieces from the attack. He picked up every last piece. Luckily, the main parts were unharmed and just the supports were damaged. He wrapped it up with some of the yarn and tied it together. Good as new.

Brant dressed his wounds as he kept his eyes on the cave. There were at least two wolfwraiths left. Three, if the one with the hacked off paw was still alive. He wiped his forehead. Hold on Alexis.

The silver sword stuck into the ground as Brant used its hilt to help himself to his feet. He slung his sword around to his bruised and bleeding back. Brant limped across the flat surface. With each step he took, the cave seemed to get farther away. Brant began to panic. He slipped and fell onto the ground. The hilt of the sword hit him in the back of his head. He fell unconscious.

Brant woke up in darkness. He heard cries for help and decided to see who it was. He noticed he was laying in a basket, wrapped inside a maroon blanket. He climbed out of the basket and looked around. Two young adults were in front of him. The man had a shaved head and a strong jaw. He was dressed in a cloak similar to Brant's. There were blue arrow tattoos on his hands and arms. The woman had long dark hair and dark eyes with a great big smile. Brant couldn't help but smile back. She was dressed in a gown that was used for marriage ceremonies.

At first, Brant thought he had run into the lost couple, but something seemed familiar with these two. He stepped closer to get a better look.

The two young adults both spoke at the same time. "Hello, son. We have been waiting a long time to see you again. Look how much you've grown."

Brant reached for his silver necklace only to find nothing. Instead, the silver necklace was around his mother's neck. He put his arms around them. "Mom. Dad." He didn't know what else to say.

Beck and Kat continued to speak in sync. "Son, we are sorry for all of the dread we've caused you. We were forced to bring you out with us that night and were foolish to believe in our faith. We are sorry for abandoning you at such a young age. You felt so lonely and were bullied all throughout schooling. All of this loneliness turned into a rage that no one soul can handle. All we can ask now is to please use this rage to fuel something positive, something that will help everyone, something that will benefit all of humanity. We love you son."

"I love you too," said Brant as his parents stepped backwards.

Two other figures appeared. It was Elijah and Phoebe. "Hello, son." They also spoke in sync with each other. "We are sorry for all the hardships we allowed you to go through. We saw you were a troubled young man and we did nothing to help. We should have been better parents to you. Maybe we just weren't ready for a child."

Under the starlight, Phoebe's long red hair was glowing brightly. "I should never have taken you in that day I found you. I was too young and took full responsibility."

They both spoke again, "We are sorry we failed you."

Brant hugged them both. "You two were perfect. I couldn't have asked for better parents. You helped make me who I am today, and for that, I thank you."

"Use that heart of yours to help people," they hugged back. "The universe is a dark place and one big heart like yours can brighten up the whole galaxy. We love you son."

"I love you too," said Brant as he regained consciousness. There were tears streaming down his cheeks. He put his head in his hands and sobbed.

After a few minutes passed, Brant got back on his feet and made his way to the cave. The fog had already started to slowly fill back into the clearing.

Brant set his hand on the wall of the cave near the entrance and wondered why there was only one cave that could be seen. Brant concluded it must be man made. There's no other reason for this being out here by itself. What is this caves purpose?

Brant took out his busted Projectocube and turned it on. The green light illuminated within. It still worked! The fog rolled past him as it came from behind. Brant sought shelter inside.

Drawings depicting the history of their people lined the walls. Brant stayed against the wall as he silently crept deeper into the cave.

There were strange symbols drawn on the wall with red paint. He didn't understand what any of it meant. On the opposite wall of the cave, something caught his eye. There was a drawing of something silver. Brant used his Projectocube to light up the wall.

There was a drawing of a person wearing a hood with a silver necklace in the shape of two crossed daggers around the person's neck. It was the same necklace he was wearing. The person in the drawing had an army surrounding them. The one with the silver necklace held a silver sword up towards the sky. Brant followed where the sword was pointing and it led to a silver planet. This was an incredible site. Could that somehow be him?

Brant continued into the cave until he smelled something horrible. As he moved closer to the smell, he found a massive pile on the ground. It was the wolfwraith who's paw he had chopped off. It must have bled out. "Serves you right," spat Brant.

A little farther down, there was an opening which lead into a bigger room inside the cave. Brant heard rustling and panting lying within. He began to move as quietly as possible, trying his best not to disturb the wolfwraiths. Brant shimmied against the wall until he was on the edge of the next room, a chamber. He peeked inside.

Both wolfwraiths were chewing on human remains. Brant was horrified. He kept on looking around the room to see if there were any signs of life.

There was something moving in the corner of the chamber. Brant looked closer to see an old wrinkly woman. It was Alexis! She was still alive. Alexis moved across the ground a few inches back, revealing two young adults leaning up against the cave wall. All three of them were wounded.

On the other side of the chamber was a huge mound of bones that piled higher than Brant.

He leaned against the cave wall, trying to come up with a plan. He wondered if there were any projections that could help him in this scenario. He thought of the perfect one.

Brant held the Projectocube up to his mouth and whispered, "Initiate holo 31-A." He tossed it in to the corner where the piles of bones were. The two wolfwraiths watched it with excitement and curiosity. The Projectocube began hovering in the air and started humming.

Suddenly, a projection of a cat sprang forth from the Projectocube. It even meowed, using a voice recording of Pandora. The Projectocube could project audio across a room using built in speakers to make it sound like the projected object was talking or making noise. The wolfwraiths perked up and growled at the feline. They stopped gnawing at the raw meat. The cat ran towards the pile of bones and raced to the top. Instinct took over the wolfwraiths and they chased after the cat.

Brant hurried to the opposite side of the cave where Alexis and the couple were sitting against the wall. "Is everyone alright?" he asked.

Alexis nodded her head and pointed at the couple. The couple's bodies were covered with mud and blood as they held on to each other. Alexis herself was in bad shape.

"I need to kill the rest before we get you back to safety," he explained. "Or else they will track us down and kill us all before we make it back inside the walls of 'The Eye.'"

Alexis nodded her head in approval.

"If I don't come back, I apologize," said Brant as he grabbed his silver sword and flung it around his body. He stealthily sneaked to the pile of bones. The wolfwraiths were on the other side, still attempting to catch the cat.

Good thing Brant recently created a training module that involved trying to catch a cat that was modeled after Pandora. It may just have saved his life. Brant climbed up the pile of bones being really careful not to injure himself on the sharp edges. He heard the wolfwraiths stumbling over the bones.

At the peak, Brant looked down at the two vicious wolfwraiths. He took his silver sword and pointed it towards the sky just like in the painting. He chuckled. Brant leapt into the air and aimed his silver sword at one of the wolfwraiths. He brought the sword down as hard as he could onto the back of the creature. The sword cleanly chopped the wolfwraith in half. Brant quickly turned around and slashed the sword upward into the other wolfwraiths abdomen. Intestines fell out on top of Brant and he fell backward in disgust.

It was over. He had defeated them all. He wiped off his cloak and got to his feet.

On his way to Alexis and the couple, he picked up the Projectocube and pressed a button. The cat disappeared and the machine stopped humming. He kept it out to light up the room.

He made it to Alexis and helped her up. "You look pale," said Brant.

"I have lost too much blood," said Alexis. "I need attention fast or else I will not make it through the night."

Brant noticed she still had the claw in her arm.

"We actually aren't that far from 'The Eye,'" said Brant as he helped the scared couple up to their feet. "Once we get to the entrance of the cave, home is straight ahead. It will take about a half hour. When we left the north entrance we traveled westward, but the dome isn't perfectly circular. The west entrance is straight ahead."

The man had trouble standing up. His ankle was twisted in the wrong direction. He had a goatee and a bulbous nose.

"How could you have seen it through all the fog?" asked Alexis.

"I'll explain on the way." Brant looked around the room for anything that might help. He took off his cloak and tied the arms together. He tied the rest of Alexis' yarn to the arms of the cloak. "Get on," said Brant to the man.

The man crawled onto the cloak and laid down. "Thanks friend," the man said. "My name is Nanoc and this is my girlfriend, Ajnos." She was short and had a red dagger tattoo on her cheek.

"Nice to meet you, I'm Brant. Alexis, you better lay down on my cloak too."

Alexis did as she was told. Brant took her handbag and pulled out the bottle of water and vegetables. He split it evenly and gave it to each of them.

"All aboard?" asked Brant. "Let's go!"

Together, Brant and Ajnos dragged Nanoc and Alexis through the cave. They made it out into the open and the fog was completely back to normal. Brant could not see the sky or the dome anymore. It was hard to see anything at all.

As they continued walking towards "The Eye," Brant wanted to keep on talking so Alexis would stay conscious and not stumble into the Eternal Darkness.

"What were you two doing out here?" asked Brant.

Ajnos spoke up. "We were out here with our group of hunters and scavengers, hunting for specterlings and gathering Intel on the..." Nanoc shushed her before she could say anything else. "On the spaceship," she said hesitantly.

"Oh, I see," said Brant with a raised eyebrow. He knew they were trying to cover something up. "And how did you end up in the cave?"

"Well, Nanoc and I went off on our own to do, you know, secret adult stuff." She blushed. "When suddenly we started walking back towards the group and they were all missing. Our yarn had been cut. We knew it would be nearly impossible to return back and we knew there was a cave nearby. We knew exactly where it was in relation to us and we knew that the cave would be the first place assassins would search for if someone went missing."

"You got that right," said Alexis grinning.

"I assume I have you both to thank," said Ajnos. "Go on, Nanoc, say thank you to these helpful assassins."

Nanoc looked at both of them. He looked grumpy. "Thank you," he grumbled.

"Don't worry," said Brant. "I think I know what might have happened. I will seek justice for you both when we get back home."

Alexis spoke up. "Brant, what was it you were saying earlier? How is it possible that you saw 'The Eye' from here?"

"I saw so many beautiful things, Alexis," started Brant. "I was being attacked by two wolfwraiths after the two others took you. All of a sudden, a giant fiery red rock appeared overhead and cleared the fog."

"Is that what that loud noise was?" asked Ajnos. "Something rumbled the cave, we thought it was an earthquake."

"I don't believe it," said Nanoc. "Why would there be a giant rock in the sky?"

Brant ignored Nanoc. "I saw sparkly white lights up in the sky and there was one green light directly overhead," said Brant. "I wonder what those things are doing up there so high. The object that flew overhead must have been going fast because all the fog cleared away. I could see farther than anyone has ever seen before. I can only describe it as a miracle. I could see the dome in the distance and you could never comprehend how massive it is."

Nanoc looked at Ajnos and rolled his eyes. Ajnos snickered.

"What? Everything I'm saying is the truth," said Brant.

Nanoc and Ajnos broke out into laughter.

"Fine, don't believe me," said an annoyed Brant.

"I believe you," said Alexis. She sounded faint.

"Hold on there just a little longer," said Brant. "We should be back home in a matter of minutes."

Brant ran out of things to say as he was lost in his own thoughts. His whole body was numb but he pushed himself forward. Brant and Ajnos continued to drag Alexis and Nanoc in the direction where he believed "The Eye" was. Maybe he made a mistake? Brant started to second guess himself.

Seconds later, Brant saw the glass wall of the dome. "We made it," he said which startled everyone. "There's no gate here so we will have to keep going until we run into one."

Brant knew the gate must be to his right because the pipes inside the glass dome angled diagonally towards him. Water flowed away from the gates. It took a minute until they found it. Brant burst through the door. "I need some medical assistance!"

Chapter 15

A team near the gate ran over to them. They had red patches around their arms, signifying their occupation. "Let us take a look," a woman from the medical personnel said to Brant.

Brant set the cloak on the ground. "This man, Nanoc, must have twisted his ankle. It looks pretty bad. As for the lady, that's Alexis. *The* Alexis. One of the greatest Master Assassins to ever exist. Please take good care of her. She has wolfwraith claws stuck in her arm and a few bad scratches all over. She has lost a lot of blood."

"We can take it from here," the medical woman said. They took hold of his cloak and dragged Alexis and Nanoc into a tent, leaving Brant and Ajnos behind.

After what felt like forever, one of the medical officers finally came over to fill them in.

"The man will be alright. We gave him some crutches and he will be up and walking normal in no time."

"As for the old woman," the medical officer trailed off, "we successfully removed the wolfwraith claws but she has lost a lot of blood. We are doing our best to rehydrate her and give her fluids. If she makes it through the night, there's a good chance she will heal and be back to normal within the next couple weeks. We may need to amputate her arm depending on how deep the marks are."

Brant looked at his feet. "Thank you for letting us know," he said.

He looked up and noticed a group talking with Nanoc by the tent. "Who are those people?" Brant asked Ajnos.

One of the guys was hanging out behind from the group, uninterested in Nanoc. He was barefoot.

"Those are my friends," said Ajnos.

"You mean the people who left you and your boyfriend behind?" joked Brant.

Ajnos fell silent.

One of the members of the group spotted Ajnos. They said something and pointed at her. The group rushed over to greet her.

Brant backed away and watched.

The barefoot man hugged Ajnos first. During their conversation the barefoot man kept on touching her shoulder and arm.

Brant noticed each of them were wearing a dagger at their waist. He silently wondered around the group, inspecting each blade closely.

Ajnos pointed at Brant. The group greeted him. "You are a true hero, sir," said the woman with red hair.

"We are blessed you had the courage to help," said the man with a yellow hood.

"It was my honor," said Brant.

A lawman walked passed them.

"Excuse me." Brant waved down the lawman. "There is a guilty man in our midst."

"Explain yourself," said the lawman.

"I am one of the people to rescue this couple who were lost in the Outside," Brant began. "When I went looking for them, I noticed a few clues at the crime scene. First, there were footprints of bare feet," Brant pointed at the barefoot man's feet, "...leading to the second clue, a yarn that had been crudely cut by a dull blade." Brant took out the frayed yarn and pointed at the barefoot man's dull dagger. "This man who stands before you as a friend, is jealous that Ajnos and Nanoc are together. He wants her for himself."

The barefoot man stood there shocked.

Brant continued, "This man is guilty for leaving the young couple in the Outside. He told the group they were behind him on the way back but in reality he left them to die. That's why you were so relived that she was still alive but didn't even care to say hello to Nanoc." Brant looked at the barefoot man. "Isn't that right?"

The barefoot man broke out in tears. It must have been true because he started to sway back and forth. Suddenly, he sprang forward.

Brant caught the barefoot man on his jaw with his fist. The man fell to the ground with a thud. He fell unconscious.

The lawman tied the barefoot man's hands together and led him away as Ajnos and the group stared on in disbelief.

Ajnos spoke up. "Thank you," she said. "You are a true Assassin."

16. FORGIVENESS

Jaylin woke up lying on her back. She had yet to open her eyes. Her whole body was sore and her muscles ached. She couldn't move. She really wished she was just having a nightmare.

Jaylin heard footsteps. She wondered where she was. She lazily opened her eyes and noticed she was in a hospital bed. *Jersey General Hospital* was written on the door to her room.

She felt like she was in a sarcophagus. The sheets were tucked underneath her body from her shoulders to her toes. Jaylin slowly moved her head side-to-side. There was someone sitting in the chair next to her.

"Akeer!" exclaimed Jaylin. She was so happy to see him, maybe for the first time ever.

Akeer jumped up from the chair. "Jaylin!" he said with a great big smile. "You're finally awake!"

A doctor walked past the room and Akeer ran after her. "Hey doc, my sister is awake," he said.

Jaylin recognized the doctor from yesterday. It was Dr. Petra Tsoukalos. "How are you feeling?" she said.

"A bit groggy," said Jaylin. "I can't move either. Not even a little."

Petra untucked the sheet from underneath her. "Don't worry, that's normal," she said. "We tuck in all of our patients who have broken bones. It's just a precaution so our patients don't roll over and fall down causing more damage to themselves."

Jaylin was processing what she just heard. *Broken bones?* She thought back to the events that occurred yesterday. *Was* it yesterday? She wondered how long she had been unconscious.

The support beams and rubble must have really done a number on her. It definitely hurt when the beams knocked into her, but it didn't hurt nearly as much as when she had broken her arm two years ago.

"Did I break a bone?" she questioned.

Petra pulled back the sheet to reveal what had happened. "One break and two fractures," she responded.

Petra pointed first at Jaylin's right forearm, which she saw was in a cast. "Your ulna bone in your arm was poking through the skin. It broke off diagonally. This will take about four months to heal back to normal."

Oh great. How was she going to swim? How would she be able to provide food for my family? This was her good arm too.

Petra pointed at Jaylin's collarbone next. "The right side of your clavicle is fractured. You will be required to wear a sling for about eight weeks. Your brother said he remembered the exact moment of impact when the beam hit your clavicle and shoulder. You're lucky it didn't hit your head."

Petra pointed to her shoulder, which was purple and yellow. "You have bumps and bruises all over your body which is why you might be aching or feeling any pain."

Petra then pointed at Jaylin's left leg, which was in a boot. "You have a shaft fracture on your fibula. Before you leave the hospital, I will give you a crutch. It will take about ten to twelve weeks for that to fully heal depending how much stress you put on your leg." Petra rolled the sheet back across Jaylin's body and tucked her in. "Any questions?"

Jaylin laid there in silence. Her mind was processing all of this information plus everything she planned on doing in the future. "So let me get this straight," asked Jaylin. "I have to wear a sling for two months, wear a boot and use a crutch for three months, and wear this cast for four months?" she asked incredulously. Karma's a bitch. She should have saved him.

"That is correct," said Petra.

"When do I get to leave this bed? When do I get to go home?" asked Jaylin. She wondered if her plan to sneak on the spaceship was still a possibility.

"You have been in the hospital for three days," said Petra. "You have all the necessary things to heal properly *here*. You can leave any time you wish, although I do not recommend it. It's late anyways. You should stay tonight to heal some more, start using your muscles, then you can leave in the morning if you insist."

Three whole days? Had she really been out for that long? She quickly did the math. If she were to stay over night, the spaceship would be leaving in

240

eight and a half days. How would she sneak on if she was in casts? She wouldn't be fast or quiet enough.

Jaylin laid there scratching her neck with her left arm. "Okay," she sighed.

"You should thank your brother," said Petra as she walked around the room. "If it weren't for him, you would have been in much worse shape. You could have easily been killed."

Jaylin slouched back in the bed.

"Let me know if you need anything," said Petra. "I have a lot of patients to tend to but I will always make some time for you."

"Thank you, Petra," said Akeer. "You are a miracle worker."

Petra smiled. She left the room and closed the door behind her.

Jaylin was left with Akeer. She didn't know what to say to him. Or at least where to begin.

Akeer was sitting again in the corner of the room by her head. His arms were crossed on his chest. His eyes fixed on her.

"Pull the chair closer," said Jaylin. "I have a lot to say to you."

Akeer did as he was told. The legs of the chair scraped against the ground making an awful sound. He turned the chair around so the back was closer to her. He sat down and leaned forward with his forearms on the back.

Jaylin looked at him with wet eyes. "Thank you. For rescuing me."

"Anytime, sis," said Akeer. He leaned forward and kissed her on the forehead. Her brother was bad at showing his emotions just as much as she was.

Jaylin smiled and chuckled. "So…" she started. "Tell me what happened. How did you find me? Tell me the whole story."

"Mom, dad, and sis are fine by the way," Akeer laughed.

This punched Jaylin in the gut. Why didn't she ask if they were alright? What had gotten into her? She was too busy worrying about herself.

"Hydronia is shaken up, but that's why we have builders," continued Akeer. "Something I wanted to be, but now I am being forced to be one of the Student Ambassadors, in case you didn't know." He chuckled.

"Anyway," said Akeer before Jaylin could say anything. "To answer your question, I was with mom and dad in one of the water bunkers under the hospital. Arkadia had been at daycare so they were prepared when the tsunami hit. We heard something loud up above. Dad said he thought it sounded like a force spear firing off with maximum pressure. We figured someone was up there, still in sub-level three, and needed help finding the water bunkers."

"Yeah, they are tricky to find," said Jaylin. "Especially when the entire room is under water."

"Mom and dad were on the same page as I was," said Akeer. "We wanted to save whoever was up there. We only had one aqua-breather in the water bunker so they volunteered me to go, since they could hold their breath longer than me. As soon as I opened the latch, water flooded the bunker. Luckily, there you were, right on top of me. It was a miracle. The support beams were already falling when I grabbed ahold of you. There was blood in the water so I knew you were injured."

"That's when you became the Achilles Heel," said Jaylin.

Akeer laughed. "I see you got that question right on the exam. I guess you really *do* know everything," he said sarcastically.

"I had help with that one," said Jaylin. "The only reason I remembered what it was called was because I kicked the girl in front of me on her heel because she wouldn't stop tapping her foot. It was so annoying."

Akeer leaned over the chair in laugher. "That's hilarious!" He regained composure and continued his story. "Anyways, when I brought you into the water bunker you had already passed out because you had over-worked yourself for two days straight. You were dehydrated and had little to sleep, plus your muscles ached from swimming for long periods of time. I gently set you down and pulled the latch closed."

"Oh, thanks for putting me down gently," said Jaylin rolling her eyes.

Akeer laughed once again. "Stop interrupting!" he said with a smile. "I pulled the lever that drains the water out and pumps oxygen back into the water bunker. Mom and dad held you until the drainage alarms ceased, notifying Hydronia all the water in the city had been drained."

"We were already in an infirmary so we carried you up six flights of stairs and found the perfect bed for you. You slept for three days because of exhaustion and trauma. At least that's what the doc said. And now here you are talking to me. I haven't left this room."

"How sweet," said Jaylin. She wouldn't have done that if their circumstances were switched.

"Mostly because my arm04 is still getting checked on. I was never released from the hospital, dummy," said Akeer.

Jaylin laughed. It hurt to laugh. Her ribs were most likely bruised or cracked. "I'm not a dummy. You're the dummy."

They both laughed together.

Looking at her brother made her realize how much she loved him. They haven't really been getting along the past few years. Jaylin thought it was because she was training so hard to become a Student Ambassador. It was time to come clean and tell her brother everything.

Jaylin raised her left hand and placed it on Akeer's good arm. "That night," she started. "During the fire…" She paused. "I was there. I was helping people make it out of the building. And then…I saw you helping others out. I saw my brother being a hero, risking his life to save others."

"At the time, I was extremely angry with you because you had been elected and I hadn't been. Your determination during the exam and endurance test made me think you really did want to become a Student Ambassador. That meant you had been lying to me the entire time and that hurt me deeply."

Akeer put his hand on hers. "I have always been on your side. I never wanted this. I still don't. I have no idea why I was chosen out of all the eighteen year old guys. Every day I ask myself, why me? What did the teachers see in me that made them think I was the one? I may never know. I still want to be a builder. That's still my goal in life. That is why I went to the school right after they announced it."

"I'm sorry I doubted you Akeer," said Jaylin. "I saw you in the room that caught on fire and I couldn't move. Something in my soul didn't want me to help you. The moment when the debris fell on you and I saw that you were hurt, I ran away. I didn't want to see my brother die." Jaylin started to cry. "I'm so sorry."

"It's alright," said Akeer. "If I didn't lose my arm that night, I wouldn't have been able to lift that beam up with my new arm04 and rescue you. Sometimes things happen for a reason."

"Ms. Britta said those exact words," said Jaylin. "Maybe things really do happen for a reason. You are always finding the bright side to everything. Maybe that's why they chose you, *brother*."

The way she called him brother had an effect on him. His face changed. He seemed to be happier. Jaylin had called him 'little brother' ever since they were young and now that she called him 'brother' made him feel respected and treated as her equal.

There was a knock at the door. Petra opened the door and peeked her head inside. "Looks like you have a couple visitors," she said.

In came Lydia, Denna, and Arkadia. Lydia went over to Jaylin and gave her a kiss on her cheek. Arkadia held Denna's hand as he went over to Akeer, who set his other hand on his shoulder. Arkadia waved to Jaylin.

"It's good to see you awake," said her mother. "We were so worried about you." She gave her another kiss. "I couldn't sleep much and haven't had much of an appetite these past few days, knowing you were in here unconscious and without a clue as to what was going on. Your brother insisted on staying. Let's not make these hospital trips a habit, kids."

She looked at Akeer and smiled. "We just had a lengthy conversation."

"Oh did you, now?" mother raised her eyebrows. "A positive conversation I hope?"

Jaylin and Akeer both nodded.

"That's good," said mother. "I have been afraid you two were growing apart. It's nice to have the family back together."

Arkadia walked over to Jaylin and poked at her cast. "Why does your arm have a hard towel on it?" She rubbed her eyes. She must not have been getting sleep either. "Will it turn into metal like Akeer's arm?"

Everyone laughed.

"This is a cast," said Jaylin. "It helps protect my broken arm while it heals."

"Oh," said Arkadia. She poked the cast one more time and walked back over to her father and grabbed his hand. She looked bored.

Denna walked around the bed. "Ms. Britta came to us the other day," he said.

Jaylin's ears perked up. Why would Ms. Britta go to them?

"She wanted to let us know how you two did on the exam and endurance test," said her father facing both Jaylin and Akeer. "Jaylin scored a perfect score on the exam. Only three others scored that high. We are so proud of you."

"Yes we are," said her mother. "Another person to receive a perfect score was Arabella."

Jaylin winced at her name.

"As for Akeer," he continued. "He received a 76 out of the 80 questions. That put him in the top 5th percentile on Hydronia. We are so proud of you, Akeer."

"Ms. Britta explained to us the reason behind the teachers decision to pick you was because you surprised them with your score," said Lydia. "But the specific reason they chose you over everyone else was because of your answer to the very last question. What would you do if you became Student Ambassador? You wrote, I would make sure everything I did was with the best..."

"With the best interest of our people," said Akeer finishing what he wrote for her.

Jaylin was dumbfounded. She thought question 80 was just a throwaway question. A question that didn't matter. Arabella must have had the answer they were looking for. Would she have been elected if her answer was better?

"I just wrote what I thought they wanted to hear," Akeer confessed.

"But I'm sure it's true," said Lydia. "You have always had a good heart, Akeer. Remember your answer when you leave Hydronia and help the human race. Never forget your answer and you will go on to do great things."

"As for you, young lady," her mother said as she turned to Jaylin. "Even though you won't be joining your brother, you can still do great things here on our planet. Keep Hydronia afloat, as they say."

"I have come to terms with my situation," said Jaylin. Her family's faces told her they didn't believe her.

Akeer leaned back in his chair and frowned. She noticed the gears turning in his head, thinking about something.

Denna scratched his forehead. "Both of you excelled during the endurance test. The teachers applauded your strategy, Jaylin, collecting all of the buoys first and then bringing up one at a time."

"Akeer was quick collecting buoys because he went for the easy ones. Another great strategy. Ms. Britta even explained how you stole one from Jaylin."

Her father laughed.

"I knew Jaylin would have a better plan than I did," said Akeer. "I watched her as I collected the first two buoys and saw she was hiding them all under the ledge. When I had the chance, I snuck over and took one. Easy peasy."

Jaylin gave Akeer a dirty look.

"The teachers liked that strategy as well. They didn't say anything about stealing buoys in the rules," said Denna. "The main reason you weren't elected, Jaylin, was because you fought your brother for the buoy he stole. Fighting another student was against the rules. You also looked at other student's exams which is a big no no. Arabella finished two and a half minutes after you, still impressive. But she didn't break any rules."

"The votes were split, but they ultimately decided on Akeer and Arabella to be the elected Student Ambassadors," said Lydia. "Even though it was your dream to become one, Jaylin, they just didn't think you were ready for the title. We don't think you are ready either."

The room feel silent.

Hearing this in person from her own mother was tough. She was denied the one thing she had wanted in life. Something clicked in her mind though. Jaylin was ready to accept that she wasn't fit for the role as Student Ambassador, but she was ready to still be the best at everything on Hydronia. She would become a strong leader in another form. Her new goal in life.

"May I speak to Akeer privately?" asked Jaylin. "I need to tell him something really important."

"Of course," said mother. "We will wait outside if you need anything." She kissed Jaylin on her cheek again.

"Come on, Kadie," said her father to Arkadia. She only allowed *him* to call her that. She grabbed his hand and her family walked out of the room. The door closed.

Akeer positioned himself on the chair like he was before. He leaned in close to Jaylin.

"Yes?" he said.

"I don't know how to tell you this," said Jaylin. "Ms. Britta told me not to tell anyone."

"Spit it out," said Akeer.

"She said that whoever goes up in the spaceship might not make it to their destination," she said.

"What do you mean?" he asked.

"The spaceship is rusted and worn down," said Jaylin. "It might not be sturdy enough to leave the atmosphere. It may have a leak so the oxygen might get sucked out once you're in space."

Akeer raised an eyebrow. "You know Ms. Britta is a conspiracy theorist, right? You shouldn't hang out with her too much. Remember that one time you came home all distraught because she told you the armored fish were growing legs and starting to live in our drainage pipes? You had nightmares for weeks."

"I have yet to see an armored fish with legs," Jaylin agreed.

"She also said your trophies had little gremlins in them. Remember that? You staid up all night one weekend to try to catch one. I will never forget that."

Jaylin smiled at this memory that had escaped her until just now.

"This spaceship has two purposes," said Akeer. "To bring us here and to take us back. Everything that has happened within the last two hundred years has been leading up to the moment we make contact again with the rest of the human race. We all have a purpose. The universe wants us to succeed."

"That was beautiful, brother," said Jaylin.

"If by any chance we don't make it," said Akeer. "Then it happened for a reason. Just remember that."

"I will," said Jaylin. She touched his hand with hers. "I also wanted to speak to you privately for one other reason, brother."

"Yes?" Akeer leaned in even closer to his sister.

Jaylin hesitated. "I want to train you. I want to teach you everything I know. I want to give you guidance for your upcoming journey."

She really had come to terms with her situation. With her broken bones and new outlook on life, she didn't have a reason to be on that spaceship anymore.

"I have prepared myself for so long and now that I am unable to do it, I must prepare you."

She rubbed his hand. It was the only embrace that she was capable of in her condition.

"Will you accept?"

"Do I accept training from the best there is?" said Akeer. "Absolutely!" Akeer stood up and did a little dance. "I can't wait, when do we start?"

"I just need some rest and we can start in the morning," said Jaylin. "I just might need some help getting around Hydronia."

They both laughed.

"It's a deal, sis," said Akeer. "I'll let you get some rest. Sweet dreams."

As Akeer headed for the door, he looked sad for some reason. Jaylin wanted to ask why, but felt it was the wrong time. She was too happy they were best friends again. Brother and sister. Twins.

Akeer opened the door.

"Thank you for everything you have done, *brother*," said Jaylin. "I love you."

Jaylin saw a smile on his face in the reflection of the window as he left the room. Something shiny streaked down his cheek. She heard him say, "Love you too," as the door shut.

17. PLAN GONE WRONG

The sun peeked over the ravine. The sound of construction filled the air. The countdown to liftoff had begun. It was the day before the Quaketownians would be boarding the spaceship to leave for *The New Frontier*. Everyone, except for Selene and Sarva.

Both hunters and miners were working on leveling the ground under the spaceship. Kelly and her team had successfully dug it out. Now, they were using the melters to slowly bring down one side to make the platform even. Kelly's hair was down, dangling by her shoulders. She didn't need to use her brain now. She had planned everything out down to the most miniscule detail. Selene could tell all of the workers respected Kelly a lot as she used her soft voice to give orders. Selene thought she would eventually make a great leader for the human race.

As for Selene, it had occurred to her that there was no place for her on the journey to find a new home. She thought about everyone's role and came up with something for everyone except herself.

Selene looked back at her time in Quaketown and tried to find something she was good at. She definitely wasn't a good hunter because she wasn't trained for that. She was a less than average miner; when the cave-in occurred, she couldn't do anything to help out. Christopherson told her to go home. She didn't know how to make jewelry like Isadora, she wasn't smart like Kelly, she didn't retrieve water like Farhad, and she didn't know how to sculpt like Miles. She wasn't a guard like Lem and Lee. She wasn't a leader like the Elders or the Council. She wasn't a parent. Everyone had a purpose. Selene was just there, living her life with no purpose. This is ultimately why she chose to go through with Sarva's plan. At least she could have a purpose if she stayed behind with him. She could be a princess like she had always dreamt of being.

Selene hopped down from the balcony and landed on the rocky ground with a thump. She looked back at Kelly and the spaceship one last time. She was going to go through with Sarva's plan tonight.

The last couple days she didn't bother to hang out with Miles. She just told him that she was busy preparing to leave.

When Selene went to Sarva after their encounter at the library, he seemed a little surprised she came. They met each other at Kelly's cavehome, because they knew she and her parents were always occupied with something else. People were too busy to notice they were at the wrong cavehome.

Once Selene told Sarva she was ready to hear his plan, Sarva described it in full detail. Since Selene was so distracted with all the details, she forgot to ask questions afterwards.

Sarva's plan was this:

The first part of the plan was for Selene to go to work in the mines. At the end of her shift, instead of turning in her melter, she would smuggle it out along with as many melters and blue crystals as she could carry. She was going to sneak out of the caves with all the supplies without anyone noticing. Sarva didn't mention how to do this. It was all up to her.

The second part of the plan included Sarva pretending to go on a hunt. Instead, he would break into a couple safe havens he knew were supplied with food. It would be the final time they were filled with food because the guards would go to the safe havens one last time on the day they leave. Sarva would take as much food as he could carry.

Lastly, they were going to meet up on top of Ceremony Hill. Sarva would then bring her to a place he knew no one would bother looking for them. He said there were wild bosas and pogo trees nearby so they would have enough supplies. The location was located by fresh water too. Sarva would teach Selene how to master the bow and arrow, so they both could easily fend off anything that could harm them.

Selene was ready to start her day. Sure, she was terrified about what was about to unfold. Mostly because she hadn't had the time to figure out her plan to smuggle the supplies out of the caves. She was going to have to come up with a plan on the spot.

Before going to work, Selene stopped at her cavehome and changed into her mining shirt. Both her parents were there. Good thing too, she wanted to properly say goodbye to them. Her mother handed her a jennybob and pogo salad for her walk to the mines.

"I'm off," she said. She didn't know how to say goodbye for the last time. She was sad, but this time she tried her hardest not shed a tear. It worked. She opened the door and looked towards the mines and then to the jungle outside. She turned back and looked at her parents.

Her mother was more beautiful than ever. Her father was preparing for his meeting with the Council. They were going to discuss the seating on the spaceship. Selene hoped he wasn't going to crack a joke. If he did, she might cry.

Selene stepped towards them. "I love you both," she said. She opened her arms. They went to her and hugged her. She held on for as long as possible, but not too long or else they would think something was up. Selene finally let go.

She took her necklace from around her neck and placed it on the table. She wanted her mother to take the necklace with her.

"Goodbye." With that, she left and didn't look back.

Selene was finished with her day of work. It was time to execute Sarva's plan. She had her melter in her hand and was headed towards the supply drop-off.

Selene saw who was at the counter and was filled with dread. It was her Aunt Luci. How was she going to steal a few melters and crystals, let alone sneak past her? She swallowed really hard, causing her throat to hurt, and walked right up to her.

"Hey, Aunt Luci," said Selene shyly.

"Hello darling. Done for the day, are we?" said her Aunt. Her eyes glowed green.

"No, I just forgot. I have to go back and break apart an area that had traces of aluminum," she lied.

Selene stepped back and disappeared into the shadows. She waited anxiously, tapping her foot.

Finally, after about ten minutes of hiding in wait, a young miner accidentally pulled the trigger of his melter shooting a laser into the rocky ceiling. Rocks crumbled on top of him as he screamed for help.

Aunt Luci, being the gentle soul she was, was the first adult to run over to help the poor young boy.

Now was her chance. Selene came out of the shadows and nonchalantly made her way to the supply drop-off. She took the bin of crystals labeled 'power' and set her melter inside. She filled the bin to the brim with metlers. Selene attempted to pick it up but it was too heavy. Her heart dropped. *Now what?*

Selene spotted a runner, which was a box with one wheel on the bottom and two handles to push it. She ran over and wheeled it over to the bin. With all her might she lifted the heavy bin and clumsily dropped it inside the runner.

Selene looked back at her Aunt Luci and said goodbye in her head. She headed towards the exit of the mines.

Now was the hard part. How was she supposed to make it past inspection? She held on to the runner and looked at the security officers up front. What were the chances of another distraction? Selene figured the chances were slimmer than domesticating a scabite. She waited, watching the people go past, hoping they wouldn't question her.

Selene formulated a plan. Instead of heading towards the inspection line, she walked to the line of people entering the mines. She turned around with her back to the entrance and began walking backwards, pulling the runner with her. She got this idea from the Little Blue Hiding Hood fairy tale. A little girl walked through the jungle backwards, turning back time to rescue her grandfather from a scabites deadly touch.

The people around her walking the correct way were young mining trainees. They came in after hours to work with some of the best miners in Quaketown, to learn safety and different techniques without any distractions. Christopherson better not be on his way in or else she would be in big trouble. The trainees didn't know how to react to someone walking backwards, which made her chuckle. All of them minded their own business and kept on walking.

Selene was close to the entrance of the mines, which meant she was getting closer to the security officers at the exit. She turned her head towards them as she continued walking. Selene never noticed it before, but the security officers looked bored. Good thing they won't have to be doing that in a few days. They did their jobs, patting down the miners at the exit. Of course they unsuspected someone going out the entrance, backwards. Who in their right mind would do that?

Selene made it out and breathed a sigh of relief. She was now near the cavehomes. Her forehead sweat was building up on her brow. So far so good. She thought of how she was going to make it through the cavehomes without anyone she knew bothering her or questioning what was in the runner.

Selene rolled the runner up to the library and went inside hoping to find a backsack to put the supplies in. To her surprise, someone left a backsack sitting on the counter. She went up to take it until a voice called out her name.

"Selene?" the voice questioned.

Selene looked to her left and saw Miles sitting at a table. He was reading a journal. She trembled. She should have known the backsack was his.

"Oh hey, Miles," said Selene. "I didn't know you were going to be here." He must have gone straight to the library after mining.

"I figured I'd finish reading about the history of Quaketown before we left," he said. "I'm on the last volume. Elias and I are going to teach all of the other humans about our history when we settle down with them on our new planet."

"I'm sure they will like that," said Selene. She grabbed the backsack as he turned his back. "I have to go. Want to hang out later?"

"Sure," he said. "Just name a time and place."

Selene went out the door because she didn't want to keep lying to him. She rolled the runner around the corner. Making sure no one was watching, she slipped the melters and crystals into the backsack. She left the runner there and put the straps around her shoulders. It was heavy. She was going to have to push herself to her limits to get out of Quaketown and into the jungle. When she was in the clear, she would be able to drag it the rest of the way to Ceremony Hill.

Selene traveled through the cavehomes. Luckily she didn't run into anyone else who wanted to speak with her.

Selene walked across the stage seating towards the exit. Before she left, she paused to look at the stage. She thought back about memories of the shows she had seen there. She remembered idolizing Claire Altaïr. She remembered her first show and how she felt. She was heartbroken she would never act again. Maybe one day when she had kids, she could perform for them.

Selene struggled past the stage and saw the security officers. The walking backwards trick wasn't going to work this time. There weren't as many people here to distract them. She decided to just act natural.

She walked up to the officers with confidence. She knew their faces well, just not their names. She smiled welcomingly at the security officer with the large chin, who was going to pat her down. He smiled back in return.

"Where are you headed to today, Selene?" asked the first officer.

"Just headed to the training grounds," she said with confidence. She was getting better at lying. She knew which muscles to relax in her face.

"That looks heavy," he said. "What's in your backsack?"

Selene said the first thing that came to mind. "Sculptures." Was this lie good enough? "Miles made sculptures for some of my hunting friends. I'm headed to the training grounds to give them to Ciri and Farhad."

The security officer felt underneath the backsack and shoved it upwards a couple times. "You're friends with Ciri now, huh?"

Shit. Selene stretched out her lie too much. She should have left her answer short and sweet. "Yup."

"I thought Ciri was reported missing. I'm glad she was found," the officer said.

Selene gave him a concerned look. Where had Ciri been this whole time? She hoped she was okay.

The objects in the backsack must have felt like sculptures because the officer let her pass.

Selene did it. She was now in the jungle. All she had to do now was make it up the incline to Ceremony Hill.

Selene hid behind a thicket of undergrowth and took off her backsack. She started dragging it. Her shoulders and back were in pain. She followed the path that she remembered walking on the day of her twenty-first birthday, around two months ago. Time had flown by so fast since that night.

It was getting dark. On the way to the hill, she started to get worried.

Selene wondered if Sarva was going to be successful pulling off his part of the plan. What if he bailed out at the last second? What if he did all of this as payback? Selene ran plenty of different scenarios through her head. She started to doubt herself. She started to doubt her decisions. Then, she spotted the hill in the distance and decided she had made it too far to turn back.

Selene spent the last of her energy dragging the backsack up the hill. She was breathing hard and heavy and looked forward to resting. She took four more steps as she reached the top. She looked out into the clearing. The stone walls were just how she remembered them.

Selene stood there in disbelief as she looked at Sarva standing in the center, where she stood during her Chosen Ceremony. By his side, were four backsacks full of meats, fruits, vegetables, and seeds.

The moon was out, shining on both of them. Was it really past midnight?

"The Five Ancients are watching over us tonight," said Sarva, a callback to the ceremony.

Selene was relieved. She let go of the backsack straps and ran over to Sarva. She took him in her arms and kissed him. "We did it."

"The plan isn't complete yet. I know of a place where we can live." Sarva noticed she was out of breath. "Let's take a few minutes to rest up. We will head there shortly."

Selene sat down and rested her head on Sarva. He played with her hair as she rested her eyes.

Fifteen minutes went by and Selene was ready to leave. Sarva put on the backsack full of melters and crystals and tied two others on his back, leaving the two lighter backsacks full of seed and vegetables for Selene.

They made their way into a thicket. Sarva took the lead as he hacked apart vines with a blade in each hand. Selene stood closely behind him, her eyes wide and scanning the area around them for any hostile creatures. She thought she saw something red move to her left but Sarva reassured her it was her mind playing tricks on her.

Scared and out of breath, Selene and Sarva entered a clearing. She saw a man-made building close by. Selene had never seen a building like this before. The walls were fifteen feet high and made of a mixture of wood and steel. There were two pillars, one on each side of the door. Selene figured this must be one of the safe havens Akira built. Selene saw a light shining inside. There must be a lost soul living there. She started to walk towards that direction.

Sarva put his hand on her shoulder. "That is not the direction we are headed," he said.

Sarva pointed across the way were there was a small cave that was hidden by its surroundings. He extended his hand towards her. Selene accepted it and they both walked towards the cave.

The cave entrance was just tall enough to walk in without ducking. The cave was damp but it would have to do. Once everyone leaves, they could start living in the safe haven across the way.

The cave had a dead end. Selene saw something sticking out of the ground. She bent down and plucked it out. It was a piece of petrified wood. She looked into the hole where she had pulled the wood out and saw some more wood. Selene knew someone must have been living here previously.

Sarva set down the backsacks by the end of the cave and offered to take the other backsack from Selene.

"It's going to be pretty cold tonight but we can't start a fire," Sarva warned her. "That would attract unwanted attention."

Sarva reached into one of the food backsacks and took out two monjaberries, which were the size of a large man's fist. He tossed one to Selene and she caught it. Selene bit into it and juice instantly dripped down her chin. Monjaberries were her favorite dessert. They were sweet and succulent.

Sarva reached into the supply backsack and took out two melters and eight blue power crystals.

Selene couldn't help but notice a look on Sarva's face that she had never seen before. It was a look of derangement. She couldn't help but say something. "What are you doing?"

Sarva was putting the blue power crystals into the two melters. Selene watched him as he put four crystals into each melter.

Christopherson told her putting more than one crystal into a melter increased its power exponentially. If a miner was caught putting more than one crystal into a melter, there would be extreme consequences; exile or even death.

Selene had never seen that happen before. There was no need for it. Melters worked perfectly fine with just one crystal.

Sarva laughed maniacally. His eyes were darker than normal. "Have you ever seen the path of destruction a melter with four crystals can leave behind?" he asked.

Selene became horrified. Why would he ask something like that? Then it all clicked. The clearing, the safe haven, and the small cave, all in one location. The petrified wood. The demonic look on Sarva's face. This is where Sarva's parents lived and gave birth to him. This is where he lived for the first five years of his life. This is where Malcolm and Darcie died protecting Sarva from their pursuers. This is where my father committed murder. It all made sense. Sarva was walking in the footsteps of his parents. Selene figured he wanted to succeed where they had failed; to destroy Quaketown.

"What do you plan on doing?" Selene asked with fear in her voice.

"We are going to destroy that spaceship right before they take off," he said.

He just said *we*. He thought *I* wanted to hurt our people. Selene thought back on her actions and wanted to go back in time to make different decisions. She never should have wanted to leave her family and friends behind. She should have listened to her parents and spent time with Miles from the start. She should have never allowed herself to know Sarva before her twenty-first birthday.

Selene got off of the damp floor and dropped her monjaberry. She instinctively ran to the entrance. She ran as fast as she could. Her legs were sore from the long walk. Selene saw the clearing when Sarva tackled her from behind.

"You're not going anywhere, Selene," said Sarva.

Selene screamed at the top of her lungs. He strapped a piece of cloth over her mouth, for fear of someone in the safe haven hearing her.

Selene struggled to get free. She punched him three times and then he punched her back right in the gut, taking all of the fight out of her.

Sarva tied her hands up in front of her and then tied her legs together, using a roll of rope he brought with him. He pushed her down in a corner of the cave. Mud splashed up in her face. Selene began to cry. Without any warning, Sarva took his bow and quiver and left the cave.

Selene was lying there with mud and tears drying on her face. She finally calmed down and started taking in her surroundings.

Chapter 17

There was a pair of chairs and a chest nearby. She rolled over to the chest and shimmied up it, so that she was sitting down. Selene opened the chest and peeked inside. She picked up a drawing of a young Sarva with his parents. They looked like a happy family.

There were a pile of letters inside, most of them about betrayal and revenge. She didn't have much time to read through them all because she heard a noise approaching. She prayed it was someone to rescue her. She set everything back in the chest, closed it, and quickly rolled back to where she was.

Sarva came bounding into the room drenched in sweat and blood. He dropped the two melters. Selene concluded he must have gone to the safe haven and murdered everyone who was inside. She imagined the poor peoples' faces when they saw someone coming to rescue them only to be slaughtered.

"How many were there?" hesitated Selene.

"Four...Four men." Sarva took a moment to catch his breath. "Four men and a woman with a child."

Selene gasped. "You monster!"

Sarva pulled her up by the rope around her wrists. Selene yelped in pain.

"Don't you ever call me a monster."

Selene feared for her life and she felt hopeless. She kept on thinking about one thing, over and over again. "Did you kill Ciri?" she asked.

"Of course I didn't," he said. "She ran off before I could. Clever girl."

She hung there in silence. "What now?" Selene knew she couldn't ask him to let her go. He might kill her.

"We wait for morning," said Sarva.

Selene woke up to the sun shining through the cave. Her head hurt. She looked around and realized she was still in her nightmare.

Sarva was sitting on one of the wooden chairs tinkering with a melter. He was also reading one of the letters that was on top of the chest. The drawing of his family was next to it.

"I have waited a long time for this," said Sarva flatly. He must have known she was awake. "I have waited patiently, blending in with my parents' killers pretending not to know the truth. I grew up being feared by everyone. I was treated like a wild animal. No one treated me with respect until I met you. Unfortunately for you and everyone else, I became a wild animal long before I met you. Not even my love for you will change me."

He is out of his mind. How was she going to get out of this situation? Had he been acting this entire time without anyone noticing? If so, he was the best actor she had ever seen. Living a lie.

"I remember what happened to my parents when I was little," Sarva continued. "Each year I escaped Quaketown to come here to pay my respects. I knew how poorly your people treated them and I had to plan my revenge." He turned towards her. "Now come. We must leave immediately to make it in time for their going away party."

Sarva set the melters he had modified into a backsack and slung his bow around his shoulder. He grabbed onto the rope strung around Selene's wrists and he dragged her outside. He continued to drag her until they reached Antilles Peak. He dragged her up and set her down on the edge of the cliff.

The view was beautiful. The sun was already above the horizon. Selene could see the spaceship across the ravine. It looked like Kelly and her team successfully built a launch pad.

People were gathered outside the spaceship, waiting their turn to go inside. Sarva propped her up and sat her down, facing the spaceship. Her family must have been down there wondering where she was.

"Enjoy the show!" he said.

Sarva stayed to the side of the Antilles Peak. He climbed down a little ways and hugged the side of the cliff. He was headed down to the thicket of trees right behind the spaceship. There, he was going to use the melters to destroy the ship with the people inside before or after it lifted off.

Selene cried out for help. With the cloth over her mouth, it prevented her from making enough noise to reach the people down the peak and across the ravine. Selene couldn't think of a way to stop him. If he went through with it, she contemplated rolling off the cliff to her death. There is no way she was going to live with Sarva after what he had done and feared what he would do to her. Her decision was equivalent to the fairy tale of Princess Bev, who drank poison after she found out her lover was actually a scabite under a body altering spell.

Sarva was getting close now. He reached the bottom of the cliff and ducked down below boulders. He headed towards the thicket of trees.

Selene continued to scream as loud as she could. She thought of her family and friends who were about to die by the hands of her murderous lover. She would scream until it was over and then scream all the way to the afterlife as she flew down the cliff. She realized this wasn't going to have a happy ending like the fairy tales. Real life had no happy endings.

Suddenly, she heard noises behind her. Of course, with her current luck, she would be attacked by scabites. She feared the worse and prepared for her end. She closed her eyes.

A hand gently touched her shoulder. She opened her eyes. Someone was untying the cloth from around her mouth. Another pair of hands untied the rope from her hands and feet. Selene turned around to emerald eyes glistened in the morning sun. It was her mother with a group of people.

"Mom!" Selene cried.

Selene gave her mother the biggest hug that she had ever given anyone. She looked around at the people behind her. Father was there, along with Kelly, Miles, Akira, Fortuna, Mr. Bradham, Farhad, Isadora, and so many others. Selene was delighted to see Ciri running behind them with a bow and arrow. She was relieved to see everyone she liked were here and not down by the spaceship. *The spaceship!*

"Hey! Listen up, everyone!" she said. "Sarva is down there! He's going to destroy the spaceship!" She pointed down towards Sarva.

Hazel and Gratius led Lem, Lee, and Ciri down the cliff. Sarva lifted up his loaded melters, one in each hand. Realizing it was too late, they quickly drew their weapons on him.

Everyone was either blocked behind trees or out of range except for Ciri. She aimed her bow towards Sarva. He was aiming his two melters towards the spaceship. Ciri pressed buttons on her bow and let go of the arrow.

Selene watched as the melters loaded with crystals began to power up with blue flashing lights. It looked like an electrical storm.

Ciri's arrow flew through the air, piercing through both of the melters. Sarva was propelled backwards as they were knocked out his hands.

Ciri's arrow must have hit the power crystals because they started to glow and shake.

Sarva began crawling away from the melters.

Selene watched as the melters violently exploded, catching Sarva on fire. Thankfully, they were far enough away that the explosion had no effect on the spaceship.

Selene heard Ciri yell, "Erespada!" to Sarva, which was the worst thing you could call someone. Sarva was still on fire, crawling away into the mountainside.

Selene couldn't help but look away, wincing. She stood there, facing everyone. The only thing she could say was, "Sorry." She curled up in her mother's arms and both began to cry.

Her father hugged them both.

Next, Kelly came to her side and hugged her.

Everyone else surrounded her on Antilles Peak. Hazel, Gratius, Lem, Lee, and Ciri eventually made it back to them.

Ciri slowly walked up to Selene and whispered into her ear. "I did it. He's finished."

Selene's parents gave them space.

"Ciri is the one who alerted us that you were missing," said Mona.

Surprised, Selene turned to Ciri and gave her a hug. "You saved us all. We all owe you one," said Selene. "But why? I thought you liked Sarva?"

Ciri laughed. "I did at first. But that was a long time ago. I found out who he truly was way before he targeted you. I tried to warn you that one night at target practice."

Selene remembered that night. So *this* was why she told her to leave.

"I wasn't going to leave you two alone, but he threatened me. I had no choice. I found out he was trying to get closer to you, so when I saw you watching us at target practice, I told him to kiss me. I wanted to make you jealous. To distance him from you. I didn't want you to suffer through what I had been through."

Selene looked down at the ground in shock. This wasn't how any of the fairy tales ended; with the unsuspecting side character rescuing the princess from a monster. Someone should make one though.

"Before he could realize what I had done, I ran away," explained Ciri. "I knew he would have killed me if I showed my face. I hid in a safe haven nearby. I felt bad leaving you behind. If he somehow managed to persuade you…"

"What I did was wrong," Selene spoke up. "I wasn't thinking. I should have listened to everyone, especially my parents."

"Good thing Ciri alerted us," said Mona. "Or else…" She trailed off.

"This morning I had a strange feeling," said Ciri. "I felt compelled to come talk to you. When I made it back to Quaketown and discovered both you and Sarva were missing, I panicked. I immediately went to your cavehome. Your parents hadn't seen you so I went to Miles. He said he saw you and Sarva talking at the library the other day."

Selene couldn't have been more overjoyed knowing Miles had seen them together.

"I had feared the worst," Ciri confessed. "We gathered a group of people to come find you. Luckily, your parents had a good idea where to search first. On our way to the cave where Sarva's parents died, we saw you on Antilles Peak. We knew we had to act fast."

"I cannot thank you enough," said Selene as she hugged her again. "Can we please be friends?"

Ciri looked at her, pleased. "After what we have been through, I don't think we have a choice. No one else will ever understand what we have suffered through." Ciri lifted up her sleeves, revealing bruises on her arms.

Selene gasped, speechless.

"Let's never mention his name ever again." Ciri lent her hand to Selene. "Come. I think we have had enough bad memories here in Quaketown. Let's board that spaceship and make nothing but good memories."

Selene walked with her family, friends, and neighbors down Antilles Hill, past Ceremony Hill, and across the ravine. She took one last look at Quaketown, before entering. She wanted to speak with her parents alone in their cavehome one last time before they all left.

After all this time, not knowing her place in the world...she finally found a purpose. Her purpose was to be a great daughter, friend, neighbor, and girlfriend. And from now on, she would never forget that.

18. NOT ALONE

Wakan woke up to a soft, familiar voice. He opened one eye and peered around the room. "I knew it couldn't have been you," said Wakan out loud to no one. He closed his eye and rolled over. He attempted to lick his lips but his mouth was too dry. As he laid down, he felt his heart pumping in his chest. Badum, badum, badum. It was beating faster than normal. A few minutes went by. It became too uncomfortable for him. The beating of his heart made his body move side to side as he laid there. He rolled back to his other side. Wakan took a deep breath before finally opening both eyes.

The sun was gone and the tan light from the mushrooms illuminated the inside of the tunnel. It was time to get up. Today was the day to reach the top.

Wakan pushed himself up on one knee. "I am definitely feeling my age today." He grabbed onto a crevice in the wall to help lift himself up. The room spun around him. "A little woozy too." Wakan sat back down and held his head.

Wakan looked towards the exit of the tunnel. "Time to get up, old man, your children are counting on you." It took all his strength to pull himself back up using the same crevice.

Wakan took off the cloak he had been wearing since the bridge and set it in his bag which was full of his friends' gifts. He then grabbed the bag, slung it over his shoulder and hobbled out of the tunnel. He looked up at the peak and the stars. There was a pathway that circled around the summit of Mount Crimson. "Nearly there."

Wakan wheezed as he headed up to the top. This time, he really was wheezing, there were no burstflies in sight. Around and around he went, following the path. Wakan grabbed the sleeve of his cloak; it was sticking out of his bag. He looked at the sleeve and to his disappointment, there was no sweat. "This isn't a good sign."

Thinking back to the plethora of stories he had memorized, a certain story came across his mind. One story told a tale of an early explorer who died from dehydration. Nicholas Jones III left the settlement that would become Dunestone to chart the desert beyond the mountain range, which would later become the Grand Dunes. Nicholas was unprepared for his journey and as he was suffering from dehydration, he chronicled everything in his notebook. Most of the symptoms Nicholas wrote about seemed just like what Wakan was currently experiencing.

A little further up the winding path, Wakan looked over the horizon and marveled at Dunestone in all its glory. It looked exactly the same as when he saw this view when he was younger with Chiyo Ito, only much smaller. "This really is truly something special. Ain't that right, Chiyo?" At any other time, this would make Wakan tear up but right now his eyes were too dry.

The spaceship was the size of a pebble from here, but Wakan could still see the flashing red light. "One more week."

Wakan continued along the path. About two-thirds of the way up, Wakan had to take a breather. He sat down. He was about to pass out until a glimmer of light a few feet in front startled him. He squinted to focus in on the bright object slowly coming towards him. It looked similar to his daughter Star, but had some noticeable differences.

"It's not like you to give up," said the beautiful glimmering object, as she came into focus. It was his deceased wife, Sapphire, still beautiful as ever.

"Hello, Sapphire, my love," said Wakan. He noticed her appearance was different from the day she passed away; filled with youth and free of scars or any damage to her face and body. This made him content. "I have been waiting for you."

With an electric smile, Sapphire gave Wakan her hand. He grabbed her soft gentle hand with his aging hands as she helped him to his feet. Her jet black hair blew in the nonexistent breeze.

"Are they with you?" asked Wakan.

"No, not yet," said Sapphire in a soothing voice. "It will be some time before they reunite with their mother." With his hands still in her hand, she led him up the path. "Star, Triss, little Zato; They are all counting on you, Wakan."

"What if I can't pull through?" asked Wakan. "What if I'm not strong enough?"

Sapphire continued to guide him. "The man I once knew, the man I loved with all my heart, could do anything he set his mind to. Your body and your leg are just obstacles. Push those obstacles aside. Clear your mind and reach your objective."

Wakan thought about what his wife just said. A moment went by. "I wish I could have done the same for you. I blame myself for what happened to you. If only I…"

"There was nothing you could have done," said Sapphire. "I was long gone by the time you made it back to me."

Wakan managed to cry through his dry eyes. "I miss you," said Wakan. "Life without you has been unbearable. Without the children…"

"You'd still have your friends," said Sapphire. "Your stories. Your followers. They all love you."

"Apparently not. At least that's not what Bruce said," said Wakan.

Sapphire looked at Wakan and held his hands tight. "Don't be so hard on yourself, Wakan."

He looked deep into her blue eyes. He missed waking up to her eyes staring back at him.

"Just know your family and friends will love you no matter what you do."

"Thank you, darling," said Wakan to his wife. "I love you so very much."

"I love you too," said Sapphire to her husband. She gave him a kiss. "I'm sorry, but now it is time for me to go."

"Can I come with you?" asked Wakan.

"Now is not your time. Look before you," said Sapphire.

Wakan looked around and to his surprise he was standing on the summit of Mount Crimson. His wife led him all the way to the top. "Is this real?" he asked incredulously.

"It's yours for the taking," said Sapphire. "Goodbye for now." With that his wife let go of his hands and right before his eyes, she disappeared.

Wakan snapped to his senses and looked around, searching for the rosena flower. He walked to the center of the summit where there was a wide hole dug out. Around the edges of the hole were shriveled up plants. Wakan stumbled up to one and fell to his knees. He cupped his hands around the flowers' shriveled up stems, devastated. No petals in sight.

"Why?" he screamed with a hoarse voice. "I came all this way for what?" Wakan threw his fists into the hard barren ground. "For nothing!"

Wakan was so frustrated, dehydrated, and exhausted, he blacked out right next to the dead flowers. He thought for sure he would never wake up again, unless it was to be with his wife and children.

———————

As Wakan went in and out of consciousness, he heard a croaking noise that surrounded him and then loud pitter-patters. He felt something wet on his face. There was a rhythm to it.

Finally, Wakan woke up from his near death slumber. His right arm and leg were underwater. His clothes were soaked. Unaware of what was going on, Wakan jolted up and wiped the water from his face. He looked around the area. It was pouring.

Next to him was a little pond that had formed in the hole. The pitter-patter sound he heard was the rain hitting the water. But there was something else jumping in the water.

Frogs!

Wakan thought frogs became extinct when he was in his twenties. He used to love eating frog leg soup. But one day after it rained, the frogs just vanished. They must have hopped their way up the mountain and lived underground. So the voyages of Stifu songs *did* stem from facts. The frogs had emerged from little holes in the ground.

Wakan looked up to the sky. He held his hands up and put them together as if he was about to pray. "Thank you, love."

Kneeling beside the pond, Wakan dug through his bag and found a purification pill. He wondered how the pill worked. With hope, he just tossed it into the pond. The greenish water slowly turned clear where the pill was. The clear water spread until the entire pond was clear. Wakan could see the frogs swimming around in the water. Unable to care, he dunked his head into the water and started drinking. He feared water intoxication so he paced himself. A gulp here, little sips there.

Wakan found five flasks and filled them up to the brim and stuffed them into his bag for his trip back.

Feeling refreshed from the water, Wakan failed to notice the water had done something spectacular. The water gave the shriveled flowers new life. He danced around the flowers until they caught his eye. Red, pink, blue, white, yellow, orange. There were flowers everywhere, how did he not notice?

"Which one is the rosena flower?" asked Wakan to himself. He paced around them a couple times with his hand on his bearded chin, deep in thought.

Remembering what his new friends gave him, he opened up his bag, picked up a journal, and opened it. It was the wrong one, Pai's stargazing journal. He put it back and picked up the other journal.

Inside Christine's medical journal, Wakan read many incredible facts. He flipped through it until he opened it up to a page that had been marked. On the page was a red flower and underneath the picture was the label: *Rosena Flower*. The description read:

> *The Rosena Flower lays dormant until it gets plenty of rain. The leaves and roots can be consumed to treat muscle pain, backache, and stomachache. They are also full of vitamins and minerals. The red petals are anti-inflammatory and antibacterial. The petals can also be used with other ingredients to treat Burstfly Disease.*

Wakan went right to the red flower and picked every single one except for two. He didn't know how much he needed for the cure but he didn't want to pick them all so it could produce more. Wakan safely wrapped the rosena flower into the empty bag, which once carried the dunelope fruit.

"I'm coming, my children," said Wakan with renewed energy and faith. "Hold on just a little longer." He slung the bag around his shoulder and headed down the winding pathway. The sun must be coming up soon and he knew he must head back into the tunnel for the long journey home.

The rain had stopped. Though his thirst was quenched, Wakan's stomach rumbled every once in a while. He ran out of dunelope days ago and he was munching on a few of the flowers and some other plants he knew were safe to eat that had sprouted from the rainfall. They just weren't currently satisfying his stomach.

Wakan had just made it out of the tunnel and he was nearing the spot where the bridge collapsed.

There was rustling to the right of Wakan. He turned to look at what was making the noise. He saw a pond roughly the size of his home. Wakan walked over to it and peered in. The water was green and muddy. The rain must have churned the silt loose.

On the side of the pond Wakan saw three crabs. Two of them were using their claws to fight each other. It must be mating season. Wakan worked his way along the pond, continuing to watch them. The bigger male crab jabbed the smaller crab in the center near its face but the smaller one retaliated and snapped its claw down on the bigger one's arm and it came clean off. Wakan grabbed a red rock that was lying on the ground. The bigger crab fled as the smaller crab went in closer to the female. The male crab moved its big claw up and down, waving at the female crab. Then, the female crab starting waving to the male crab. Their waving became synchronous after a few seconds. Wakan raised the rock and lowered it onto the male crab, crushing its shell. The female crab ran into the pond.

Wakan grabbed the back of the crab and pried off the shell. He ripped off the gills and tore out the guts. The underbelly came off so smoothly. Using his fingers, Wakan split the rest of the crab in two, making two even slabs of meat and legs.

He easily started a fire and set the meat on the flames until it was thoroughly cooked. Wakan blew on the meat to cool it down. To his taste buds and stomachs delight, the crabmeat was juicy and cooked to perfection. One by one, Wakan ate the leg meat.

Reaching into his bag, Wakan grabbed the crab net Copper had left him. He was still starving. He unraveled the net and tossed it into the pond. It dragged along the bottom as Wakan pulled it in. There were five crabs caught in the net. Wakan cracked open three of them and let the other two go. He cooked all three and ate them one at a time until he was completely satisfied and ready to continue down the mountain.

Wakan packed up his crab net and set four cooked crab legs into his bag. This should last him for a while. He stomped out the fire.

Continuing down the path, he saw the fallen flamerod bridge and the dangerous terrain he was about to traverse. Four days had passed since he crossed the bridge and was separated from his friends. Ever since, he wondered how he would travel back across.

Wakan walked to the boulder on the edge that once held up the flamerod planks. He looked down and saw the bones from his fallen enemy. The skull of Bruce was positioned so it was looking directly up at him. He could have sworn it looked angry.

Wondering how he was supposed to climb down the steep side, Wakan remembered Tobias had put rope in the bag. He looked inside and at the very bottom of the bag was the long coiled rope. Wakan took it out and fed it over the edge. Lower and lower the rope went as Wakan used both hands, right, left, right, left. Finally, and to Wakan's amazement, the rope was long enough to touch the bottom. He even had enough length at the top to tie it around the boulder.

Wakan shimmied around the boulder and tied two double knots. "That should do it," he said to himself. "The more knots, the better." Wakan tugged on the rope to see if it was safe. He stomped on his bad leg a couple times to make sure he could support his weight.

Feeling ready, Wakan inched to the side while holding the rope. Stepping off the ledge and setting his foot on the steep surface was the hardest part for Wakan. Once he was fully off the edge he wrapped his left leg around the rope and easily repelled down the side. "Impossible, they said."

After Wakan reached the bottom, he unwrapped his leg. He cut off six feet of rope and set it in his bag just in case he needed it later.

Now came the hard part. Wakan looked at the steeples popping out of the ground. They were a lot bigger than he thought. Nine feet straight up in the air. The shortest steeple was two feet, so Wakan had to be careful not to poke himself. It would be tough to make it back home if he were to poke an eye out. Some steeples were so close together Wakan couldn't make it through and had to find a different path.

After starting over for the sixth time, Wakan thought he had finally found the right path. He was squeezing through the steeples until one of them poked him right in his bad leg. Wakan screamed out in agony. The tip of the steeple pierced through his skin of his shin but thankfully did not reach the bone. He pulled his leg away from the steeple and blood squirted out. He could not reach down to apply a bandage so he would have to hurry to the top.

In pain, Wakan hobbled up the side of the hill, maneuvering through the obstacles. To his relief, he could finally see a clear path to the top. He pushed through the pain and climbed forward. Once he reached the top, he looked down at his leg. There was a lot of blood on his shin and foot but he noticed the bleeding had slowed down considerably. He tore out a blank page in one of the journals and applied it to the wound. The paper soaked up some blood. He sat down near the edge and sighed, relieved. He made it.

The footprints of his friends were still there. It must not have rained here. "I'm so lucky," he said. "That rain cloud could have missed the peak. "

As soon as Wakan entered the tunnel, he noticed little green sprouts coming up out of the red and black gravelly ground. There was one here, and one deeper inside the tunnel, and then another one even deeper. "These sprouts look familiar," said Wakan. "I have seen these around home. But why are there so few of them? They seem to be evenly spaced out too."

Eventually, Wakan reached the end of the tunnel and he noticed the sun would be down soon. He was very tired. He decided to take a nap to rest up his legs and lungs. He dreamt about his reunion with his kids.

After he woke up, he was empowered to finish this journey. He ate some more crab legs and drank purified water. Wakan wiped his dirty sleeve across his mouth.

Stepping out of the tunnel and into the open, Wakan took a deep breath in as he looked up into the stars. There was the Venerable Spirit in all of its glory.

Wakan drew his finger into the sky, outlining the constellation. He stopped at the west corner because he saw a tiny bright blue planet. "Simply amazing," said Wakan.

Wakan searched through his bag for Pai's stargazing journal. He took it out and searched through it. He found the page titled Venerable Spirit. There was a hand drawn picture of the constellation. On the spirit's left hand was the planet. Underneath the picture was a name for the planet: Hydron.

He looked back up into the night sky, specifically at Hydron. "Some day, I am going to travel there and take a vacation," said Wakan. "There will be oceans of fresh water inhabited with billions of crabs. There will be warm beaches where everyone can relax and the sun won't be too hot. That's the life."

As Wakan was closing Pai's stargazing journal, he dropped it by accident. The pages flipped open to the Aureole constellation. Wakan picked up the book and looked at it. He angled it in different directions while looking at the picture. "Christine was right," said Wakan. "It does look a lot like Tobias." He chuckled and then stored the journal back inside his bag.

After a while, Wakan noticed everywhere he was going, he was following the little green sprouts.

"These definitely weren't here coming up the mountain," said Wakan. "I wonder what they could be?"

Wakan knelt down and dug up the sprout. Underneath the stem was a dunelope seed.

"Of course!" said Wakan. "The dunelope Bruce was eating. He would suck on them and spit out the seeds constantly. Thank you, Bruce. You may have turned out to be a real jerk, but you have made my journey back a whole lot easier."

Following the path of the dunelope sprouts, Wakan made his way closer to Dunestone, with the ingredients for the cure for his children.

Wakan heard a loud noise begin in the distance. The ground rumbled. Wakan hoped it wasn't an earthquake, but he also hoped it wasn't the spaceship about to leave without him. He was so close.

There was a gray cloud of smoke forming small clouds in the dark sky. It had to be the spaceship starting. Wakan ran as fast as he could around the bend. The wound on his bad leg hurt. He turned the corner and saw a hundred people standing outside. There were bonfires and people dancing with their loved ones.

Wakan looked northeast towards his home where the spaceship was supposed to be. Luckily, it was still there, but to Wakan's disappointment, the engines had already started. He realized the smoke in the air was actually dust. The spaceship had lain dormant in the same place for two hundred years and had been collecting dust all this time. Wakan noticed there weren't any flames coming out from the bottom exhaust. In fact, to his wonder, there *was* no exhaust. Wakan has been living next to this spaceship his entire life and he didn't even know how the thing worked. Somehow it was linked magnetically to its mother, *The New Frontier*.

"Wakan! Over here!" It was Memphis. He was standing over by the strip of land between the gardens and the caves. "I have been patiently waiting for you."

Waken didn't know whether he should trust Memphis. He didn't know who he could trust in general besides his close friends. But he needed to see his children. "Where are my children?" he asked "I have the rosena petals." Wakan reached into the bag and gathered the ingredients. He handed them to Memphis. "Here."

"They are inside my home. Come," said Memphis.

Memphis led Wakan into his cave.

"How are they doing?" asked Wakan.

"They are about the same as you left them. Just a touch worse," said Memphis.

"Thank the spirits," said Wakan. "I left them in good hands."

"Hey, Tobias told me everything. I apologize for what my actions have done," said Memphis. "I should have never invited him to go with you. Forgive me."

Wakan nodded, unable to test Memphis of his loyalty.

The earth continued to shake.

Wakan saw Star, Triss, and Zato all lying down in separate beds. He rushed to them as Memphis went to the table to mix the ingredients.

"My children!" said Wakan. He went to each one and gave them a hug and a kiss on their forehead. He then knelt down next to Star. He grabbed the rest of his water from his bag and gave the flask to her.

"Ta-da! I made it," said Wakan. "How are you feeling? How are your brother and sister? I missed you so much."

Star gulped some water out of the flask. "I still have a fever but other than that I'm fine. Triss is still in bad shape. She passes out daily. Memphis keeps on making her drink liquids to keep her hydrated. As for Zato, he has been an annoyance."

Wakan laughed.

"I think he is feeling better than he shows us," said Star. "He talks my ear off all day when Triss is trying to get some shuteye. He has been here for us though. We have one very empathetic blaze raiser, poppa."

"It's good to hear your voice, Star," said Wakan. He gave his eldest another kiss on her forehead. "Let me talk to the other two."

Wakan got up and knelt beside Zato. "Hey Z, how are you doing, big man? I heard you have been very brave."

"You told me to stay brave for Triss and Star," said Zato. "Did I do a good job, poppa?"

"Of course you did, son." Wakan kissed his youngest on his forehead. "You did a wonderful job being the man of the cave while I was away."

"Did you find the petals?" asked Zato.

"Yeah, Memphis should be done making the cure soon," said Wakan. "You will be back to full health shortly." Zato smiled as his father patted him on his head.

Wakan looked at Triss bundled up in rags. She was fast asleep. He went over to her and kissed his middle child on her forehead. He put his hands together and prayed. He prayed to the spirits to guide her back to full health. He prayed to Sapphire to keep their daughter in this world. As Wakan prayed, the ground shook even faster.

"You better go, poppa." Triss opened her eyes. "The spaceship is going to leave without you if you don't hurry."

Wakan gasped because she had woken up. "Hey, little one." A wave of emotion surged through him. He used his finger to get the hair out of her eyes. "I think I'm too late. The spaceship is ready to go. I needed to come straight here to see that you and your brother and sister are taken care of. You are all that matter to me."

"You have done your part here," said Triss. "Now, your people need you out there." She pointed up towards the sky.

Wakan couldn't believe what he was hearing. "Triss, even if I hurried I would never make it."

"You'll find a way," said Triss. "You always do."

Suddenly, the ground shook even faster. A loud noise filled the room. Wakan heard people cheering outside. The spaceship must have finally taken off.

Triss sighed and closed her eyes. Wakan knew she had looked up to him as a leader and she really wanted him to be the one to unite humanity.

"Sorry, honey," he said.

Memphis brought over a beaker containing green liquid, some small bits of yellow powder, and crushed up red rosena petals.

"It's done, Wakan," said Memphis. He held out the beaker to Triss. "Drink up."

As Triss was drinking the burstfly cure, Rufus barged into the room and was shouting something. Wakan limped over to his friend and calmed him down.

"What is it, Rufus?" asked Wakan.

"I need to speak with you privately," said Rufus out of breath. He pulled him aside. Wakan noticed his friend was unwell. He must have the burstfly disease from their encounter.

"I may have a way to get you on that spaceship," said Rufus.

Confused, Wakan stared at him in disbelief. "That was the spaceship that just left right?"

"Yes, but I can get you up there if we just hurry," he said.

Wakan turned around to his three children sitting up in their beds. Color had already returned to their faces and they were looking much better already.

"Go, poppa," all three of them said.

"This is the moment you have been waiting for," said Star.

"Don't worry about us, we'll be fine," said Triss.

"Say hi to mom for us," said Zato. He was told that she was living up in the stars.

Wakan nodded and he started crying. "I love you all."

"We love you too, dad," they said. "Now go! Have fun!"

Before they left, Memphis made Rufus drink the rest of the burstfly cure. Rufus refused at first because he was rushing but finally took a swig.

Wakan and Rufus ran out of Memphis' home. He saw the spaceship high in the sky.

"How in the inhospitable blazing dunes am I supposed to make it all the way up there?" said Wakan.

"Well, you see…" said Rufus.

19. FAMILY

The room was pitch black. The musky smell Brant had grown to love filled the air. He could feel a hand on the middle of his back as he slowly maneuvered around the barrels towards the east end of the first floor. Brant stopped once he felt the two walls meet and then he turned around to face the center.

The hand on his back belonged to Alexander. Brant felt his hand move across to his right shoulder. A new, gentler hand now rest on his back, which belonged to Elise. Her hand moved across his left shoulder.

Brant now put his left hand on Elise and right hand on Alexander and he pushed off gently. He had been signaling them to move off into separate directions. He would go straight to the middle of the room.

Brant had been cooperating with his teammates for the past four months. He had come up with new ways to communicate in the darkness without making a sound.

As Brant scurried from barrel to barrel, he heard Elise on his left take down someone heavy. It was Ulysses, complaining as usual. Elise didn't make a sound and must have tapped him out of the game.

Brant heard a single footstep a few feet from where he was crouched. Either the person heard Brant moving towards them or they heard Ulysses lose. Brant waited for a minute or so before he heard whoever was in front of him start walking to his right. Brant took a giant footstep for every step the person took. Eventually, Brant was on top of the enemy.

Thwack! Brant jabbed the foam dagger into the person's side and slashed their legs. He tapped the person on their head. Whoever it was had long frizzy hair. It must have been Blythe.

Continuing to slither through the first floor of the building, Brant kept silent and vigilant. He defeated two more enemies before he reached the other corner.

Alexander and Elise met up with him. Alexander put his hand again in the middle of Brant's back. Brant lead his team stealthily up the stairs to the second floor.

The team of three unleashed the same plan. Brant lead them to the closest corner and they fanned out, with Brant taking the center again. This time, Brant didn't hear a noise from Elise or Alexander. Brant weaved his way across the room. This time, he defeated Carpenter, Peebles, and Faruk. With each slash of his dagger, he tapped each on their head. They dubbed it the *Brant Double Tap*.

Once Brant made it to the other corner, he sensed another person there. He couldn't tell who it was so he snuck up on them and struck the person on their neck.

The person went down and Brant tapped them on their head.

"Brant?" the person asked. "It's me, Alexander." Brant felt Alexander stand back up.

"Oh, sorry," whispered Brant. "I could hear you, leading me to believe you weren't yourself or Elise. I taught you better than that."

"You boys better be quiet," whispered Elise as she crept up on the two of them. "How many do we have so far? I have four."

"Three for me," whispered Alexander.

"Seven," whispered Brant. "No wait, six." He had to subtract Alexander from his list. "Good job. Thirteen so far. Almost half. Let's hope our other teammates are doing just as well. Let's wait a few minutes before we do it again in reverse."

"Gotcha," Alexander and Elise said together.

Brant gave his two teammates the signal as he made his way back across the second floor. He leaned up against a wall and waited a moment. He then heard a strange noise coming from the opposite side of the wall. It took a few seconds for Brant to realize the sound was someone's stomach growling. Brant formed a smile but was trained enough not to laugh. He had a pretty good idea who it was, considering how this had happened before and not too long ago.

Brant leaped up, grabbed the ledge of the wall, and transferred to the other side. He held on with one hand as he grabbed for his dagger. Brant dropped down from above to where he thought the hungry man was and struck his dagger through the air. To his relief, Brant knocked down someone large. "Sorry, Hanks," said Brant. "I think it's about time you quit."

Hanks sighed and pounded the ground as Brant patted him on his head.

Brant knew if Hanks was posted here, Patches and Tarjeel weren't too far away. Immediately after Tarjeel won over Brant many months ago, Patches took a liking to him and promoted him to second in command of the Greasy Gangsters. Hanks was pissed but he had nowhere else to go, so he stuck around, still wearing his purple leather jacket proudly.

Continuing on, Brant came up to a pair of barrels that were stacked two high. He bumped into both of them with so much force, they almost toppled over. That would have been the end for him. Brant held them both up and gently set them back to their original position.

"What was that?" someone whispered. To Brant, this question sounded like it was aimed towards someone else, not to him.

Brant hid behind the barrels. Once he realized a pair of footsteps was headed in his direction, he crept around the barrels footsteps. Brant grabbed a small object he had found earlier and tossed it into the direction of the barrels. The object met one of the wooden barrels with a loud *clang*. The footsteps immediately stopped.

Someone from Brant's right side put their hand in the middle of his back. Brant turned around and touched the person's head; it was Elise. Brant turned back around and guided Elise toward the two enemies. He took his left hand and touched her hand signaling her to take out the person on the left.

They both stealthily positioned themselves behind the two enemies. Brant took the lead in striking the person in front of him. He then immediately heard Elise bring down the second person. Brant tapped the one he brought down on their head.

"I figured you needed my help," whispered Elise.

"Thanks," whispered Brant. "Let's keep going. This game is almost finished."

Elise placed her hand on Brant's back as they continued to the other side. When they reached the corner, Alexander was already there. Alexander placed his hand on Elise's back.

At least sixteen down.

They each brought down one opponent and headed towards the stairs.

Brant halted as he heard a faint tapping at the bottom of the stairs. Brant whispered to his teammates, "I'm going to slide down the railings. Get ready for a fight. Follow me down." Brant heard Alexander snicker.

Brant sat on the railing and slid down as quick as lightning. The person at the bottom had no clue what hit them. Brant heard another body fall to the ground beside him.

All the lights in the building came on. Once Brant's eyes focused, he noticed he was sitting on top of Tarjeel. To his right were Alexander and Elise standing over Patches who was on the ground rubbing his shoulder.

"What is wrong with you people?" whined Patches, "You're all crazy!"

As Brant approached, the people laying on the ground stood up. Brant, Elise, and Alexander gave each other elbow bumps as a sign of respect. His other teammates congratulated the trio.

Ashe, one of the senior instructors, came up to them. "How is this even possible?" she asked. "Did my timer stop working? The three of you collectively took down eighteen opponents in less than six minutes." They looked at each other excitedly. "That's a new record."

There was a faint clapping behind Brant. He turned around and saw Alexis standing in the doorway. She was clapping her right hand on her left bicep. Her left arm had to be amputated from the wolfwraith attack.

"It's nice to see you back on your feet," he said.

"I see you're still winning," said Alexis.

Brant said goodbye to his teammates. He walked up to Alexis and hugged her.

"Let's talk," she said. She held the door open for him and they walked to her house. She pulled up a chair for him. He sat down.

"A new record, huh?" said Alexis, visibly impressed. "I see you are working well with your team now."

"I guess they weren't all that bad," said Brant.

Alexis laughed like an old lady. She grabbed something off of her mantle. It was a dark red pair of fingerless gloves. She tossed them on Brant's lap.

Brant looked at her confused. "What are these?"

Alexis sat down across from him and leaned forward. "There is something I have been meaning to tell you Brant. Ever since the first time I met you, you have reminded me of a great apprentice I once had over a few decades ago. This young man broke all the records in Sneak. He still holds the highest recorded takedowns in a single game. Sixteen."

Brant felt the surface of the gloves. He had wanted to beat that record ever since he started playing Sneak. He came close a couple times.

"Those gloves you have in your hand belonged to that young man, but I am not giving you these gloves just because you remind me of him. That young man's name was Beck. Your father."

Brant gasped and looked up at Alexis. "You knew my father?" He sat up in his chair and grabbed the hilt of a sword by accident, forgetting it was hidden within the chair. He realized what he was holding on to and let go. Alexis noticed this and laughed. She *did* have weapons hidden everywhere.

"He was my greatest apprentice," she said. "I ended up getting to know him pretty well. After a few years, Beck ended up marrying my daughter. Your mother."

Brant looked at Alexis, dumbfounded. "But, then that makes you my…" He stood up and gave Alexis a hug. The best hug he had ever given anyone.

Alexis patted him on his back with her hand. She was crying.

Brant felt tears well up within him. "Why didn't you tell me sooner?"

"I didn't know until you told me that story about your parents," said Alexis. "You looked a lot like Beck and my Kat but I couldn't be too sure. Unfortunately, I lost touch with them a few years before they were lost in the Outside. I knew they had a baby but I thought it was lost with them. The only thing that was brought back to me was the empty basket full of blankets. I wanted to wait for the right time to tell you this."

"That silver necklace that you always wear with the dagger on it…" She looked at Brant, but he wasn't currently wearing it. "That silver necklace was your mother's. Your father had given it to her right when they had you. Only elite assassins get the honor to wear that necklace. You came into this world wearing that necklace and it seems you have grown into it," she said as they still hugged.

Brant let go of Alexis. "I appreciate everything that you have done for me, grandma." He smiled.

"You're welcome, grandson," she said.

"I wish I could stay and talk some more but I really have to get going," said Brant. "I promised Persephone I would make it on time for dinner tonight."

"Of course," said Alexis. "We will have all the time in the universe to talk some more when we leave on the spaceship."

Brant gave his grandmother one last hug before he left.

Once out the door, everything shined in a new light for Brant. He felt like a new man. A happier man. He found himself walking at a different pace. He took the alleyway to the southwest and danced through it because of muscle memory.

Brant headed south towards the spaceship construction zone. He quickly decided to check on their progress since he hadn't looked in three weeks.

He walked towards the edge of the construction and saw the spaceship was completely excavated.

Only two weeks away until he would be sitting inside, blasting off to a new world to better the future of the human race. He was actually excited for once.

The spaceship was shiny and metallic. It had a strange shape to it, almost like an upside down 'T'. The wings were smaller than he imagined and he wondered how it was even aerodynamic.

There were steps circling down towards the entrance of the spaceship. There were people going inside, cleaning it out and making it livable. Brant saw a person taking soil inside, probably to start a garden.

Brant saw enough and turned around.

Nanoc and Ajnos were kissing each other over by the gate. Nanoc saw him and ran over.

"Hey, Brant," said Nanoc. "Thanks again for saving our lives." It was the first time he had seen them since that day four months ago.

"It was no problem at all. Really," said Brant. "Looks like your ankle has fully healed."

Nanoc laughed.

"If there is anything we can do, just let us know," said Ajnos.

"Anything," said Nanoc. "We owe you so much."

Brant waved his hands in front of him. "Thanks, but I was just doing my job. I won't accept any payment."

"Dinner, then?" asked Ajnos.

"Sure," said Brant. "I must get going though, I have dinner plans with a special someone."

"Okay then," said Ajnos.

Nanoc waved at Brant. "Have a great time!"

Brant headed west towards Persephone's house. He skipped down another alleyway. On the other end was an old friend.

"Where are you headed in such a good mood?" It was Lizbeth. Her hair was now hot pink.

"Lizbeth. Hey," said Brant. "I'm headed to see my girlfriend, Persephone."

"You have a girlfriend?" Lizbeth laughed. "How did you manage that?"

"I have changed," said Brant. "For the best. I see you have changed too. You're not protesting the excavation anymore?"

"It was a losing battle from the beginning. We Pretty Poisons have moved on to better things."

"Pretty Poisons, huh?" he said. "Didn't I come up with that name?"

"No, I think you overheard me saying it," said Lizbeth. She laughed. "Now get going, your cheeriness is going to rub off on me. Shoo!" She waved goodbye to Brant.

Brant hopped up the steps to Persephone's door. He knocked three times.

Persephone opened the door and greeted him with a smile. "You're on time," she said surprised. A wonderful smell was coming from the kitchen. He stepped inside.

"It's nice to see you again," said Brant. He set his pouch on the table and gave her a hug.

"It's nice to see you as well," said Persephone. "And so soon."

Pandora jumped up on the table and looked at Brant with her big eyes. She lifted a paw and began licking it.

Brant pet Pandora on her head. "I see Pandora is joining us for dinner."

Persephone laughed. "She is allowed to do anything she pleases." She scratched Pandora on her chin. "Isn't that right, princess?"

"Oh, she's royalty now?" asked Brant. "Princess Pandora. Does she get her own crown and dinner menu?"

Persephone set down the food on the table. Mashed potatoes, carrots, and radishes lined the right side of the table. On the left were twenty cooked specterling legs.

"You have outdone yourself," said Brant. "Everything looks delicious."

Pandora licked her chops. As she stepped towards the specterling legs, Persephone stamped her feet on the ground trying to scare her away. Pandora snatched a specterling leg, jumped to the ground, and ran into Persephone's bedroom.

"I better not find bones hidden away in my mattress," said Persephone. She looked at Brant eyeing the table of food. "Don't wait for me. Dig in."

Brant shook his head. "I can wait." He walked over and helped her by pouring two glasses of water. "Anything I can help with?"

"Not at the moment," she said.

Persephone plated the dessert. It just happened to be Brant's favorite. Carrot cake. She set it down on the table.

Brant pulled out the chair on the end of the table for Persephone. "Quite the gentleman you are turning into. I think I like it." She laughed. "Thank you."

Brant pulled out the chair next to Persephone and sat down.

Starting with the mashed potatoes, Brant made a sound of approval. "So good," he said. "I'm glad you're coming with me." He laughed.

"I wouldn't miss it for the world," she said.

Brant ate everything on his plate and cut himself a slice of carrot cake. He ate it in four mouthfuls. He wiped his mouth and hands with a cloth.

Brant looked at Persephone still eating and smiled. "I'll be right back," he said. He stood up from the chair and grabbed his pouch from the table. He walked into Persephone's bedroom and closed the door.

"Where'd you go, Pandora? I know you're in here." Brant looked around clothes that were laying on the ground. He looked behind the dresser. No sign of Pandora. He picked up a scent of specterling meat and followed it to the bed. Brant looked under the bed and he could see her glowing eyes. She started to purr. "There you are." He reached underneath the bed and held on to the cat. He brought her out and set her on the bed.

"I have something very important to ask you," Brant said to the cat. She looked at him with her big green eyes. "I have fallen in love with your mother. Ever since she took me in the night my adoptive parents died, she has cared for me and treated me as somebody special. No one outside of my family has ever treated me that way. I am thrilled we were paired with each other so long ago and lately I have come to understand why. She is my opposite and we complement each other, but somehow we still have a lot in common. I couldn't think of a better person to spend the rest of my life with." Brant took Pandora's paw in his hand. "This is why I have come to you, to ask for your mother's hand in marriage."

Pandora started purring and rubbed her head on his arm.

"I'll take that as a yes," he said. "Thank you."

Brant pet Pandora and then reached into his pouch. He took out a silver wedding ring and held it in his hand.

Brant heard a noise behind him. Persephone was leaning against the wall.

"How much did you hear?" asked Brant.

"I heard every single word," said Persephone. "That was very cute of you."

"Cute? No one has ever called me cute before." Brant blushed.

Persephone saw the silver ring in his hand. "Well, are you going to ask me or what?"

Brant slowly got to one knee and held on to Persephone's hands. "Earlier today, I parted with something I have treasured my entire life. The silver necklace I always wear is the only thing I had left from my parents. I decided to melt down my necklace and form it into this." He showed Persephone the silver wedding ring. "I wore that necklace every day of my life and as a symbol of how much I treasure you, I now hope that you wear this ring for the rest of your life." Brant took a deep breath and exhaled. "Persephone. Will you marry me?"

"Yes!" Persephone outstretched her arm and jumped up and down. "Of course I will marry you."

Brant put the silver ring on her finger. He stood up and gave her a kiss.

Pandora jumped down from the bed and laid next to them.

"Welcome your new daddy to the family, Pandora," said Persephone. She lifted Pandora up and set her in Brant's arms.

"Does this make me the king of the household?" asked Brant.

"Nope," said Persephone. "This just makes you Princess Pandora's servant."

Brant looked at Pandora. She was purring. "Can I retract everything I have said within the past few minutes?"

"It's too late," said Persephone. "I already said yes."

Brant set Pandora on the ground. He then jumped in the air and kissed Persephone again. "She said yes!"

20. TEACHER

The sound of construction filled the air. Jaylin awoke to the sound of pounding and hammering. The builders must have been hard at work, making repairs following the tsunami's path of destruction.

Jaylin felt much better this morning. She was able to turn on her side, only to find no family members waiting for her. She laid there in the quiet, all alone. A sling and a crutch sat next to her bed. Petra must have came in early to give it to her. She was ready to leave.

Jaylin sat up on her bed and set her feet on the ground. Her shoulder ached in searing pain. She used her left hand to wrap the sling around her casted arm and strapped it around her shoulder. She reached for the crutch and was ready to stand up for the first time since her injury. She used her knees to stand as she put the end of the crutch under her left armpit. It was awkward at first because her left leg was in a boot so it was higher off the ground. She placed the base of the crutch in front of her and stepped with her good foot. One step at a time.

Remembering she was on the third floor, Jaylin was aware she would have to go down a few flights of stairs. She hobbled out of her room and looked around.

The doctors were busy running from one room to the next. A lot of people must have been injured.

Jaylin began hobbling towards the end of the hall closest to her.

Petra exited a room just up ahead. "Good morning, Petra," said Jaylin. "Busy day?"

Petra saw her and smiled. She reached for her with both hands. "Here, let me help you," Petra offered. "Wait here. I will be back in just a moment." She left and came back with a chair that had eight small wheels on the bottom.

Jaylin had seen these climbchairs in action before. The smart wheels detected changes in surface height. The person in the climbchair could press a button to slowly move forward. When the wheels detected the stairs, the first set unlocked and dropped down until it hit the step below. It then locked in place. The person in the climbchair moved forward again until the second set of wheels unlocked and dropped to rest on the step below. The process continued for the third and fourth set of wheels. Depending on the width of the steps, the wheels could span anywhere from two to three steps at a time.

Petra rolled the climbchair to Jaylin and motioned for her to sit down. Petra held her crutch for her as she used the motion button to wheel forward. Petra had to manually turn the climbchair so it would face towards the steps. Jaylin pressed the button and the climbchair worked its way down.

When she reached the first floor, Petra handed Jaylin back her crutch. "Thank you for everything you have done," said Jaylin.

"Don't think too much about it," said Petra. "It's my job after all." She winked at Jaylin. "Take care," she said as she waved goodbye.

Jaylin hobbled down the hall and into the lobby. The same receptionist was there from the other day. She recognized Jaylin as she walked past. "Jaylin!" exclaimed the receptionist. "I have been waiting for you. Your brother, Akeer, told me to let you know he is working right outside." Her knotted hair swung around her head. "Tell him I said hi."

"Thanks," said Jaylin. "I will." What was *that* about?

Jaylin opened the doors and breathed in the fresh oceanic air. She took her first steps outside Jersey General Hospital and took in the view.

The buildings she had familiarized herself with were different; many of the tall skyscrapers were destroyed. Rubble covered the streets. It would look like a wasteland if it wasn't for all the people joined together rebuilding the floating city.

The cleanup crew was sweeping off the streets and salvaging materials. Scaffolding scaled the façades of almost every building with builders lined up to help.

Akeer propelled down the side of the infirmary's walls, startling Jaylin.

"Arc you dating the receptionist?" she asked, arms crossed. "She told me to tell you she says hi."

Akeer scratched his head. "No, Felicia and I are just good friends." He blushed as he unstrapped himself from the harness. "Are you ready?"

Jaylin looked down at her injured body. "Ready as I'll ever be."

As Jaylin hobbled along the street, Akeer matched her pace. "So what do you have in mind?" he asked.

"Where do you think you will need the most improvement so I have an idea where to start?" asked Jaylin.

"Speaking to women," said Akeer seriously.

Jaylin laughed. "Sorry, I can't help you there, buddy. Try again."

Akeer changed his answer. "How about using force spears? We are going to bring them into space for protection. They are proven to be good weapons in and out of water."

"*That* I can do," said Jaylin proudly. She thought of how she could help him to improve with the force spear. "Let's go to the training grounds." She turned around and starting heading west. "I can teach you a few tricks of my own."

The twins made their way to the training grounds. On the way there, they passed the rusted spaceship. It had no signs of damage from the tsunami. Maybe it *was* capable of space travel.

They made it to the training grounds, a large stadium with an open area in the center. They chose a spot in the corner. Akeer moved a bench over for his sister to rest on.

Jaylin had him pick up a training spear at the service desk. "Show me how you would normally hold the force spear," said Jaylin.

Akeer held up the training spear, his arms straight as if he was ready to whack her with it. His hands were close together on the hilt.

"For the first lesson, I will teach you how to have the perfect stance," said Jaylin. "Start from the top and place your dominant hand about a third of the way down the shaft. Go another third and place your other hand on the hilt."

Akeer did as he was told.

"A little bit further down," she instructed. "Good. Now slightly bend your elbows and hold the spear closer to your body. Bend your knees and place your right foot slightly in front of you. This stance allows you to attack or defend yourself from any direction."

Akeer was in the stance and pretended he was being attacked, swinging the training spear around.

"Remember," said Jaylin. "The force spear is a deadly weapon and should be treated as such. Don't be swinging it around and pointing it at people. It is always ready to fire at any moment. This is the most important thing to keep in mind while you wield a force spear."

Akeer looked down at the training spear and looked frightened. "You know, maybe this isn't such a good idea," said Akeer.

"You want to be able to protect yourself up there, don't you?" asked Jaylin.

"Well, yeah. Of course," responded Akeer.

"Then let's continue," she said. "The next thing I will train you on is combat. Get back in your stance."

Akeer held his training spear out in front of him as he was taught. He bent his elbows and knees.

"In this position you will be able to guard yourself. Use the force spear to block oncoming blows. Just extend your left arm towards the area the strike is coming from. You may also attack from this stance. You can step forward and jab or swing the force spear."

Akeer jabbed and swung the training spear around. After each movement, he returned back to his stance.

"Each have their advantages and can catch the enemy off guard," she said. "Fighting with a force spear takes practice. Unfortunately, there's no one here to practice against, so let's move on."

"Easy enough," said Akeer. "I'll be good as you in no time."

"You wish," Jaylin laughed. "A big reason we use these spears is because of their power. This pressure build up, or force, is useless if you are bad at aiming. Accuracy is one of the most important things that I can teach you. Hand me the spear."

Akeer walked over to Jaylin and handed his training spear to her. She balanced the spear on her cast and grasped it with her left hand.

"While aiming, you must always be aware of where your target is," Jaylin tried her best to point at a beam across the way. "Hold the spear close to you as you extend your dominant arm while bringing your other arm up towards your chest. Place the hilt between your arm and chest."

Jaylin did her best to show her brother how to do it step by step. "Pretend the force spear is an extension of your body," she instructed. "You want to point it directly at your target. Use your dominant eye to look down the shaft and line it up with your target. When you are ready, hold down the button. Breath in just like you would when you are going to dive deep without an aqua-breather. Right before you let go, release your breath slowly for the best accuracy."

Jaylin let go of the button and the training spear shot out a short burst of air. The force of air found the beam and made a dent right in the middle. "Just like that."

Akeer had seen how good she was over and over again but he never knew *how* she was continuously good. His jaw hung open as he watched in awe. "I'm impressed you still can shoot that well even with broken bones," said Akeer. "May I try?"

Jaylin gave Akeer back the training spear. He followed every step as best as he could. He aimed down the shaft, held down the button, and let go. The beam of air missed the target by a couple feet and struck the padded wall. Akeer looked disappointed.

"Nice first shot," said Jaylin. "Try it again."

Akeer's second attempt ended with the same result. "Am I doing something wrong?"

"It looks like you are aiming too far left," said Jaylin. "Try aiming just to the right of the target."

Akeer followed her instruction and on his third attempt, the burst of air found its target. "Woohoo!" Akeer celebrated. "I never knew I could be so good at this stuff!" His words echoed off the walls of the training grounds.

"Easy there, brother," said Jaylin. "You're just getting started."

————————————

The next week flew by as Jaylin taught Akeer how to improve his skills; swimming, breathing, hunting, and surviving. Jaylin even persuaded Ms. Britta to show Akeer how to use the Lean Mean Spear

Machine 7000. They planned on possibly sending it up with the spaceship to use as a space vehicle.

Jaylin expanded and improved on what Akeer already knew. He learned how to improve things he was already good at. This would not have been possible without his sister.

The citizens of Hydronia were gathering outside the auditorium; its walls had been knocked down. Jaylin was in the middle of the crowd with her parents and little sister.

The 108 Ambassadors were on stage making speeches. They were going in order from oldest to youngest, male then female. All of them seemed to know exactly what they were getting themselves into. All of them talked about their upcoming journey. Half of them made their speeches yesterday.

Principal Jeffrey Edison was at center stage as he announced the next Ambassador. "May I have Akeer Robbins up here?" *Finally*. It had been a long wait.

Jaylin and her family clapped proudly as Akeer made his way up to center stage. He was holding on to a training spear.

"Hello Hydronia," said Akeer. "How is everyone doing today?"

The crowd was a little tired from clapping all day. Most of them clapped but it was more so out of obligation.

From where she stood, Jaylin could tell Akeer was nervous.

"My name is Akeer Robbins and I was elected as the eighteen-year old male Student Ambassador. I can tell everyone here wants this show to wrap up so I will keep it short and sweet."

Akeer looked towards Jaylin. "Much like many of these Ambassadors, I didn't even want to be elected. I had been going to builder school because that's all I wanted to do with my life. But I was picked because the teachers believe I will do what's best for our people. If anything goes wrong up there on *The New Frontier*, we will be prepared to stand, fight, and defend ourselves. That is why we are bringing force spears with us even though this defies direct orders from the Sleepers."

As Akeer made his speech, he performed his technique with the training spear, demonstrating how he would protect his people with it. Just how Jaylin taught him.

"We will return back home once we have learned what our plan is and fill everybody in. In the mean time, just continue being you."

Akeer received some applause from his speech. Principal Edison was about to cut him off until Akeer spoke up again.

"Before I end my speech I would like to have everyone here give my twin sister, Jaylin, a round of applause."

At the mention of Jaylin's name, the crowd seemed to perk up.

Akeer motioned for her to come up on stage. "My big sister has taught me so much in life. She was born sixteen minutes before me and she managed to learn everything before me and be better than me at everything."

Jaylin made it to the stage. Akeer grabbed her left arm as he hoisted her up on the stage. "These past couple weeks I had to watch her suffer because all she wanted in life was to be a Student Ambassador. The rejection had been hard on her. But through all of this pain, I learned she has a strong heart. She came to terms with her situation and decided that she would leave her dreams behind to train me, to make me a better, stronger person. Without her help, I wouldn't have been prepared for this journey." Akeer put his hands on her shoulders. "Let's hear it for Jaylin!"

The crowd must have gotten a second wind because everyone was clapping and cheering for her. Some people even whistled.

Akeer stood behind her and whispered in her ear. "These people love you, Jaylin," he said. "Look how much they care about you. I am a nobody and that's why they are sending me away."

"That's not true," she said. "You are the best of all of us. Better than me." She just realized what she had said. All her life, people had said that she was the best at everything. She grew up believing it and soon she would put it to the test. When she did realize she was the best at everything, she started telling it to all of Hydronia and they believed her and put her up on a pedestal, literally.

Acknowledging Akeer was the best of all of them was a huge step up in Jaylin's life. She realized she needed to be open to people because she never knew who might surprise her.

The crowd applauded during Jaylin and Akeer's entire walk back to Akeer's seat. He let her sit in his chair while he knelt next to her. The teachers allowed it because it would be mean to have someone who's healing from broken bones have to jump off the stage or to not have somewhere to sit.

"Thank you, Akeer." Principal Edison announced the next Ambassador to take the stage. "Please welcome Arabella Huang to the stage!"

The girl sitting next to Jaylin stood up. It suddenly dawned on her that this girl standing in front of her was the girl helping Akeer rescue the people during the explosion. She didn't know why she hadn't noticed before. "Good luck, Arabella," said Jaylin, as Arabella walked to the stage. She actually meant it. She wasn't jealous of her anymore. She saved her brothers life and deserved the spot over her.

"Um, hello," said Arabella. "I'm Arabella Huang and I too am one of your Student Ambassadors." She stood there facing the enormous crowd.

Jaylin could tell she was shy. She wasn't prepared to give a speech. To top it off, she had to go after she and Akeer were just wildly applauded. Jaylin felt sorry for her.

"I don't really know what I can say that my peers already haven't," said Arabella. She was looking at the floor, playing with her hands. "I promise everyone here I will try my absolute best out there. My fellow Ambassadors and I will help each other to strengthen our relationships with the other human beings and forge a new world…together." Arabella stood there trying to think of what else to say. "Thank you," she finished.

People in the crowd cheered for her light-hearted speech. Mostly because it was short.

As Arabella walked towards her to sit back down, Jaylin stood up and clapped for her.

"Hey, Arabella," said Jaylin. "May I speak to you backstage after the last person speaks?"

Arabella looked shocked. She pointed at herself and mouthed the word, "Me?" She took a seat and said, "Sure?"

After the last person, a fourteen year old girl named Kaya who was escorted by her parents, gave her speech, Jaylin took her crutch and walked around backstage. She worked her way down the few steps and turned around, waiting for Arabella. About three minutes went by until she came down the steps.

"What is it you want?" asked Arabella. "Came to mock me?"

Jaylin was surprised with her irritated tone of voice. "What? No," she said. "Why would you think I would do that?"

"You have before," said Arabella. "When we were seven you laughed at me because I couldn't swim. I was humiliated in front of the whole class."

Jaylin didn't remember this. "I am truly sorry," she said.

"I never wanted to feel that way again, so I taught myself to become the strong swimmer that I am today," said Arabella. "Come to think of it, I probably wouldn't have become Student Ambassador if you didn't make fun of me that day."

"Sure," said Jaylin. "Rub it in my face."

"There has also been a rumor going around that you have been campaigning against me to take my spot as Student Ambassador," said Arabella.

"I admit, I did want to take your place," said Jaylin. "I had always dreamed of becoming one."

"I'd let you take my position if I could," Arabella softened. "I already tried, but the teachers wouldn't let me. Like your brother, I didn't choose this path. I wanted to be a doctor. Maybe I can still be one wherever we end up, but my first priority is to find a better future for humanity."

"I am really sorry for the way that I've acted," said Jaylin. "But now I am trying to be a better person." She reached out her hand towards Arabella. "Forgive me."

They shook hands.

"I forgive you," said Arabella.

"I just wanted to say I'm glad you get to go instead of me. I wanted to go for the wrong reasons," said Jaylin. "If you, my brother, and all of the other Ambassadors are the people our teachers have put faith in for our future, then I couldn't be happier. Take good care of my brother while you are up there."

Arabella gave Jaylin a hug. "Thank you," said Arabella. "It really means a lot coming from you."

Arabella waved goodbye as Jaylin turned around.

Akeer was leaning up against the wall. "That was fascinating," he said. "I didn't think you had it in you."

"I have changed," said Jaylin. "Walk with me, brother. I am getting achy. Let's go home."

Akeer put his arm around Jaylin to support her as she walked.

"I am going to miss you, Akeer," said Jaylin.

"I won't be missing you," said Akeer. He laughed as Jaylin frowned at him. "Just joking with you. I will miss you more than you know, Jaylin. Thank you for everything you have done for me. I will pay you back one day."

Jaylin and Akeer met up with Lydia, Denna, and Arkadia.

"Was there any reason for it to be that long?" said her father.

"Respect your Ambassadors," said her mother.

"I'm tired," said Arkadia as she rode piggyback on her father.

They all laughed.

"Ok," her mother confessed. "It *was* definitely too long."

They walked home together as a family. Jaylin and Akeer side by side. Akeer would be leaving in a matter of days. In the mean time, they were going to spend as much time together as possible.

21. FAREWELL

Selene was packing up her belongings for the journey to *The New Frontier*. She stuffed her four outfits into a backsack and jammed her diary on top. She closed her backsack and watched as her parents gathered their belongings.

"I appreciate you guys," she said. "I'm not going to lie to you, so I will come right out and say it. Sarva came to me a while ago and told be he had a plan. He wanted me to stay with him here. At the time, I was deeply in love with him and had pictured myself with him throughout all stages of my life; getting married, raising kids, and growing old together; all alone. It was my chance to become the princess you told me about when I was little. Sarva was offering me what I thought was the chance of a lifetime. I was actually more afraid of leaving Quaketown and journeying into the stars than leaving everyone behind. I was afraid I wouldn't have a valuable part in all of this. Obviously, I was wrong and I am sorry. I completely understand if you have to punish me."

Mona and Aqib finished packing and looked at Selene.

Mona said, "We can talk about this later."

Aqib put on the backsack and opened the door. "Time to go," he said.

Her mother picked up something off the table and handed it to Selene. "Don't forget this." It was her necklace. She forgot she left it on the table before she left. Deep down, she thought she had left the necklace behind so her parents would notice she was missing, but Ciri noticed something was wrong first and alerted her parents. Of course the first place her mother and father would look was the cave by the safe haven because they believed that was the perfect spot for Sarva to take his revenge. Selene put on her necklace.

The three of them stepped outside of their cavehome for the last time. Selene stopped and turned to look back at the place she grew up in. She had fond memories of her childhood in this cavehome. She was going to miss it. They walked through Quaketown for one last time.

They came upon Kelly's cavehome. Kelly, her parents, and baby brother, Jack, were walking out. "Heya Selene," said Kelly.

"Kelly," said Selene. "How are you? You must be exhausted from all the work."

"That I am, Selene," responded Kelly, looking at the ground.

They both seemed distant. They didn't know how to talk about the events that just occurred.

Kelly spoke up. "I thought I was excited for this journey but now I'm not quite sure...What if I did planned or did something wrong to mess this all up?"

"Listen to you," said Selene. "You've fought so hard for this. Take a deep breath."

"You're right, Selene," said Kelly as she followed her friends instructions.

"Let's go take one last look at Quaketown," said Selene. "I'm looking forward to spending time with you on the way up to *The New Frontier*."

Kelly smiled and gave her a hug.

Selene, Kelly, and their families walked together on the final stretch of town. They came upon the stage.

"Wait here," said Selene.

Selene ran up on the stage and looked out into the empty seating area. A different future flashed across her mind; she was acting on stage to a packed audience. She was doing the Camilla Quaketon bit she once saw Claire Altaïr do. Selene was dazzling in the lights while the audience roared. She knelt down and touched the stage floor, trying to commit every detail to memory. She said her goodbye to the place she loved and headed back to her group. Ciri had joined while she was on stage and greeted her. Mona, Aqib, Kelly, and Ciri clapped as she approached.

They made their way outside. Stepping forward into the ravine, all seven of them looked back at their home. There were dozens of other families doing the same thing. Selene noticed a lot of people crying. Not her, she had gone through too much lately to cry. She noticed Kelly and Ciri weren't crying either. Maybe they were looking forward to this endeavor.

Selene walked the path towards the spaceship, holding hands with her friends, Kelly and Ciri. Selene saw the thicket of trees right near the spaceship. No one has found Sarva's body. She didn't know if he was dead or alive and she didn't really care. He got his wish, he was being left behind.

Miles was waiting at the spaceship. He waved at Selene and her family. His parents were already inside. Selene walked up to him and he gave her that awkward hug she hadn't gotten used to yet. She hugged him back. At one point in her life, Selene wouldn't have been caught dead hanging out with Miles, but her life had been on fast forward these past two months and she felt different.

"Beautiful necklace," Miles said to Selene.

Selene blushed and gave him her hand. They walked into the spaceship with her family and friends. They didn't look back.

The spaceship was zooming up into the sky; almost out of sight.

"How the inhospitable blazing dunes am I supposed to make it all the way up there?" Wakan asked desperately.

"Well, you see," said Rufus, "Remember that invention I said I was working on that would have made it easier to get to the top of the mountain?"

Wakan thought back to the conversation they had on the mountain. He nodded.

"Well, I *just* finished it," said Rufus. "I was about to use it to come find you until I overheard nosey Mrs. Berenstein telling her husband you already made it back."

"What is it?" asked Wakan.

Rufus hurried over to the gardens. There was a large oddly shaped bag on the ground. It had two shoulder straps and a hood with a facemask and microphone clumsily attached to it. Wakan noticed it was made out of the coolant cloak Bruce and Tobias had given the group.

"May I present to you," announced Rufus, "...the spacebag!"

"What am I supposed to do with that?" asked Wakan, confused.

Rufus demonstrated it for him. "You put the straps over your shoulders and put the hood and mask on. The microphone allows you to communicate with the spaceship. When you are ready you just pull this lever on the side and the magic begins." Rufus jumped up into the air with one arm pointing towards the sky like some sort of super man. "Zoom!"

Rufus handed him the spacebag. "Come on! Put it on! We are running out of time!"

Wakan put on the spacebag. "Are you sure about this?"

"One hundred percent!"

Wakan knew Rufus didn't use percentages lightly.

"Here I go," said Wakan. "Tell everyone I said goodbye. I hope the cure works fast for you, Rufus."

Rufus waved at him as he pulled the lever. Wakan instantly flew into the air. He was traveling so fast but he didn't feel any G's or wind resistance.

"Can anyone hear me?" Wakan asked into the microphone. "Is anyone able to hear me?"

"Wakan, is that you?" said a familiar voice. "I'm sorry but we can't turn around. This thing is moving on its own."

"Open the hangar doors," Wakan commanded.

"I'm sorry, what did you say?" said the person on the other end.

"You heard me right," said Wakan. "Open the hangar doors. Now!"

Wakan was catching up to the spaceship. He would be there in a matter of seconds. If he missed his opening, he would either fall out of the sky or fly right into space and he guessed that would *not* end well for him.

"Do you read me?" asked Wakan. He was closer to the spaceship now; close enough to grab on. He pulled on the lever to stop the propulsion of the spacebag as he shimmied to the side of the hangar door. "Is anyone there?" Wakan was feeling light-headed as the oxygen in the air began to deplete. It was only a matter of time until they reached the outer atmosphere. Wakan began to pray.

Finally, the hangar doors opened. Wakan hurried inside. "I'm in!" said Wakan. The hangar doors closed and Wakan knew he was finally safe.

Another door opened from within the spaceship. Wakan stared inside. His people stood in front of him. They were clapping. "Wakan! Wakan!" they cheered.

Christine and Copper were surprised to see him. They both ran up to him to give him a hug.

The man who was on the other side of the microphone walked over to Wakan and gave him his hand. It was Copper's older brother, Silver. He had graying hair, a short beard, and wore gray overalls. He was a gardener and crabber on Dunstone. "You were on the mountain. How the inhospitable blazing dunes did you make it all the way up here?"

Wakan smiled, "Believe me. It's a long story."

On cue, the people gathered around Wakan and sat down to relax. Wakan knew exactly what they wanted. "I guess we have plenty of time for a story."

The audience cheered him on.

As Wakan started the telling of his adventure, he smiled. He had been telling stories for years but not once did he tell a story about himself. Wakan was now part of Dunestone's history. He was a legend. Now it was time for him to relax and enjoy himself, at least for a while.

Brant took Persephone's hand as they left her house. The silver ring on her finger shone brightly in the illuminated lights of the street. They both carried their luggage; they were able to fit most of their belongings. Pandora was curled up inside a basket.

"Goodbye, house," said Persephone. "Thanks for giving me shelter and keeping me safe."

Without looking back, Brant and Persephone walked through the streets of "The Eye." This was the first time in his life where Brant didn't take an alleyway. They headed straight to the spaceship.

Alexis was waiting for them at the steps in front of the spaceship. She had already unpacked and was carrying a single pouch. "Are you two ready for this exciting adventure?"

"I don't know if it will be exciting…" said Brant.

"Of course we are," interrupted Persephone.

Alexis had two men grab their luggage for them. Persephone still held on to Pandora.

"Persephone, why don't you go with them to your new cabin," said Alexis. "I have something important to tell your husband."

"Yeah, no problem, grandma," said Persephone. She followed the two men onto the spaceship.

"Congratulations on your marriage," said Alexis. "I'm sorry I couldn't stay after your wedding. I had to run."

"We were just glad you could make it," he said.

"It's important for me to see you here," said Alexis. "You have done extraordinary things here. I've taught you in the ways of the assassin and you have excelled every time. You have improved in your skills and you have become a better human being. I am proud to call you my grandson."

Brant hugged Alexis. "I'm proud to call you my grandmother."

"On this day, the day we leave this planet, I am now granting you the title of Master Assassin."

Brant looked at her in shock. He couldn't believe what he was hearing.

Alexis continued. "You are now among the ranks of the elite." She pulled a maroon cloth from her pouch and wrapped it around Brant's arms. "Your duty now is to protect us all, as we journey into the Up Above. I am honored to be by your side." She cut the maroon cloth in half and took one of the pieces.

"I too, am honored to be by your side," Brant responded. "I will do my best." He strapped the maroon cloth around his waist.

"I know you will," said Alexis. "Before you head inside, I have one more thing to show you." Alexis reached into her pouch and pulled out a cloak with a hood. "I want you to have this. I made it out of the blankets you were found in as a baby. I even ripped off the arms and sewed on a hood for you. I was never a fan of hoods, but I knew you missed wearing one ever since you ripped yours off to bandage up my arm. I am giving this to you as a gift for saving my life."

"Thank you so much," said Brant. He took off his old ragged cloak and put on his new one. He recognized the material of the cloak. He hugged Alexis again. "Shall we?" He looked towards the spaceship.

"I'm ready if you are," said Alexis.

Brant put on his hood and walked with Alexis into the spaceship, ready to conquer any challenge that awaited him.

The spaceship on Hydronia would be leaving in the morning at approximately 3:19. The flight path was already pre-scheduled into the spaceship's system. Some civilians had already said goodbye to their families and spent their first night onboard. Akeer wanted to stay with his family until the last minute.

The Robbins family were eating dinner at the table. Jaylin still had the sling, cast, and boot on, so Akeer was the one to go out to the docks and catch some armored fish. Akeer was now skilled in fishing with the force spear. He used Jaylin's techniques to be successful.

"This is damn tasty, Akeer," said Denna.

"Watch your language," said Lydia.

"Kadie is twelve years old," he said. "She should get used to that word. It's not like her classmates don't use it."

Lydia turned to Arkadia who had an entire foot long armored fish on her fork as she tried to bite it.

"Is this true?" asked her mother.

Arkadia finally put down the armored fish on her plate. "They say a lot worse too," said Arkadia.

Jaylin and Akeer snickered.

"There's nothing funny about this," said Lydia. "Kids these days…it better not be like this when we find a new Earth to live on."

"Don't worry, mom," said Akeer. "I promise if I become a leader in the future, I will make sure kids will be able to," Akeer paused, "swear as much as they like."

Everyone laughed except Lydia, who gave Akeer a dirty look.

"We will miss you, Akeer," she said sadly.

Akeer looked down at his empty dinner plate. The room became silent.

"I'll miss you all," said Akeer.

No one took another bite after this. Akeer had to get up early so they each said their goodbyes and went to bed.

Jaylin was sound asleep when her bedroom door creaked open. She opened an eye and peered into the darkness. It was Akeer.

"What time is it?" asked Jaylin.

"It's two-thirty," answered Akeer.

"Couldn't help but to say goodbye to me one last time, brother?" asked Jaylin. "I must be special."

Akeer put a finger up to his lips and shushed her. "Don't let them hear," said Akeer. "I snuck in here to take you with me."

Jaylin slowly sat up in her bed. "I must be dreaming," she said.

Akeer picked up the crutch from next to the bed and handed it to her. "I know of a way to get you on the spaceship without anyone noticing. I'm sure others will be sneaking family on board too."

Akeer threw her a pair of clothes. "Hurry up and get dressed. I'll help pack your belongings once you finish. I'll wait outside." Akeer went outside her bedroom to wait. He came back a couple minutes later. Jaylin was still in bed. "What's wrong?" he asked.

"I'm not going," she said. "I have done my part already. I have proven myself to our community. Now, it's *your* time to shine. Make us proud."

A tear formed in the corner of his eyes. "You better do a good job here then," he said.

"You better come back to find out," she said.

Akeer hugged Jaylin. "I love you, sis."

"Love you too, big brother."

Akeer disappeared into the darkness. Jaylin heard him sobbing. She heard the front door close.

Jaylin tried to go back to sleep but she couldn't. All she could think about was her brother. She heard a loud noise erupt from the center of Hydronia. She got out of bed and hobbled outside. Jaylin saw the spaceship take off. Her family joined her as they watched the spaceship leave the atmosphere and into space. "Good luck," they all said together with tears in their eyes.

22. THE FIRST CONTACT

As the air escaped five large tubes, a loud noise filled the chamber. A machine popped and crackled as it powered on for the very first time in nearly two centuries. Gears rotated counterclockwise, moving the tubes upwards out of the metallic floor. The screens on the desks powered on and glowed blue. Coding appeared on screen.

Each of the five tubes had a window at the top. A layer of frost covered the inside of the windows. A computer-generated voice announced the cryosleep was being deactivated while the heating units were gradually warmed to 75 degrees Fahrenheit. The frost on the windows slowly thawed.

Inside each tube laid a person. All of them visibly under the age of 45, but their bodies have been alive for over two-hundred years. The tubes were still defrosting as more machinery powered on. The navigational system, communications, safety lights, warning systems, oxygen supplier, and automatic food dispenser all powered on.

The first tube on the far left began to open. The blue screen updated and turned to black. The green text read:

Name: Vladimir Kingston.
Age: 36.
Race: Malayan/Brown.

Vladimir Kingston was a General for the Eighth Battalion in the Pangaean War. He led his troops to victory for his race, gaining the northern half of Asia. Vladimir, along with other leaders, including Chief Cersei Tonawanda and President Anakin Volkov, held a peace summit at the Grand Hotel in Egypt to end the Pangaean War because of the oncoming threat of the asteroids.

Vladimir used the same war machines he used on the battlefield to help create The New Frontier. The war machines were easy to disassemble and put back together. They had many uses and would provide the five new colonies with this technology in their new worlds.

Vladimir became the third General because of his battle experience.

The second tube next to the first starting opening. Mist escaped out of the tube into the chamber. The green text on the screen read:

Name: Kiki Chung.
Age: 29.
Race: Ethiopian/Black

The General Kiki Chung was working as a medic in the Pangaean War. She was stationed all over South America as the war spread. Kiki earned the Red Cross from Vladimir Kingston for saving many people's lives on the battlefield.

After the Pangaean War, Kiki was stationed at the Library of Knowledge. There, she studied medical practices.

Towards the end of the construction of The New Frontier, Kiki was elected by American President Anakin Volkov to run the medic station on board and be the fourth General. Kiki Chung is the youngest and kindest General.

The next tube in line started opening up. The green text on the screen read:

Name: Cersei Tonawanda.
Age: 41.
Race: American/Red

General Cersei Tonawanda was a Chief and Captain of her Tribe. During the Pangaean War, Cersei fought across both land and sea in Europe. Cersei was Captain of Our Lady's Voyage, a massive metal ship that she brainstormed herself, which traveled across the Mediterranean Sea gaining land for her people. The opposing soldiers knew her as The Red Witch.

After the Pangaean War, Cersei used her knowledge of mechanics, architecture, aerodynamics, and engineering to draw up a blueprint for The New Frontier.

Cersei was appointed as the second General because of her wisdom and knowledge of the spacecraft.

The fourth tube opened. The green text read:

Name: Jonathan Quaketon.
Age: 30.
Race: Mongolian/Yellow.

The General Jonathan Quaketon avoided the Pangaean War. While his people were fighting in North America, he traveled back and forth between continents avoiding any conflict. There were many like him, but Jonathan specifically caused trouble for the stationed troops wherever he went. His picture was displayed on five continents and was named a deserter. Jonathan grabbed this opportunity as a way to travel the world.

When the Pangaean War was over, President Anakin Volkov found him vacationing in Australia, a continent that was left behind by the human race.

Anakin elected Jonathan as the fifth and final General because of his escape and survival tactics. Jonathan's sister, Camilla, was also chosen to lead her people to a new world on The New Frontier.

The fifth and final tube started to open. The green text on the screen read:

Name: Anakin Volkov.
Age: 33.
Race: Caucasian/White.

Anakin Volkov was named President of his people. During the Pangaean War, Anakin was under protection at the New White House in South Africa. He commanded his army from his desk using new tactics he created himself. Anakin's Army fought north into Egypt and began spreading into Western Europe. Anakin knew the Apocalypse was looming and proposed a peace summit to be held at the Grand Hotel in Egypt.

At the summit, Anakin announced to the other leaders that humans should put aside their differences for a short period to build a spacecraft to escape Earth before it was destroyed. After that, they would separate and travel to five different worlds until they found a new Earth.

Anakin chose one person of each race to institute the Generals as the leading world power. The Generals would hold meetings to gain knowledge to save the human race.

The five tubes came to a halt and the computer-generated voice announced the cryosleep awaken parameters were set and complete. All five humans opened their eyes.

Vladimir was the first to attempt to stand up. His legs wobbled as he pushed himself away from the tube. Vladimir had a brown widows peak, pointed chin, and long fingers. He looked around as the others took their turns standing up.

Second was Kiki, with long straight black hair flowing to the middle of her back and freckles on her cheeks; followed by Cersei, with short black hair and bangs, a stoic look, and was the tallest of the

Generals, Jonathan, with black hair sticking up in the back, bushy eyebrows, and a big grin, and finally Anakin, with blonde wavy hair, double chin, and weight north of two hundred pounds.

"That was quite the nap," Jonathan, still smiling, joked as he yawned and stretched out with his arms.

"Let me check your vitals before we start moving around," announced Kiki. She picked up a device that detected heart rate, blood pressure, oxygen levels, and other information. She tested it on Vladimir first.

Once Kiki moved on to Cersei, Vladimir walked over to the navigation table. "*The New Frontier* is right where we left it," he said. "Perfect. That's one thing we don't have to worry about."

Cersei tested out the communications systems. She heard the speakers turn on. "Testing, testing," she said. Cersei pressed a few buttons to display the connections. "The spaceships are out of reach. I can't contact them just yet." She typed in some coding. A screen appeared which displayed a measurement. "It appears they are coming in fast. Let's hope the magnetic dampeners kick in before they arrive."

"How are you doing, sir?" Kiki asked Anakin.

"Still a little sick," he replied. Anakin contracted a cold before he was put in cryosleep.

Jonathan patted Anakin on his back. "Just don't get near me, ok?"

"Always the one with nothing to say," said Anakin. "Go to your post."

"Aye aye, sir," said Jonathan. He walked over to look at the warning screen. There were no red lights. "No red lights, Anakin. Looks like my job is done."

"I guess we just have to wait now," said Vladimir.

"Anyone else excited?" asked Kiki. She was confirming all her medical equipment was where she left it, ready to treat anyone who might be injured from their journey.

"I'm looking forward to seeing my people," said Cersei. "I want to see how much they have evolved."

"Does anyone want to make a bet?" asked Jonathan, as a hot dog popped out of the automatic food dispenser. No one was interested. "How many spaceships are we going to see today? Huh?"

"We will see all five," said Anakin. "I have faith." He put on a headset and listened to the space around them as he looked through a telescope.

The five Generals worked at their posts waiting for the five spaceships to arrive. The air ventilation turned on and fresh oxygen filled the room. Huge metal doors opened, revealing the living quarters.

A red dot flashed on the navigation table. Then another appeared. "We have contact," said Vladimir. "Two bogeys approximately ten minutes away."

"Attempting to communicate," confirmed Cersei. She picked up a walkie-talkie with a universal translator and held down a button. "New Frontier to bogey one, do you read? Over." She let go of the button. Static. "I repeat, New Frontier to bogey one, do you read? Over." More static.

Then a voice spoke. "This is the people of The Eye, Alexis speaking," said the voice. "We read you loud and clear, over."

"Please standby for more information, over," said Cersei. She put them on mute and turned a dial. She pumped her fists in the air due to excitement. "New Frontier to bogey two, do you read? Over."

"Yes, we read you," another voice spoke over the speaker.

"Who is this? Over." asked Cersei.

"This is Jeffrey Edison of Hydronia," he said.

"Good. Please standby, over," said Cersei.

"We have two more bogeys inbound," said Vladimir as two more red dots appeared on screen.

"New Frontier to bogey three, do you read? Over."

"I do read," said another voice. "This is Stephano Bradham by the way, the people of Quaketown are pleased to…"

Cersei cut him off. "Please standby, over."

Jonathan jumped out of his seat. "Did that man just say Quaketown?" He laughed and slapped his knee. "Oh boy, I wonder what my sister did to have the entire nation name their home after her."

Cersei turned the dial again to communicate with the fourth spacecraft. "New Frontier to bogey four, do you read? Over."

"All of these overs are giving me a headache," said Vladimir as he messaged his temples.

Another voice spoke on the speakers. "I read, but I mostly do the storytelling," joked the voice.

"State your name and place of origin then," said Cersei.

"The name is Wakan. As for the place of origin, we are originally from Earth as you know. But our new civilization originated in Dunestone."

"Please standby, over."

A fifth red dot appeared on the navigation table. "The last one has arrived," said Vladimir. "The one from Dunestone arrived slightly behind schedule but *this* one is behind by a full nine minutes, Anakin."

"We'll have to see why once they get here," said Anakin.

"New Frontier to bogey five, do you read me?"

Static.

"I repeat, this is New Frontier to bogey five, do you read me?" She looked at Vladimir to see his reaction to her next word. "Over."

Vladimir momentarily stopped messaging his temples and gave her a dirty look.

A minute went by as static filled the chamber. Suddenly a strange voice cut through the static.

"I…We hear you…New Frontier," said the voice. "Can you hear…us…?"

"Copy," said Cersei. "State your name and place of origin."

The strange voice answered. "I am…Mikhail… from planet…Duskeloid…"

"Something must be wrong with our signal Mikhail, please standby."

Cersei turned all five dials to the right and spoke into the walkie-talkie. "Cersei speaking. I am one of the five Generals of *The New Frontier*. Please do not speak as I am using full power to contact all five of you. I will be in direct contact with you until your arrival. Estimated time is under ten minutes. Once you are all here, we will open the bay doors and welcome you to your temporary home. Please prepare to disembark." Cersei let go of the button on the walkie-talkie. She gave a thumbs up to the other Generals.

"Everyone seems to be accounted for," Anakin confirmed.

"Now we wait," said Kiki as she set up her medical tent.

Shortly after, the five spaceships came into view outside the chamber windows. The Generals looked on in awe at the carriers of the human race. To them, only four years had passed since the last time they saw the spaceships detach from *The New Frontier*. It had been two hundred years for everyone else.

The magnetic dampeners worked and the five spaceships slowed down as they closed in on *The New Frontier*. Arms reached out and attached to the spaceship. Once the fifth spaceship moved into place, a loud noise came from each door. *The New Frontier* shook as the bay doors opened on each spacecraft.

The people boarded *The New Frontier*. Each group of people looked on at the other groups. The biggest group had come from Selene with around six hundred. Mikhail's group had the least amount with around fifty.

Selene walked into the chamber and saw the others.

Gratius turned to her and whispered, "Look at all the Jambos and Sirfates."

"Be careful what you say, old man," said Selene. "You don't want to give the Ancients a bad first impression."

Mona and Aqib steered her away from him.

Wakan walked into the chamber surrounded by his followers. "I could have never imagined this. Just think of all the stories I can tell when I get back. I miss Star, Triss, and Zato so much already."

Copper and Christine stood behind him, walking at his pace.

"You will see your family soon enough," said Christine. "Hey look, the spirits are up ahead."

Brant walked into the chamber next to Alexis and Persephone. He was holding his hand in front of his face, trying to let his eyes adjust to the bright lights. "Let me know if you see any trouble, Master."

"I find the Up Above so mysterious," said Alexis, looking at the Others.

Akeer walked into the chamber by himself. He was the last one out of Hydronia's spaceship. He looked around at the architecture and then turned his attention to watch as the five people walked towards him. "So these are the Sleepers," Akeer said to himself, amused. "Doesn't look like they are sleeping anymore."

The Generals started handing out translators. They demonstrated by sticking it to the side of their neck. Once everyone had one applied, they gave an announcement.

"Gather around, everyone," announced Cersei on the speakers. "I noticed that you all call us by different titles. Please call us Generals, or by our names. Now, proudly stand with your group and we will discuss our situation."

The Generals were gathered in the center of the chamber.

Vladimir joined Akeer's group and started shaking hands with people in the front row, introducing himself. He quickly realized there was one of each gender per age group. Not nearly enough as he was expecting.

Kiki joined Brant's group. She was greeted with caution as she asked if any of them needed medical attention. She was intrigued by their fashion; black clothing with neon colors.

Cersei joined Wakan's group. Wakan introduced himself to Cersei and started telling her all about his journey there.

Jonathan joined Selene's group. He announced that Camilla was his sister. Selene ran up to him and started talking to him about his sister.

Anakin stood with the other group of people. The man named Mikhail, who was awkward looking and disheveled, was talking to Anakin. They did not shake hands and Anakin seemed distant.

Anakin made his way to the center to make an announcement. "Can I please have ten to fifteen of your top leaders of each group to stay with us," he asked. "The others can go to the living quarters right down the hall. I have already put up color coordinated signs to show which group belong in which quarters."

The groups started to decrease in size as they decided which people to stay.

In the group from Quaketown, the candidates were: Elders, Akira, Fortuna, Hazel, Christopherson, and Elias. The Council members, Aqib, Mona, Gratius, and Mr. Bradham. The young protégés Kelly, Lem, Lee, and Ciri. And finally Selene and Miles.

In the group from Dunestone, the candidates were: Wakan, Copper and his brother, Silver, Christine and her brother, Tobias, Pai, and six others.

In the group from "The Eye", the candidates were: The Master Assassins, Alexis and Brant, Persephone with Pandora, partners, Alexander and Elise, Greasy Gangsters, Patches and Tarjeel, and four others.

In the group from Hydronia, the candidates were: Akeer and Arabella, and thirteen other Ambassadors. The ages ranged from fourteen, a little girl named

Kaya, all the way to sixty, a fit old man named Hobbes.

Selene was looking around at the other people. "I couldn't have imagined how diverse humanity is. I'm scared how some of our people will act."

Wakan was writing in a journal he had been taking logs in. *We are so much alike*, he wrote. *The only difference is our skin color, language, and clothing.*

Brant had his hood up as he held Persephone's hand. He held Pandora in his other arm, protectively. Alexis was in front of him so he could keep on eye on her in case anyone attacked. He kept an eye on Akeer because he was holding a spear and Selene's group because they were holding bow and arrows. Brant looked around at the fifth group who were acting very suspicious. His daggers were ready to unsheathe.

Akeer held on to his force spear tight to his chest. He didn't trust these strange people. The Hydronians were all on the same page. On their ride up, they had prepared themselves for a potential attack.

Mikhail and his group did not interact with each other. They just stood there and didn't move a muscle. They must have been nervous or scared.

Since Cersei had been doing all of the talking thus far, the Generals decided she should continue.

"You must be the best of your people," said Cersei. "Look around at each other. You will be working together a lot and should get acquainted with each other. We have scheduled daily sessions to get to know each other as we prepare ourselves to begin our journey. As of right now, Anakin has discovered two Earth-like planets in this solar system."

"What will the weather be like?" asked Wakan.

"It depends where you are on the planet," said Anakin. "It could be dry in one place, snowing in another."

Everyone else looked at each other wondering what snow was.

"There are forests and caves," said Anakin.

Selene liked the sound of that.

"Mountains and lakes."

Wakan felt at home already.

"Deserts and shade."

Brant perked up.

"Oceans and seas."

Akeer eyes sparkled.

"Any landscape you can think of, it is on these two planets."

"And that's what Earth was like?" asked Selene.

"Every bit of it," answered Jonathan.

"Your Generals are about to finish scanning the two planets," said Cersei. "If it is true they are habitable, we will send out the self-replicating 3-D printers to start building cities and gardens. We could be moving to our new Earth in as soon as a six months. Then we will send the spaceships back t your homes and start bringing the rest of your people here once we get a community started. For now, you can get situated in your new temporary home. Get some rest and we will contact you in the morning to discuss more plans."

Selene, Wakan, Brant, and Akeer left at the same time and walked silently beside each other. They separated once they got to their designated living quarters. It was time for them to rest.

23. SABOTAGE

Back in the control chamber, Vladimir pulled up an image of two planets on the navigation table.

The first planet was 58% water and 42% land, with all sorts of environments. It had two large continents.

The second planet was smaller in size. It had 73% water and 27% land. There were nine continents.

Vladimir pressed a button and started scanning their environment.

"Is it just me or are my people acting strange?" asked Anakin. "Everyone here had been acting human, even though we have been separated for two hundred years. From a glance, little has changed from your groups. But mine…" He paused.

The other four Generals nodded in agreement.

"They were acting out of the ordinary, I did notice," said Jonathan. "They didn't talk to each other and they barely moved."

"They moved slowly when instructed to do something," said Kiki. "Almost as if they had no clue what we were saying. So they waited to see what the other groups did first."

"I would keep an eye on them if I were you," said Vladimir. "We have made it this far. That's the last thing we need right now, something or someone screwing up our main mission."

"Agreed," said Cersei. She yawned. "Anyone else tired? You would think being in cryo for two hundred years, we wouldn't need sleep ever again."

Anakin yawned. "The machines must have woken us up too fast. Usually when people wake up from a deep sleep, they just want to fall back to sleep." He walked around the control chamber in a trance. He placed a sensor on the door to the hallway. "Alright, let's take turns on overwatch. Two at a time. Might as well file paperwork in the meantime."

Everyone on *The New Frontier* had moved in. Their sleep cycles were mostly aligned. It was getting to be that time.

The Generals were in their own living quarters. Only Jonathan had fallen asleep. Anakin and Vladimir scrambled around the room, making sure everything was neatly organized, refusing to rest until they were finished. Cersei was filing away paperwork and Kiki was watching the monitors of the hallways.

In the Quaketown living quarters, Selene was sound asleep with her family, without a care in the world. The Elders were huddled together trying to think of a way to approach these new people. They had thought about it on their way there, but now that they have seen what they look like, they had to modify their plans. There were just so many of them. It was overwhelming.

In the Dunestone living quarters, Wakan was up telling stories he knew about the four other groups. The children gathered around him listening intently. Copper and Christine cuddled up with one another on the ground, listening to Wakan.

In "The Eye" living quarters, Brant was sitting up on his new bed, twirling his daggers. His silver sword was strapped to his back. Persephone laid awake next to him. Pandora was curled up on her chest. Alexis was pacing around the area. "Something is up," she said. "I can feel it in my bones."

The Hydronians were standing around with their force spears in hand. They were skeptical of the position they were in. Akeer was wondering what Jaylin was up to as he practiced his training.

After several hours, *The New Frontier* became eerily quiet. Everyone became exhausted from the long day full of new horizons. Most were asleep, including the Generals. The cryosleep had gotten the better of them.

Down at the furthest living quarters, Mikhail and his entire group snuck out of their room. Mikhail was holding a thin metallic weapon, which unlocked the doors to the chamber and led them in. His group broke off into five subgroups, scattering around to four of the five spaceships.

Mikhail led the fifth group to the navigation table. Mikhail sat down at the command center and started speed typing on the screen. He was hacking into *The New Frontier*'s system. He halted all scanning of the two planets and set an explosive under the table.

The four other groups placed explosives on the outside of the doors leading to the four spaceships.

Mikhail started a timer.

All five Generals had rushed into the chambers, as well as a few people from each living quarters.

Mikhail and his group set off a motion alarm when they came into the chamber that could be heard in the General's quarters.

Everyone wanted to know what was going on.

The door to Mikhail's spaceship closed as he waved goodbye with an evil grin on his face.

But that wasn't the only thing different. Mikhail and his group's skin had changed to a different color. Their skin was not white anymore. It was green.

Their body didn't resemble a normal human body anymore. They were all equally approximately five feet tall, and had big heads, long arms extending past their knees, and tiny feet. They also lacked ears and a nose.

"Shapeshifters!" yelled Jonathan. "I used to love those from the old comics I read back on Earth when I was a kid."

"Shut up," said Cersei.

Mikhail said something in an alien language that the translators couldn't translate. "Inta qualizar nifiratus."

Once the door shut, the spaceship detached itself and took off in one direction. Suddenly, one explosion went off after another.

The Generals laid on the floor from the impact of the explosions. It had ignited fires in every corner.

"Back up," Anakin instructed the people behind him. Anakin pressed a button on the outside of the control chamber. A heavy metal door slammed down, sealing off the room.

Anakin and Vladimir typed in a code on each side of the door. All the oxygen left the chamber, extinguishing the fire. They waited for a green light and Anakin pressed the button to open the door back up.

The Generals went through first, assessing the damage.

"It seems the main command console is offline," said Cersei, as she checked her station. "This can't be good."

"I'm not getting a reading on anything," said Vladimir as he hit the monitor. "I'm going to try a full system reboot." He entered a shortcut command on the keyboard.

Kiki and Jonathan were at the spaceship doors that had been blown open. They looked inside and it was a mess. They both ran diagnostics on the spaceships.

"Sir, one of the spaceships is completely destroyed," said Kiki referring to the spaceship from "The Eye".

"The one from Dunestone has sustained extensive damage," said Kiki. "It will take a long time to repair it. That's if it is repairable…"

"It doesn't look good on my end either," said Jonathan. "Hydronia's spaceship is completely destroyed as well. Although, there is a mini spacecraft that was unharmed." It was one of the spear machine prototypes like Ms. Britta's Lean Mean Spear Machine 7000.

Jonathan looked at the other diagnostic for the fourth and final spacecraft. "The one from Quaketown is fine though. Some light damage. To be honest, we should be able to repair it in less than an hour."

Some more people came rushing into the control chamber.

The Generals received a lot of, "What happened?" and "What are we going to do?"

"Please go back to you living quarters while we straighten this out," advised Cersei, calmly. "We will fill you in momentarily." She escorted them out and locked the door.

"Is anyone going to point out those aliens were shapeshifters?" asked a fascinated Jonathan. "We just had our first contact with an alien race! And they can resemble us! How wild!"

"Don't' forget, they are unfriendly. They nearly blew us up," said Vladimir. "We need a plan of attack."

"We need to analyze the situation first," said Anakin.

The system had finally finished rebooting. Anakin was searching on the computers for what the shapeshifters were up to.

"It appears they stopped the scan of the two planets," said Anakin, deep in thought wondering why. "Vladimir, take a look at what direction their spaceship came from."

"I don't have to," said Vladimir. "They came from the same direction of planet number two."

"Do you mean…?" gasped Kiki.

"The shapeshifters are from one of the new Earths," said Anakin. "That's why they wanted to delete our scans and destroy our transports. They didn't want us to invade them."

"Why didn't they just take us out?" asked a confused Vladimir.

"Or ask us politely," added Jonathan.

"Maybe they didn't know how advanced our technology was?" said Cersei. "Maybe they were just scoping us out. Reconnaissance. That's why they retreated. They are delaying us while they go back home to prepare themselves for war."

"War?" asked Jonathan. "Just what we need." He rolled his eyes. "I'm getting tired of that word."

"Now they know what they are up against," added Kiki.

"Everyone calm down," commanded Anakin. "We need to come up with a plan. Let's gather the leaders again to go over what we think happened and see what plans they come up with."

"We're going to place our fate in their hands?" asked Vladimir.

"That's what all of this has been about," Cersei pointed out.

Cersei unlocked the door and opened the control chamber. She asked for the same people they met with earlier to come join them.

The four groups of chosen leaders came into the control chamber and stood in a circle. They briefly introduced themselves to each other. The Generals filled them in as to what happened. They asked if any of them had any plans.

"We need to strike back," said Brant. "That is our only option."

Akeer agreed with him. "We must prepare first, before we strike."

"I say we are already prepared. We have everything we need right here," said Brant. "We have an army." He showed his daggers.

Akeer raised his force spear.

"*You* have an army," said Selene to Brant and Akeer. "Most of us were miners back home. We do have hunters that are highly skilled with a bow and arrow, but we don't have many." She pointed to Ciri.

"We are just crabbers and inventors," said Wakan. "We are not experienced fighters."

"Well then what do you suggest, old man?" asked Brant.

Wakan stood there with a hand to his bearded chin. "Well," he started. "Since we were brought here to work together for humanity's future, we can stockpile our resources."

Wakan turned to Selene. "This young lady said most of her people are miners. I'm sure we can use what they mined to fuel the spaceship."

"You mean go back to Quaketown?" said Selene.

"I think this man is on to something," said Akeer. "What types of resources do you have on each of your planets?" He pointed to Selene first.

"Like the man said," offered Selene. "We have different metals we can use for fuel. Melters too. Maybe we can even build machines or something out of the metals? We are hard workers but we are not skilled with constructing things."

"That's fine," said Akeer. "A lot of our people are builders." He smiled. He then pointed to Wakan. "What resources can you contribute?"

"My people are scientists with brilliant minds. They have many inventions that would improve our chances of survival," said Wakan. "Some of them could be used for offense and defense if we are really going to war."

"Great," said Akeer. "And you?" He pointed at Brant.

"We have trained assassins," said Brant. "And battle tactics. I also have some projection tech if anyone is interested."

"We have weapons," added Akeer. "*Powerful* weapons and vehicles. Builders too. We could help the scientists of Dunestone build new war machines. If they live underwater, we have strong swimmers."

"Well I think we have a plan then," comfirmed Anakin. "First, we need to make sure the spaceship has everything for it to function. We need to go to Quaketown first for fuel. Good thing you mentioned that Wakan. Since the spaceship is directly connected to *The New Frontier* magnetically, it was only capable of running to and from its destination. That fuel we can obtain in Quaketown will allow us to break that magnetic hold and travel to the other planets using coordinates."

"From Quaketown, we will travel to Dunstone for the scientists and their inventions. They can work with the builders to build the war machines."

"Next, we will travel to "The Eye" for the assassins. We need them for their battle tactics. Brant said he had projection tech, which sounds promising."

"Finally, we will then travel to Hydronia to get the builders, powerful weapons, and special vehicles. The builders can start doing what they do best. Hydronia is also the closest planet to Duskeloid."

"Hopefully by then, we will be prepared for the inevitable war. We will also pick up more people along the way, since we will have the room. Luckily, the biggest spaceship was the one to survive."

Anakin looked around at everyone. "Does this sound like a good plan?"

"Yes," said Selene.

"Absolutely," confirmed Wakan.

"I guess it's the only one we have," added Brant.

"Sounds good to me," approved Akeer.

"Then let's get to work," commanded Anakin. "Let's prepare to kick some alien ass and find a new home for humanity! This will be the most important battle ever recorded in human history. Even greater than the Pangaean War."

"I'm Akeer by the way," introduced Akeer. He reached out his hand to greet the new faces.

"Selene," she said as she started to go around the circle shaking each of their hands. "These are my parents," she said as she introduced her parents to the group.

"The name is Wakan," he said. "It's a pleasure to meet you all." He used two hands to shake everyone's hands.

"Brant," he said as he nodded his head.

The four people from different races greeted each other as equals. They knew there was bad blood between them from the two hundred year old stories of their ancestors back on Earth. All four of them were willing to forget about the past and forgive what their ancestors had done. They knew they had to stand up and unite to fight off this new threat. They needed to join *together* to save the human race from extinction.

Selene, Wakan, Brant, and Akeer continued talking to each other, already forming a lasting bond with each other.

The five Generals looked at the four brilliant people in front of them and they knew the human race was not going down without a fight.

Cover Art:

Green Planet Image:

Artist: Goran Ličanin, Gileryd @ deviantart
Title: Grass Planet Resource
(https://www.deviantart.com/gileryd/art/Grass-Planet-Resource-29825198)

Red Planet Image:

Artist: Morgan, B-SquaredStock @ deviantart
Title: Planet 5 PSD
(https://www.deviantart.com/b-squaredstock/art/Planet-5-PSD-161993774)

Black Planet Image:

Artist: Colin Capurso
Title: Blue Planet
(https://github.com/FinnStokes/orpheus/wiki/Asset:-planet)

Blue Planet Image:

Artist: Martin Kornmesser, ESA/Hubble, and NASA.
Title: Artist's impression of the deep blue planet HD 189733b.
(https://www.spacetelescope.org/images/heic1312a/)

Whether you enjoyed this book or not, I always like hearing back from the readers. I would appreciate it if you visited my website:

www.BooksByBills.com

or directly contact me at:

michael.bills@booksbybills.com

or follow me on Facebook by searching:

Michael Bills: Books By Bills

<u>About the Author</u>:

Michael Bills has always enjoyed writing, but this is his first attempt at writing a novel. After high school, he went to college for media production and fell in love with scriptwriting. Having an active mind, he comes up with ideas constantly. One day, Michael came up with the idea for The First Contact and knew it couldn't be written as a screenplay. It had to be a novel! He sat down and immediately wrote a detailed outline of the planets and characters. The story nearly wrote itself once he had the building blocks set in place. It took him about two years to complete. Michael currently has a full time job in Upstate New York. Even though he is busy, he predicts that writing book two of The Contact Trilogy, titled The Next Contact, will take far less time than the first. Book three will be written shortly after, titled The Final Contact.